# SCORCH

# SCORCH

STEEL BROTHERS SAGA

BOOK TWENTY-FOUR

HELEN HARDT

This book is an original publication of Waterhouse Press.

This is a work of fiction. Names, characters, places, and incidents either are the product of the author's imagination or are used fictitiously, and any resemblance to actual persons, living or dead, business establishments, events, or locales is entirely coincidental. The publisher does not assume any responsibility for third-party websites or their content.


Cover Design by Waterhouse Press, LLC
Cover Photographs: Shutterstock



ISBN: 978-1-64263-340-5

*For everyone who follows a dream . . .*
*only to find another.*

# PROLOGUE

## Brock

"It's more important that we find out who's been hijacking our property and moving . . . cargo."

"Cargo, Dad? Really?"

"It's just an easier word to say, son."

"I suppose. But we can't let ourselves get easy with this, Dad. It's a harsh reality. I don't want to get comfortable with it."

"This has nothing to do with getting comfortable, Brock. You know that."

"Yeah, I know that."

"All I can tell you is this. I understand that Pat Lamone means more to you because of what's going on with you and Rory. I get that, and I understand. But we really need to find out who left that information for Donny. Someone wanted us to find out what's happening on our property. Whoever it is, we have to consider them a friend at this point."

"Do we?" I ask. "That's pushing it, in my opinion."

"In mine as well. But whoever has hijacked our land for these horrific purposes is the enemy for sure. Someone wants us to know, and you know what that means. The enemy of my enemy is my friend."

"Maybe, Dad. But if they're a true friend, why didn't they

just come to us? Why sneak around and leave shit in Donny's bathroom? Who the hell does that?"

"Someone who doesn't want to—or can't—reveal themselves to us. Which means—"

"They're probably working with the enemy," I finish for him.

"Exactly."

My mind races. "There's got to be a connection, Dad. That ring. That ring that belonged to your mother. With the initials LW on it. That's got to be some kind of clue, right?"

"Yes, but I haven't been able to figure out what. We have to look deeper, Brock. Whoever wanted us to have that information, those GPS coordinates, also left the ring. But why? I've been racking my brain to try to figure this out, and I haven't yet. But I will, and you're going to help me."

"I will. Donny and Dale will too. But do we keep it among the four of us for now?"

"I'm going to bring Talon in. After all, he was shot, and at this point I think we have to assume that his shooting is related to the rest of this."

"Is that a reasonable assumption?" I ask.

"Reasonable? Hell, I don't even know what reasonable is anymore. But my brother gets shot in a place where he almost never goes? And the next thing you know, all this other shit comes to light? The puzzle pieces have to fit together somehow, Brock."

"But there's more, Dad. The stuff Brendan Murphy uncovered under his floorboards."

"I'm not completely convinced that is related," Dad says. "But it is something else we need to figure out."

"Hell yeah, we need to figure it out. Because whatever

else was left under those floorboards is no longer there after Murphy's place got trashed."

"I know, son. I know."

"We need to go back, Dad. Tonight. Rory's going to be involved with her father for a few days. That gives me the chance to deal with some of this stuff. We'll check out Doc Sheraton's land. Talk to him about the guard dogs. We have to figure out who's behind this. We *have to*."

"I agree with you. And we will."

"Except..."

Zach and Dusty waggle up to the deck to have their ears scratched. I oblige, stroking their soft heads.

"I have to take care of the Pikes' dogs."

"We can get someone else to take care of the Pikes' dogs. What about your brother? Or Dave or Henry?"

"Yeah, I suppose Brad could do it. Someone just needs to come over here in the morning, feed them, and let them out, and then do the same thing in the evening."

"Perfect. Call your brother and get that all arranged. If he can't do it, get Henry or Dave. I'm going to talk to Bryce about taking a few days off. Let's get started as soon as we can."

"I'm in. All in. At least while Rory's occupied with her father." I sigh. "I just wish..."

"So do I," Dad says. "I get it, Brock. It's a tough thing. But at this point, it's ride or die, son. We figure this out or we go down."

"I understand."

I end the call.

*Ride or die.*

I breathe in and hold it, drawing strength for what I must do. What I must do for my family. For Rory. For the future of the children she and I will have someday.

They deserve everything I have to offer, everything my name has to offer.

The Steel family will *not* go down on my watch.

# CHAPTER ONE

## Rory

My father has always been my hero.

I don't look much like him. Neither do my sisters or my brother. We all seem to favor our beautiful mother. Maureen Antonia Sebastian Pike—local beauty queen and homemaker extraordinaire.

Though I may look like my mother, I'm nothing like her. Not on the inside.

She's a good mother. Rather, she does the best she can. I believe she'd give her life for any one of us.

But my father?

He gets me. He understands me in ways my mother doesn't.

He's the one who looked me in the eye and told me he would support me whether I became an operatic mezzo-soprano or not.

Whether I chose to settle down with a man or a woman.

He's the one who told me—after two and a half years of New York auditions—that it was okay to stop. It was okay to stop putting myself through the hard work and determination only to have my dream crushed again and again.

*It's okay,* he said.

*It's okay to look for a new dream.*

My mother, of course, wanted me to keep trying. After all, I was her firstborn daughter—Aurora Maureen Pike. I carry her name as my middle name. I'm known as the great beauty of the family—as she was. Even though both my sisters are beautiful as well, my mother expected greatness from me.

But the great things she expected of me? They all had to do with my beauty. She wanted me to be an operatic mezzo not because of my talent or because of my love for singing, but because I would be on the stage, showing my beauty to the world. She wanted me in local pageants, as she had been, and was visibly disappointed when I refused. And of course . . . she wanted me on the arm of the handsomest man in town.

At least I've given her that one—Brock Steel is not only one of the handsomest men in the world but also one of the richest.

But as for visibility? She didn't get her wish. I'm not onstage. As a music teacher in Snow Creek, Colorado, I'm seen by no one.

But my father sees me.

He has always *seen* me.

The person below the polished exterior. After all, I did nothing to earn my beauty. I was born that way. And that is one thing I *do* have to thank my mother for.

But I am not my face. I am not my body.

My father was always the one person who knew that. Who understood that. Who saw what lay beneath the pretty face.

He is, and always has been, my hero.

My hero—with a tube down his throat, his eyes still closed, hooked up to machines, and a huge dressing on his chest covering the incision the surgeons made to heal his heart.

He's doing wonderfully, all the nurses say.

It's not that I don't believe them. I do. But this is my father. My big strong father.

Seeing him this way? Intubated and hooked up to machines?

It breaks my heart.

I let out a quiet and ironic chuckle at my own thought. A broken heart. People throw that term around as if it has some kind of literal meaning.

But the only literal meaning of the phrase is what I'm looking at right now.

My father, who had a broken heart.

The doctors assure us it's fixed now. He's recovering nicely, and he's shown signs of waking. In a few minutes, they will extubate him.

Maybe I should have waited until then to see him.

He'd still be hooked up to the machines, of course, but at least he wouldn't have that horrible plastic thing shoved down his throat.

My brother, Jesse, stands with me.

Callie and Maddie are outside the room. So is our mother. They couldn't take seeing Dad like this. I'm not surprised at my mother, but I'm a little disappointed in Callie and Maddie. My sisters are strong.

But apparently not strong enough to see our father in such a state of weakness, completely dependent on machines.

In truth? I'm not either. It's heartbreaking.

God, that stupid phrase again!

It will never have the same meaning for me.

A nurse in green scrubs bustles in. She takes notes of Dad's vitals and then turns to Jesse and me. "I'm going to extubate him now. Do you want to leave?"

Jesse and I look at each other. My brother lifts his eyebrows, and I nod.

"I'll stay," he says.

"I will too."

"Are you sure?" the nurse asks. "It can be uncomfortable for the patient."

I grab hold of my father's hand. "I'm not leaving."

"Neither am I," Jesse says.

Jesse is as close to our father as I am. Partly because he's the only boy, and partly because he's the oldest.

But partly because Jesse, like I am, is a musician. We get our musical talent from our father. He plays the guitar and the piano, and he started teaching us both when we were four years old. Dad also has a beautiful singing voice.

When I was small, I asked him why he decided to be a rancher and a winemaker—I mean, the man doesn't even drink—rather than a musician.

His words struck me.

"Because my music is for me, Rory. Only for me. It's not for anyone else, and if I make it my work, I will no longer enjoy it."

Funny how Jesse and I both went into music as our vocation when our father so clearly never wanted to. But as I look at him now, his body broken and hooked up to machines, I wonder if he wasn't right.

Neither Jesse nor I have had the success we wished for at this point in our lives. We both do fine, make a decent living, but we're not in front of audiences drawing huge crowds.

Jesse's at least still singing. As a rocker, he can easily find gigs at local and regional venues. Not too many of those venues are interested in an operatic performance. I sing with his band when he asks and when I'm available, and it's fun and I'm always well-received. A rocker at heart, though? That's not me. At least, I never thought it was.

The nurse removes the tape holding the tube in place.

I jerk at how harshly she rips it off. My God, she must've taken some of Dad's stubble with it. I desperately want to say something, but I keep my mouth closed. Surely she knows what she's doing.

Dad's eyelids twitch.

"Looks like he's waking up," the nurse says. "I'm getting this tube out of him right on time."

With a brisk movement, she pulls the tube out of Dad's mouth. I gawk at the sight of it, at how long it is. That thing was in my father.

Jesse and I still stand there as the nurse wipes Dad's mouth with a moist cloth.

His eyelids flutter once more.

When he opens them, his gaze meets mine.

And his lips curve upward. Only slightly, but I notice.

"Hey, Daddy," I say. "Don't try to talk."

"He'll probably be hoarse from the tubes," the nurse says.

"Hey, Dad." Jesse smiles.

I don't take my gaze from his as I squeeze his hand. "You're okay, Daddy. Everything's going to be okay."

# CHAPTER TWO

**Brock**

"Hey, Donny," I say into the phone after I call my cousin. "I just wanted to check in with you to see if you came up with anything for that number. The one who called Rory and said, 'You won't get away with this.' With everything else going on, I forgot to ask you about it."

"Nothing," he says. "Totally untraceable, which is unsurprising. It's obviously a burner phone. Why? Did she get another call?"

"No. Not that she's told me, anyway. I just got a text from her. Frank is awake. Sort of in and out."

"Yeah, I got a text from Callie with the same news."

"Dad and I are taking a few days off," I tell him. "Going to go back to Wyoming to check out Doc Sheraton's land. Maybe talk to him if he's there."

"You want me to come along?"

"Can you? With Callie out of the office and you being the only city attorney right now, I'm sure you're needed there."

"Yeah… I guess I could ask Mom to come out of retirement and take over for me, but…"

"No, just do what you need to do, Don. I'll keep in touch with you and Dale and let you know what's going on and if we find out anything of importance."

"Damn . . . I really just wish this would all go away."

"Me too, bro. Me too."

After ending the call, I pack a small bag for our trip. Dad says we may be gone for a few days. I got my cousin Dave Simpson to take care of the Pikes' dogs, and now I just need to tell Rory.

She'll understand. Still, I hate to leave her when she's in Grand Junction with her father. I should be there, supporting her.

I sigh and tap my phone to call her.

"Hey," she says into the phone breathlessly.

"Hey, sweetheart. How are you holding up?"

"I'm better now that that horrible plastic tube is out of his throat. Seeing him like that . . ." She laughs. Sort of.

"What?"

"I keep wanting to say that it broke my heart. But I swear I may never use that phrase again. Not when my father has a literal broken heart."

"It's not broken anymore, Rory. The doctors fixed it. He's going to be fine."

"I know. But a heart attack, Brock. My big strong father who eats healthy and hardly ever touches alcohol. I don't understand."

"Unfortunately, there's a lot in this life none of us will ever understand."

If that isn't the damned truth.

"I'm glad he's doing well," I add.

"Thank you. Me too."

"Do you need me there with you? Because I will drop everything if I have to, Rory. I will be there to support you."

"I'm fine. My entire family is here, and I know you have work to do."

"Actually, Dad and I have plans to be gone for a few days. We're going to head back to Wyoming, maybe talk to Doc Sheraton. At the very least check out his land."

"A few days?" Rory says.

"Yes."

She's silent for a few seconds, but then, "I understand. You need to go. The world doesn't stop just because my father had a heart attack. I mean, we both have so much else to deal with."

"Listen to me," I say. "You deal with your father right now. He is your sole focus. I'm glad he's doing well, and you stay with him as long as you need to. Anything you need, I will make sure you have it. The rest of this crap? Pat Lamone and everything else? You don't need to give that a thought. You let me bear that burden for now."

She sighs softly. "I'm not sure what I ever did to deserve you, Brock."

"Are you kidding me? I'm the one who doesn't deserve you. I'm serious, Rory. You focus on your father, and you call me if you need anything."

"All right. Thank you for everything, Brock. And you call me too, okay? I want to know everything you find out, but more than that, I want to know you're okay."

"I'll be fine, sweetheart. I promise."

After ending the call, I grab my bag, hustle Sammy into my pickup, and make the short drive to my parents' house. I drop Sammy off with Mom, who will be taking care of her while Dad and I are gone.

I give Mom a kiss on her cheek.

"You two be careful," she says. "I don't like any of this."

"Neither do we, baby," Dad says.

"Have you heard from Rory? How is Frank?"

"He's doing well, Mom."

"And Rory and Callie? How are they?" she asks.

"As well as can be expected. Rory is concerned. I think she has a hard time believing the doctors."

"Who are his doctors?" Mom asks. "I can check them out for her. I still have some pull at that hospital."

"That's kind of you, but I'm sure the doctors are fine. Frank is out of the woods. For now, anyway."

Mom nods. "I feel for Maureen and all her kids. It's always difficult seeing someone you love vulnerable like that."

"This may sound rude," I say, "but I'm glad I didn't go see Uncle Talon in the hospital."

"Not rude at all," Dad says. "And yeah, that totally sucked. I'm glad you didn't have to see it."

"It was hard on his kids," Mom says. "Especially Dale, because the two of them are so close."

My phone buzzes.

"Excuse me for a minute." I walk into the kitchen.

"Hello?"

"Brock, it's Gordon Jackson."

"Hey, any news?"

"Yes, and I'm sorry for not getting back to you within twenty-four hours as I promised."

"Not a problem. My girlfriend's father had a heart attack, so I've been pretty busy."

"I'm sorry to hear that. Is he okay?"

"Things look all right so far. What do you have? Anything?"

"I have good news and bad news," Jackson says. "The good news is, the speck of blood on the stem yielded a DNA sample."

I gulp. "And the bad news?"

"It matches the bones, Brock."

My stomach turns. “I see.”

“I know you were hoping those bones didn’t belong to the young woman.”

“Well, they had to belong to somebody. Human bones on our property aren’t a good thing, no matter who they belong to.” I scratch my forehead, but the throbbing itch doesn’t go away. “At least now we know. That poor young woman—who was in love and had her whole life ahead of her—was killed, and somehow her bones ended up buried on our property.”

“You said she disappeared from a hotel?”

“I believe the story goes that she was out shopping in Snow Creek and never returned.”

“I see. I wish there were something more I could do for you.”

“I appreciate everything you’ve done, and I appreciate your discretion. Send me a bill, and I’ll be sure that you’re compensated well.”

“I appreciate it. Thank you. And again, I’m sorry it took so long.”

“Not a problem.”

I end the call and walk back into the foyer.

Mom and Dad are embracing, kissing.

They still kiss like newlyweds.

I clear my throat. They separate.

Mom blushes. “Sorry.”

“Don’t be. It’s an amazing thing to have such passion after twenty-five years of marriage.”

Dad gives Mom one more kiss, this time on the cheek. “Ready, Brock?”

“Yeah. Let’s go.”

# CHAPTER THREE

### Rory

Dad is alert now, and Jesse and I have left the room to allow Mom some time with him alone.

Callie and Maddie are down in the cafeteria, and Jesse and I are in the sitting room at the end of the hallway.

My brother and I are the closest to Dad. I love Jesse, but the sibling I'm closest to is Callie because we're only two years apart in age. My brother and I are four years apart, he being the older, so he's always treated me like an annoying little sister.

At least he did when we were kids. Now, we work together a lot when I sing with his band. We've gotten closer over the years, but we tend to talk only about work and music. Other than that, our conversations are a bit stilted.

So I'm surprised when he says, "So... you and Brock Steel."

"Yes."

"I've got to tell you, sis. I didn't see that one coming."

I smile, feeling the warmth spreading over my cheeks. "I didn't either. And I'm pretty sure Brock didn't."

"I don't know him very well," Jesse says. "He's so..."

"Young?" I finish.

"Yeah, young. And... not the guy I really want with my sister."

I shrug. "Well, he's the one you've got."

"Right. I'm not used to Donny Steel yet, and you give me Brock?"

"At least Brock wasn't your high school rival," I counter.

"I suppose." Jesse shakes his head. "But he's the worst of the lot. Of him, Donny, and Dave Simpson? Brock was the biggest playboy of them all. I swear to God, if he ever hurts you..."

"He won't," I say with conviction.

And that conviction? I feel it in every bone of my body.

"He'd better not."

"Or what?"

"You know exactly what. He'll get what Pat Lamone has coming to him."

"Just..."

"I'm serious, Rory. I'd like to strangle the motherfucker."

"Keep your aggressions focused on Lamone, then. Leave Brock out of it."

"Fine."

"I get that this is hard for you. First, watching Callie fall for Donny, and now me with Brock."

"Are you sure, Rory? I mean, you and Raine seemed pretty serious."

"Raine and I were serious at one time, or at least I thought so. I'm not sure she ever was. But I have to be honest with you, Jess. What I feel for Brock... It's so much stronger than anything I ever felt for Raine, or anyone else. It's the real thing this time, and believe me, no one is more surprised than I am."

"And you're sure he shares these feelings?"

I smile as the warmth of a soft and cuddly blanket envelops me. "I'm sure."

Jesse rolls his eyes. "Now I guess I just have to wait for Maddie to fall for the one remaining Rake-a-teer."

I drop my jaw open.

"Oh shit," my brother says. "Do you know something that I don't?"

"Maddie kind of has a crush on Dave," I tell him.

"You've got to be fucking kidding me."

"Yeah. But it's nothing, really. They flirted a little at Murphy's a while back."

"Crap. I remember that. He was helping her with her pool game."

"And you allowed it?"

"Hell yeah, I allowed it. I was glad she wasn't focused on Dragon. I love him like a brother, man, but no way is he getting near any of my sisters."

"What's the story with Dragon anyway?" I ask.

"Not my story to tell, sis. Suffice it to say that if you knew, you wouldn't want him anywhere near Maddie."

My brother's words aren't new. He's cautioned us all away from Dragon Locke in the past. Funny thing is, I almost ended up in bed with Dragon after a fight with Brock.

The only thing that stopped me? A phone call. Brock calling me in a drunken stupor.

"Is Dragon his real name?" I ask.

"He says it is. But I'll be honest. I've never seen his birth certificate." Jesse smiles.

"It does seem to fit him."

"He's been Dragon as long as I've known him."

Jesse and Dragon met in college. They were in a music business class together, and Jesse recruited him for the band he was starting with our cousin Cage Ramsey.

That's really all I know.

That and the fact that Dragon is something of a dark prince.

Someone coined that term a long time ago. I'm not sure who it was.

Jesse sighs. "Maddie's twenty-one. She's way too young for Dave Simpson or anyone else."

"I agree with you that she's too young for Dragon," I say. "He's your age. But Dave Simpson is twenty-four, Jesse."

"So? He's a grown man. Maddie's a kid."

"You just said she's twenty-one." I chuckle.

"Twenty-one is a kid, Rory. Don't you agree?"

"No, I do not agree. Eighteen is a kid."

Except eighteen is *not* a kid. Just the mention of that age makes me think of the whole Pat Lamone situation. That's how old I was when he took those compromising photos of Callie and me. While he can be convicted of child porn if he publishes Callie, who was sixteen at the time, he won't face any criminal charges if he publishes the photos of me.

Damn.

Why did I have to start thinking of that?

I need to be focused on my father.

"I suppose I should talk Maddie out of the whole Dave Simpson thing," Jesse says.

"It was one night of flirtation at Murphy's. There's nothing to talk her out of—at least not yet."

"Yeah? Well, I'll be watching him like a hawk."

I roll my eyes. "I'm sure you will."

"Yeah, and I'm going to be watching Brock Steel like a hawk too."

"There's a big difference between Maddie and me," I say.

"And what's that exactly?"

"Well, seven years, for one. I have several serious

relationships under my belt, and I know how to handle myself."

"There's a big difference between Raine Cunningham and Brock Steel."

"One big difference." I lift my eyebrows.

"Don't gross me out," he says.

"I can't help it. You just made that way too easy."

"I'm serious, Rory. Isn't it just a little too convenient that two of the Steels are suddenly involved with two of my sisters?"

"Come on. You're not really thinking that the Steels want something from us?"

"It's possible."

"No, it's not possible at all. The Steels *have* everything they could want."

"Yeah? And my sisters are the only women in Snow Creek who are more beautiful than Steel women."

I love my brother, but did he *really* just go there?

"That's why they want us? For beauty? You think they're looking at us as breeding stock?"

"Don't be crass."

"You're the one being crass. You basically just called Callie and me egg donors. Incubators for gorgeous Steel children."

"Those are your words, not mine."

The irony of my own words isn't lost on me. For a hot minute, I actually looked at Brock as a potential sperm donor.

But no longer. I'm in love. So very much in love with him. I'll get his sperm the old-fashioned way.

"Look," I say. "I didn't set out to fall in love with Brock Steel. It seriously just happened. As for Callie and Donny, you'll have to ask them about their own story." I rise from the uncomfortable chair that has my ass aching. "I'm done with this conversation. And I don't care what Mom says, I'm going to see my father."

# CHAPTER FOUR

**Brock**

Dad and I reach Doc Sheraton's property before noon. Dad parks the truck pretty far down his driveway so as not to alert anyone here.

"Now or never," Dad says, opening his driver side door.

I say nothing. Simply open the door and place my feet on the solid ground.

A small ranch house is visible in the distance, and two cars are parked near the garage. Good. That means Doc Sheraton is most likely here.

Dad and I walk, our boots making prints in the gravel, toward the house.

Until—

A fierce Doberman pinscher jumps in front of us, stands and growls, baring his large and sharp canine teeth.

Dad jerks backward.

"Easy, Dad," I say. "These dogs feed on fear."

"What the hell do you know about any of it?"

"There's a reason why certain breeds are trained as guard dogs. They're the more fearful breeds. It's because of fear that they attack."

"You always did have a way with animals," Dad says.

"I do love them, especially dogs." I keep my voice low and

calm. Sudden sounds will only add to the dog's fear.

"No one needs an alarm system with this damn thing here," Dad says.

"Hey, fella." I keep my voice composed and soothing. "No one's going to hurt you."

"Brock—"

"Quiet," I say to Dad. "Let me handle this."

I step a few inches toward the dog.

The growling intensifies.

From the corner of my eye, I see Dad begin to open his mouth again. I shake my head at him slightly.

"Don't move, Dad."

"That dog is looking at me like I'm a fucking pork chop," he says.

"I told you to be quiet."

I step another couple inches toward the dog.

Again, his growling intensifies.

"It's okay," I say again.

"Brock?"

"Dad, I told you. Be quiet," I say, this time in a hissing whisper.

"Brock . . ."

Damn it! What does my father not understand about *shut the fuck up*? I turn my head slowly to look toward him, and—

Oh, shit.

Another dog.

This one stops on Dad's other side, stands and growls.

"Why aren't they attacking?" Dad says, without moving his lips.

I force myself not to be too rigid in my stance. Tension will alarm the dogs. "Because they're guard dogs, not attack dogs. Now be quiet."

I'm at a loss, though. I can't keep edging toward the first dog and ignore the second dog. I have to somehow keep my eyes on both of them.

The second dog growls, and his is louder and fiercer than the first's.

"Jesus Christ," I say under my breath.

I mentally tell my dad to be quiet. We're both big men, but these dogs... Are they trying to guard, or are they trying to attack? I told Dad they were guard dogs, but in truth I have no clue.

I'm probably right. If they were going to attack us, they would've done it by now.

These two dogs are Doc's alarm system.

And it's a damned good alarm system.

Better than Monarch Security for sure.

How do we get past them? How do we get to the house?

"Let's go back to the car," I say to Dad.

"Seriously? You want to go without finding anything out?"

"Keep your voice low, Dad. Do you have a better idea?"

"Well... not really."

"Do not turn your back on these dogs. We're going to walk backward toward the truck. Inch by inch."

"All right."

"Follow my lead." I move backward a few steps.

More growling.

They growl every time we move. Of course they do because movement is a threat. But they don't come any closer to us.

Interesting.

I glance around, and then I see why. They *can't* move. There's an electric fence around the perimeter of the house. If the dogs go past the barrier, they get a shock.

My God. Doc is a veterinarian. How can he shock an animal?

"We're good now, Dad," I say. "They can't come near us. There's an electric fence."

"How can you tell?"

"There's a beacon on their collars, and the wires are underground. If you look closely, you can see where the ground has been disturbed."

"That's inhumane," Dad says.

"I agree."

"We let our livestock graze. We've never even thought about keeping them fenced in with anything that could harm them."

"I know, Dad."

"Bryce and I made the right choice all those years ago," Dad says. "I'm glad we didn't hire Sheraton as our full-time vet."

"I agree." We reach the car, and I place my hand on the door handle. "What the hell do we do now?"

"I don't know. We could call Sheraton. I have his cell phone number."

"We can try, but what if he doesn't want to talk to us?"

"He will."

"How can you be so sure?" I ask.

"Because I'm going to make an offer he can't refuse."

# CHAPTER FIVE

## Rory

"Hey, Daddy," I say to my father.

He's the most alert I've seen him since he woke up.

"Hey, baby girl," he says, his voice hoarse.

"Don't make him talk, Rory," Mom says. "It hurts his throat."

"Maureen, let her be." Dad smiles at me. Sort of. His lips are dry and chapped, and his skin so pale.

I place my hand on his shoulder. "Are you in a lot of pain?"

"They've got him pumped full of drugs, Rory," Mom says.

I won't be short with my mother. She's trying to protect the man she loves, of course. This is her husband, her life mate, and it's not like I can kick her out of this room so I can spend some time alone with my father.

Besides, Jesse and I spoke to the doctor before I came into the room, and Dad's prognosis is excellent.

"I hear you're going to get out of here in a few days," I say. "It'll be really good to have you home."

"Yes," Mom says, "and we will not be eating any more saturated fat."

"What about the cattle we raise?" I ask.

"Just because we raise beef doesn't mean we have to eat it."

"For God's sake, Maureen," Dad chokes out. "We make wine for a living, too."

"Which Dad doesn't even drink," I add.

Dad is great at making the stuff, but he doesn't drink it. He's not all that fond of alcohol, which makes his heart attack all the more bizarre.

"Right now we have no grapevines, thanks to that fire," Mom says. "But maybe you *should* drink wine, Frank. I've heard that red wine especially is good for the heart."

"Did you read that in *Cosmo*?" I ask snidely.

I instantly regret my snarky words. I've heard the same thing from various sources, but there are just as many other sources that say avoiding alcohol is best for the heart and circulatory system. Still, though... Why did Mom have to mention the fire and how it destroyed our vineyards? Our livelihood? We've always done more wine business than beef business.

I'm feeling pretty pissy toward my mother these days.

I breathe in and out slowly. Time to get a grip.

I squeeze Dad's shoulder. "Don't try to talk."

"We'll be eating a lot more fish." Mom smiles, ignoring my *Cosmo* comment. "That salmon en croûte I made the other night turned out beautifully."

"That's one of your best dishes, Mom," I say. "But you know what else is one of your best dishes? Beef stroganoff."

"Maybe I can make it with chicken," she says.

Dad laughs, but then he winces. "Damn. That hurts."

"Easy, Daddy."

"Right. But chicken stroganoff? Jesus, Maureen."

"We will do what's best for you, Frank."

"Reenie..."

Uh-oh. When he calls Mom "Reenie," he wants something.

"Yes?"

"Would you mind? I'd like to spend some time with Rory."

That's what he wants? To spend time alone with me? Sounds good from where I'm standing.

"Wait a minute." Mom wrinkles her forehead. "You're kicking me out?"

"Only for a few minutes."

She huffs and leaves the room.

"You're going to pay for that one," I say to Dad.

"No. She's so freaking scared, she won't dare say anything to me."

"I'm as scared as she is, Daddy."

"I know you are, baby girl. I'm going to be all right. I promise."

"Yeah, you will be. Did you want to talk to me about something? It can wait. I don't want to make you talk, Dad. I know it hurts."

"It's okay," he cracks out. "I'm sorry that this happened. That I had to put your mother and you kids through this."

"None of this is your fault."

"I know." He sighs. "I did everything right. I don't drink, and I eat well."

"Maybe it's the cigars," I say.

"I don't inhale the smoke, Rory."

"Not intentionally. But the smoke is there, and some of it gets in."

"Fine." Dad lets out another sigh. "I'll give up the damned cigars. You'll be happy to know Brock didn't like the one he had the other night."

"Didn't he?"

"No. He did his best, but he looked kind of green."

I laugh. Brock Steel is such a big strong man, and the fact that he was felled by a little cigar smoke . . . It's endearing.

"Speaking of Brock, I want to talk to you about him."

"Okay. What about him?"

"I like him, Rory. I like him a lot."

"I know that." I smile.

"I like him because I see the way he looks at you. It's not a look of lust, and it's not a look of longing, even. It's the way I look at your mother, Rory. I noticed it with Donny and Callie as well. The man loves you. Surprised the hell out of me, to be sure, but he loves you. Only a man in love recognizes that in another man."

"I love him too, Daddy."

"Do you?"

"I do. I know it's difficult for someone who isn't bisexual to understand someone who is. But it's truly an either-or thing. It could've been a woman, or it could've been a man. Turns out it's a man, Daddy. It's Brock."

"You have my blessing, baby girl."

"It's still a new relationship. It may not last."

Ouch. Those words cut me, but I have to face their truth.

"I believe it *will* last," Dad says. "I may be wrong, but I doubt it. I like him, and not because he's a man and not because he's a Steel."

"That's what Mom likes."

"It's *part* of why Mom likes him," Dad says. "Rory, your mother wants you to be happy above all else. She has a few preconceived notions, and she is who she is. I can't change her, and I don't want to. I love her. But I want you to know that I like Brock. I've always liked the Steel family. But I like Brock because of the way he looks at you, my daughter. He looks at you the way you deserve to be looked at. He loves you the way you deserve to be loved."

"I don't know how you can tell all that from a look."

"Like I said, only a man who has looked at someone else that way can see it."

I'm not sure I believe my father, but I don't have to talk anymore. He made his point. He likes Brock, and he believes Brock loves me.

"I want you to rest now," I say.

He nods and closes his eyes.

I squeeze his hand and give him a kiss on his cheek. "I love you, Daddy."

But he's already asleep.

I leave the room, where Mom is waiting in the hallway.

"He's asleep now," I say.

"What was all that about, Rory?"

I don't want to share the conversation with my mother, but I have to give her something. She'll be relentless if I don't.

"He was just giving me his blessing," I tell her. "For me and Brock."

A huge smile splits Mom's pretty face. "That's wonderful, Rory. I hope you know that you have my blessing as well."

"I know, Mom. It means a lot to me."

My mother is who she is, and I know she tries and continues to try. She's come around a lot since I came out to her years ago. I can love her for who she is and because she continues to grow. I can give her the gift that she has trouble giving me.

And I will be a better person for it.

"Now that Dad's doing better," I say, "I think I'll go home.

Brock had to leave town, and Dave Simpson is looking after Zach and Dusty. But I don't want to put him out."

"I understand. Maddie's going to stay here with me. She can keep up with her classes online. But Callie and Jesse are going to go home as well."

"You call if you need anything, Mom. We'll come right back."

"Thank you, Rory," Mom says. "Thank you for being the strong woman that you are."

"I learned from the best." I give my mother a hug.

She is a strong woman, in her own way.

And I do love her.

I'd be lost without both my parents.

# CHAPTER SIX

## Brock

"Let me see your phone," Dad says to me when we're back in the truck.

"Why?"

"Because I'm pretty sure Doc Sheraton knows my cell number. I don't want to give him a chance to ignore the call."

I nod and hand him my phone. He taps in the number and puts the phone on speaker.

Sure enough, the man answers. "Doc Sheraton here."

"Doc," Dad says, "Jonah Steel."

"Joe?" Doc clears his throat. "I didn't recognize the number."

"Listen," Dad says, "my son Brock and I are here, outside your home in Wyoming. I've got some things to talk to you about. Seems we have an opening on our staff for a veterinarian."

"Oh?"

"Yeah, and we'd sure like to talk to you about it."

"How did you know I was up here?"

"Your daughter's boyfriend, Pat Lamone, told my nephew. Brock and I are up here to check on some other things, and we thought we'd stop by."

"Where are you now?"

"In my truck. We tried to come up to the house, but . . . we were waylaid."

"My dogs. Yeah. Come on up to the house. I'll call them off."

"Thanks, Doc. We appreciate it."

"See you in a few minutes."

"Absolutely. Looking forward to it." Dad ends the call.

"You didn't answer his question about the phone number," I say.

"Of course I didn't. It's none of his damned business whose phone number it is."

"You're not really thinking of hiring him, are you?"

"Of course not. It's just a ruse, son. I'd never hire a man who electrocutes animals as my veterinarian."

I leave the truck, walk slowly up the gravel driveway, keeping my eyes out for the dogs.

True to his word, though, Doc Sheraton seems to have called them off. We make it to the front door and knock.

Doc answers, dressed in jeans, cowboy boots, and a long-sleeved black T-shirt. "Welcome, Joe. Brock."

Dad tips his hat. "Doc."

"Hey, Doc," I say.

"Come on in." He holds the door open for us. "Brittany! Could you get some lemonade for Mr. Steel and Brock?"

"I didn't realize Brittany was here," I say.

"Oh yeah. She helps me."

"Who's manning the business in town?" Dad asks.

"I have a list of veterinarians in neighboring towns who I keep on call when I have to be here."

"That works out well for you," I say.

"I do the same for them when they go out of town. Small-town vets like us need side hustles."

"Indeed," Dad says.

"Which is why I'm interested in what you have to say, Joe," Doc says.

"Absolutely," Dad says, "but before we get to that, Brock and I want to talk to you about buying some guard dogs from your business."

"Oh?"

"Yes," Dad says. "We're very unhappy with our present security company. We're looking for a new one, and we'd like to add to our security as well. We've never used dogs before, but we're animal lovers, as you know, and clearly your dogs are well trained."

"I can certainly help you out there. You saw how well Jaws and Ferdinand reacted when you tried to come up to the house."

"Jaws and Ferdinand?" I say.

"Guard dogs have names, of course."

"Right," I say. "I just thought the names were… interesting. I mean, Jaws makes sense. But Ferdinand?"

Doc laughs. "Brittany named him. She loved that cartoon about the bull when she was a kid."

Interesting. If I recall from my own childhood, the story of Ferdinand the Bull has several themes, one of which is the ethical treatment of animals.

Which, in my humble opinion, doesn't include electrocution.

Brittany arrives then, carrying a tray with a pitcher of lemonade and three glasses.

Doc smiles. "There you are, sweetie. Brittany makes wonderful lemonade. Just the way her mother used to."

"Hello, Mr. Steel. Brock." Brittany sets the tray on the small coffee table.

"Hello, Brittany," Dad says. "It looks refreshing."

Where the hell is my father? Not sure I've ever heard him use the word *refreshing*.

Of course, he's playing a part, and I need to do that as well.

"Looks amazing," I say. "Will you be joining us?"

Brittany's cheeks redden.

She's Rory's age, or a year younger. At any rate, she's older than I am.

"No, I'm busy in the kitchen."

I give her my dazzling smile. "You should join us."

"Well . . ." She glances at her father.

"It's fine, sweetie. If you'd like to."

"All right. I'll get another glass." She disappears back into the kitchen.

Doc Sheraton pours the lemonade into three glasses and hands one to Dad and then to me. "Please, sit down."

"Thank you," I say, taking a seat on the blue suede couch. Interesting decor.

Dad joins me and takes a drink. "Absolutely delicious. Thank you."

"I told you." Doc sits in an armchair adjacent to us. "I don't know what I would've done all these years without my Brittany."

"I'm sure it must've been difficult for you," Dad says. "I can't imagine having to raise my children on my own."

"It's been difficult, for sure," Doc says, "but Brittany turned out great. I couldn't be happier."

*Yeah, Brittany turned out great all right. Stealing drugs from your veterinary clinic, drugging Rory and Callie Pike, and then . . . Putting atropine in a baby's diaper . . .*

I draw in a breath and smile again. I've never been an actor, but I'm going to have to be one now. If only Rory were here to give me some pointers.

Brittany rejoins us, pours herself a glass of lemonade, and sits next to her father in another chair.

"So, about the dogs," Dad says. "My security advisor says we should have about ten, and he says males are superior to females."

Is Dad pulling this stuff out of his butt? But I've got to hand it to him. He's a damned fine actor.

"That depends," Doc says. "Female dogs tend to be better for personal guard dogs, due to their maternal instincts. Males are usually better for guarding property because they're more territorial. But in truth, most dogs can be trained to do what you want them to do, regardless of their sex."

Dad clears his throat. "I see. We're more interested in guarding property, of course. So I'm thinking male dogs."

"Of course. You have two options available to you, then. You can purchase fully trained dogs, or you and I can work together to train your dogs to your specifications."

"I like that idea," Dad says. "Tell me more . . ."

I know what Dad is doing. He chose that option because it will require him to work with Doc Sheraton closely. It's a way to see what's going on here on this property. It's also a way to get Doc talking so I can deal with Brittany. Yes, my father is using me as bait with Brittany. I should be offended, but I know I can get what I need out of her.

I turn to her. "How are you?"

She blushes again. "I'm just fine. How are you?"

"Good. I'm seeing Rory Pike."

I mention Rory not to show Brittany I'm off the market but to make her think about what she did ten years ago to the Pike girls.

Brittany looks down at the glass of lemonade. She grips it with white knuckles. "How nice."

She knows I know.

I know she knows.

I need to get Brittany alone, but I'm not sure how to do that.

I can rely on Dad to keep Doc Sheraton occupied, but I need a reason for Brittany and me to leave the living room.

Of course, I can't think of one at the moment.

"How is Pat?" I ask, still smiling.

God, I must look like the Joker with this fake smile pasted on my face.

"We . . . We're kind of taking a break."

"Are you? Isn't he house-sitting for you and your father?"

"Well, yeah. But he's *just* a house sitter."

I don't for a minute believe they've broken up, but this might be my chance to find out more.

"I had no idea you were available." I smile.

I glance over at Dad. He and Doc are still talking about male versus female guard dogs.

"I guess I am."

"Maybe we could get a drink sometime."

"You mean you, me, and Rory?"

"Yeah. That would be fun, don't you think?"

"Sure."

I'm blowing this big time. Where the hell are my womanizing instincts? Granted, I don't want to use them on this particular woman, but what choice do I have? I need to get her alone. Get her talking. Except I already volunteered the information that Rory and I are seeing each other.

And that's the whole problem. My womanizing instincts were tied to my womanizing. I'm in love now, devoted to only one woman. No more womanizing means no more womanizing instincts.

I need another tactic. Coming onto Brittany isn't going to work. Besides, the idea nauseates me anyway.

"I'm really interested in the dogs," I say. "Could you show me the kennels?"

"I suppose . . ."

"Great." I stand. "Let's go."

"Brock?" Dad says.

"Brittany's going to show me the kennels." I raise my eyebrows.

He nods slightly. "Wonderful. When Doc and I are done talking, we'll come out to take a look too."

"Sounds good."

I follow Brittany through the house and out a back door. Beyond the small backyard is a series of fenced-in dog runs.

A couple of dogs are in the runs, and in one of the fenced areas, a litter of puppies plays. Rottweiler puppies, and they're adorable.

Beyond the dog runs lies a large building that I presume is the kennel.

"These are the training areas out here," Brittany says. "We train in the mornings, and they come out here to play and roughhouse in the afternoon."

I follow her through the pathway, and I stop when we get to the puppies. "These guys are so cute."

"Aren't they?" She scoops one into her arms. "I just love

them. Sometimes it's so difficult to think about them when they're this size and this playful. They will grow up to be vicious guard dogs."

"Vicious?"

I pick up a puppy. He's so cute—black with some brown markings—and he squeals and licks my chin. I can't even imagine him being vicious.

"Not vicious on purpose or anything," Brittany says, kissing her puppy's nose. "They do what they're trained to do."

My puppy wiggles in my arms, and I scratch him behind his tiny ears.

"Do you not like training?" I ask.

"I do very little of the training. My dad and I have a few employees who work here with the dogs when we're not here."

"They live here on your property?"

"Some of them do." She nods to the right where a few small houses stand in the distance.

"Interesting." I put Rufus—yeah, I already named him—down and turn to her. "I'm going to need you to level with me, Brittany."

"About what?" She raises her eyebrows as her own puppy wiggles out of her arms and back into the pen with his brothers and sisters.

"You know what. You know exactly what I mean."

"You mean . . . the dogs?"

I narrow my eyes. "No, I don't mean the dogs, though I have to say I hate the fact that you use those electric shock collars."

"I—"

"But I can't get into that now. I'm talking about the emails you sent to Rory and Callie from your father's email address.

The phone call Rory got. And of course, the drugs."

"I don't know what you're—"

I raise a hand to stop her. "Please. Don't insult my intelligence. What the hell is going on here?"

Brittany picks up another puppy and snuggles it to her cheek.

Nice try.

I take the pup from her, give it some love, and then set it back down with its siblings. "We're moving away from the puppies. Come on."

I walk toward the kennel building, and to my surprise, she follows me. I stop several yards away from the pups. "Now. Tell me what's going on."

"It's… It's Pat, you know? He's just really worried about his grandmother."

"Grandmother?"

"She's mentally ill. She's in the hospital."

"You must be talking about Mrs. Smith."

"Yes. Sabrina Smith."

"Wait, wait, wait." I shake my head. "Her last name is *actually* Smith?"

"Yes. That's what he told me, anyway."

"Okay. Tell me everything. Right now, and don't leave out a single dirty detail."

Brittany darts her eyes around. "Daddy!"

"He can't hear you out here."

Brittany lets out a strange sound, kind of like a squeak. "You're scaring me, Brock."

"Am I?"

"Yes, you are."

I take a step backward—but only a small step. "I haven't

raised a hand to you. I haven't even raised my voice to you. You have nothing to fear from me—nothing physical anyway. Besides, even if I did raise a hand to you, I'm sure you could call a dog on me."

Her lips tremble.

"I won't hurt you. I promise you that I won't. But I need to know everything you know about Pat Lamone. About his grandmother. About those emails and calls to Rory and Callie. And about all the drugs you stole from your father's clinic."

"You'll never understand," she says.

"Try me."

She shakes her head. "You won't. You have everything you need. Everything you could possibly want. Plus, you have your mother. My mother was taken from me when I was just a little girl. My father..."

"What about him, Brittany?"

Brittany pauses a moment and then drops her mouth open. "Your father isn't interested in guard dogs, is he?"

"Sure he is."

"No, he's not. You're here for other reasons."

"Maybe. Maybe not. That's not any of your concern." I rub the stubble on my jawline.

"I never wanted to do any of this stuff," she says.

"So you're going to pass the buck."

"No. I'm not passing the buck. I'm just..."

"Protecting Pat?"

"No," she says. "Pat is not the person I'm protecting."

# CHAPTER SEVEN

### Rory

Home.

Jesse and I arrive, and after being assaulted by Zach and Dusty, and after I text Dave to let him know he doesn't need to check on the dogs this evening, we sit on the deck.

"Will you make it to your gig?" I ask.

"Yeah. I have to. It's a lot of money for us, and the band needs me. Especially if they don't have you."

Envy for my brother jolts into me. To get away for a few days sounds pretty wonderful.

"You know what? Maybe I will come along," I say. "Brock is gone for a few days with his dad."

Jesse stares at me. More like glares at me. "I'm going to fucking kill you, Rory. Can you ever make up your mind about anything?"

"Honestly, I just need some time away from everything."

"What about your lessons? Didn't you just get back from England?"

"It's a weekend gig, right?"

"No, Rory, it's a small tour that begins this weekend. We're playing a few shows in Grand Junction and outside Salt Lake City, where agents tend to hang out."

"Well . . ." I sigh. "I guess I really shouldn't join you, then."

"For God's sake . . ." Jesse shakes his head. "You will be the death of this family, Rory Pike."

I frown. "That's not even remotely funny when our father is lying in a hospital bed."

"You're right. I apologize. I didn't mean it literally."

"I know you didn't."

"Hey." Jesse squeezes my forearm. "Dad's going to be okay."

"Until he's off that hospital bed and home doing regular stuff, I just can't bring myself to believe that."

"He's strong," Jesse says.

"Yeah, he is, and this still happened."

"I know." My brother sighs. "We should probably all get our cholesterol and blood pressure checked."

"I already do. I get all that stuff checked when I have my annual gynecological exam."

My brother covers his ears. "Jeez, Rory, I don't need to know about that."

"It's a fact of life," I tell him. "And it keeps women honest. We get the plumbing checked once a year, and while we're there, the doctors check everything else. So if my blood pressure or my cholesterol were getting out of hand, I would know. How would you know, Jesse? How would Dad know? Men are so infuriating sometimes. You all seem to think you're bulletproof, that you never have to go to the doctor just to get simple blood work."

"I'm thirty-two years old, Rory. I'm the picture of health."

"But that's my point. So was Dad, Jesse. So was Dad."

My brother purses his lips. Good. I've made him think. Thirty-two is still a young man, but it's not exactly eighteen. In fact, I'd better make sure Brock has a physical as soon as he gets back in town.

"You win. I'll make an appointment with the doctor."

"Good."

"*After* this gig. I don't have time right now."

"That's fine. I'll take it," I say.

The gig.

I really do want to go. With Brock out of town for a few days, I need something to take my mind off Dad.

Of course, I'd never forgive myself if something happened to Dad and I wasn't there.

"You're really going to take the gig, huh?" I say to Jesse.

"I don't have a choice, Ror. The band has a contract. And you know what? Dad would tell me to go."

He's right. Dad *would* tell him to go. And if I wanted to go? He'd tell me to go too.

"Jesse . . ."

He scoffs. "Really? You changed your mind again?"

"I think I need to do this," I say. "It's something I enjoy. Making music. I know I have that Christmas recital to plan, but planning doesn't give me the euphoria that being onstage does. And right now, Jesse, I really want to feel that high."

"I get it. Why do you think I'm going?"

"Because the band needs you. At least that's what you said."

"That was the truth. We're under contract, but I'm also going because I *need* this as well."

"Is there time to get my lodging?"

"We've got two rooms. I can check."

"Well, if they can't, would Cage, Jake, and Dragon mind staying in one room? You and I could share the other."

"Yeah, we could." Jesse grabs his phone and starts tapping. "I'll check on everything. We may be able to get you your own room."

"You know what? Don't. You and I will just share a room. As long as there are two beds, we'll be fine. I don't want to add any more to the band's expenses."

"Fair enough. It'll be easy enough to request a cot or rollaway bed so the guys don't have to share one. They won't mind because they all want you involved in the first place."

"Do they really?"

"Of course, Rory." He gives me a good-natured punch on my upper arm. "We're a good band. We know that. But you? You make us better."

I nod and smile. I'm going. Although I may end up without any students by the time I return at the rate I've been canceling their lessons.

But it's like Jesse said. We *need* this.

And sometimes you have to see to your needs.

# CHAPTER EIGHT

**Brock**

I resist the urge to curl my hands into fists. I will never harm a woman. I'm not that guy. But right now that pledge is as tough as it's ever been. Brittany Sheraton deserves to be pummeled.

"Who, then, are you protecting, Brittany?"

She backs away slowly. "I . . . I can't. I can't talk about this anymore."

"You *will* talk about it."

"You can't make me."

I have to physically stop myself from grabbing her arm. I will not turn into that guy, no matter how hard it is.

"How much do you know?" I demand.

"More than I want to," she says.

"Is Pat related to the Steel family?"

"I can't . . ."

"I can make sure you're taken care of," I tell her. "I can see that no one harms you."

The words make me ache. This is a woman who has been harassing Rory and Callie. A woman who most likely injected them with something and then stood by and watched as Lamone took pictures of them in compromising positions.

I don't want to give her the protection of my family, but if it can get information out of her, I will make that promise.

"How long has he known?" I ask.

"It was only a suspicion for a long time," Brittany says.

"How long?"

"I don't know."

"Don't lie to me."

She sighs. "Since high school."

"Did he poison Diana Steel on purpose?"

"You can't prove any of that."

"No, I can't, and the statute of limitations has passed, so even if I could, it would be a dead end. But I want to know. If he suspected that he was related to the Steel family, why on earth would he try to harm us?"

I already know the answer to my question.

Jealousy, pure and simple. If he truly believed he was related to this family, he would have wanted all the benefits that came with the name. Diana had those benefits, and he was jealous of her. Can I even blame him for feeling that way?

I've never *not* known the benefits of being a Steel. I've never had to worry where my next meal was coming from, and I've never had to live paycheck to paycheck or wear hand-me-down clothes.

My family is far from elitist. We understand the value of a dollar and the value of a hard day's work. My father taught me those values, and I will teach them to my children someday, as will my brother and all my cousins.

But there is one thing we don't think about a lot.

How we must look to the others in town.

Especially now that I know that we actually *do* own the damned town, as was the rumor for years.

What if Lamone's claim is valid? What if this Sabrina Smith, his grandmother, had a child with William Steel? I can easily put Callie on that. She has access to all the databases. She can trace Pat's lineage, find birth certificates.

"Listen," I say to Brittany. "I can't ever forgive Pat for what he did to Rory and Callie. That's beyond what I'm capable of. But I might be able to forgive you. If you level with me."

Big lie, but what the hell?

She bites her lower lip, wrings her hands together. "I never wanted to do any of it."

"Why did you, then?"

"Pat. He can be very . . . persuasive."

"So he persuaded you to steal the drugs from your father's clinic?"

"I researched it thoroughly. I made sure that Rory and Callie would not be harmed."

I hold back a scoff. She's ready to talk, so now is not the time to piss her off. But damn . . .

My father taught me when I was a young man that you never harm a woman. Never. She can be beating you black and blue, but you do not strike her back. Ever. It's the law of being a man.

I really want to break that law at this moment.

But I won't. I will *not* be that guy.

"Well, that's good," I say. "Exactly what kind of research did you do?"

"I asked my father."

I keep my jaw from dropping. "So your father knew what you were up to?"

"Oh, no, of course not. I just asked him how the substance would affect humans of a certain weight."

"All right." I draw in a deep breath and hold it for a few seconds, counting to ten. I exhale and draw in another one.

This time I count to fifteen. When I finally feel like I can speak without anger, I meet Brittany's gaze. "Tell me what you know about atropine, Brittany."

Her eyes widen. "You know about that, too?"

Oh God…

"How could you?" I say. "How could you use an innocent baby like that?"

Her mouth drops into an O as she gasps. "What are you talking about? I would never hurt a baby."

I don't want to give this woman any credit, but she looks absolutely horrified.

If I had to bank my fortune one way or the other in this moment, I would bet that Brittany doesn't know about Janine Murray and her baby.

I don't want to give too much away, but I have to know. "My uncle was poisoned while he was in the hospital recovering from the gunshot wound. A nurse poisoned him."

Brittany gasps. "A nurse?"

"Yes. A nurse. She was forced to. Her child was threatened."

"Oh my God. Oh my God, oh my God."

"You supplied that atropine, didn't you?"

"I… I don't know, Brock. Please, you've got to believe me."

"What do you mean you don't know?"

"The atropine. Pat *did* ask me for some. But I told him no. We had a huge argument about it."

"You didn't give it to him?"

"I didn't."

"Then why did you ask if I knew about the atropine?"

Brittany grips the sides of her head. "Oh God. Oh God oh God."

"Who, Brittany?" I take a step forward. "Who the fuck are you protecting?"

She steps back. "I can't. You won't understand."

She's got that right. I don't understand any of this. But I will play my part, and I will play it well. "Try me. Maybe I will understand. After all, you're talking to a man who will do anything to protect the people he loves."

"My father and I . . . All we have is each other. He worked so hard to make a life for us after Mom died."

"Are you telling me—"

"I'm telling you that I would do anything for him."

"Is he the person you're protecting?" I say through gritted teeth.

"I can't . . ."

"Tell me, Brittany. What the fuck is your father up to?"

"Just his veterinary practice. And his guard-dog business here in Wyoming."

"What might we find on our leased land? That tract of land that is adjacent to your property?"

Brittany shakes her head, chokes back a sob. "I don't know. I'm sorry. I don't know what you're talking about."

"You didn't know that your father leases property from the Steel family?"

"No, I swear, Brock. I didn't know."

I look over my shoulder. My father and Doc Sheraton are still in the house. Good.

Barking comes from the kennels. Low mostly, but sometimes shrill.

The sound makes my ears ache.

"Brittany, has your father made any large purchases lately?"

"What do you mean?"

"Cars? Jewelry? Anything like that?"

She scrunches her forehead. "I don't know. Nothing that I've noticed."

"How about expensive dinners?"

"I cook for my father. I always have."

She doesn't know. And all of this shit started about ten years ago, when my father and Uncle Bryce did not offer Doc Sheraton a full-time job with our ranch.

Right around the same time Pat Lamone and Brittany Sheraton formed their own grudges against our family.

That feeling again...

That shadow of impending doom...

If only...

"Brittany, does your father own a gun?"

She sniffs. "Yes. A couple of shotguns and a pistol."

"What kind of pistol?"

"I don't know. I don't know anything about guns. I hate them."

Surely Doc Sheraton wouldn't be stupid enough to shoot my uncle with his own gun. That would be suicide. So really, any guns he owns that Brittany would know about have no bearing on the situation.

"Is he a good shot?" I ask.

"What do you mean?"

"Does he ever go to the shooting range? With his pistol?"

"No. But he does have his own shooting range here. On the property."

"Does he practice a lot?"

She chews on her lip again.

"Brittany?"

"Every day," she says. "He practices every day."

Damn.

I'll never know for sure. Not unless we can link the bullet to Doc Sheraton somehow.

This is madness. The small-town vet? Who I always thought was such a stand-up guy?

But then . . . Would a stand-up guy raise a daughter who's capable of injecting two girls with veterinary drugs just to please her man?

No.

No, he would not.

All this time, when we found out atropine had veterinary use, we thought Brittany was the person behind it.

Was it Doc all along?

Doc . . . who's probably supplying guard dogs to whoever is . . .

No.

Just no.

He's a veterinarian. He cares.

Or does he? Shock training animals is common, so Doc isn't alone there. Still, how could someone who loves animals harm them in such a physical way?

What is the real reason my father denied Doc Sheraton the position on our ranch?

I know one thing about my family—we like to take care of our own. We love Snow Creek, and we do a lot for our small town.

My father wouldn't have denied Doc Sheraton the job unless he had a good reason.

And here we are. On Doc's land, pretending to do business with a man who clearly is *not* a friend.

"Brock?"

"What?"

Brittany crosses her arms. "Nothing. I mean, you just haven't said anything for a while."

"I'm processing."

"That's what I was afraid of."

"What is going on?" I ask her.

"Please." She gulps. "You have to protect my father."

"From what? Why would you even say that?"

"He's a good man, Brock. I swear to you he's a good man."

I let out a scoffing laugh. "I'm supposed to take your word for that? The word of a woman who injected drugs into two high school girls?"

"I was a high school girl myself then. You can't hold me accountable for everything I did back then. Isn't there anything *you* did in high school that you're ashamed of?"

"No."

It's a lie, of course. Everyone does stupid shit in high school. But I did draw the line at drugging people.

"What if one of them had an allergic reaction to the drugs?"

"They didn't."

"No, they didn't, thank God. What if they had? Did you do your"—air quote—"*research* on that possibility?"

"Part of me wishes..." Brittany uncrosses her arms and fidgets with her fingers.

"What?"

"To be honest? Part of me wishes Pat had never come back to town. Everything's going to hell now."

"I think, Brittany, that everything has been going to hell for the past ten years."

# CHAPTER NINE

## Rory

"I guess I should call Brock," I say to my brother.

"Sure. Where is he, anyway?"

"I told you. He and his dad went to Wyoming for a few days to check out some of the Steel property there."

"They own Wyoming too?"

"Jesse, for God's sake. They don't own Wyoming. They don't own Colorado."

"But they own Snow Creek."

I open my mouth to refute his words, but I don't. I'm not even sure if they're correct. Plus, I can't tell him what Callie and Donny uncovered.

"That's just a rumor," I say. "I'm going to call him and let him know I'm going on the tour with you guys. I also want to find out how long he and his father will be gone."

"All right." Jesse rises. "I'm going to head in."

I nod and give Brock a call. The phone rings several times before he finally answers.

"Hey," he says, sounding a little out of breath.

"Are you all right?" I ask.

"Yeah, fine. How's your dad?"

"Everything looks good. What are you up to?"

He pauses a moment. "Just hanging out with Doc Sheraton on his property."

His voice sounds a little . . . off.

"Are you sure everything's okay?"

"Yeah, we're good. Just in the middle of stuff. Did you need something, sweetheart?"

I warm at his endearment. He sounded so weird, I was afraid he wasn't happy to hear from me. But the "sweetheart" negates that.

"Yeah, I just wanted to let you know I've decided to go on that mini tour with Jesse and the band. It starts this weekend."

"That's tomorrow," he says.

I blink. "You're right. That *is* tomorrow. My days have kind of blended into one another."

"Believe me, I get what you're saying." He pauses for a few seconds. "I support you, of course, if you want to go. But are you sure you want to be away from your dad?"

"It's just a short tour of some venues in Grand Junction and outside Salt Lake City," I say. "We won't be that far away. Besides, Jesse has already committed, and the band needs him. And I . . . Well, I need to focus on something, Brock. Something other than my problems."

"I hear that one. So how long will you be, then? I thought it was just a weekend gig."

"So did I. Turns out it's longer, but less than a week."

"I'll be back in a day or two."

"I know. I'll miss you."

"I'll miss you too. Send me the itinerary, and maybe I can come to one of the shows."

"I would love that," I gush. "I'll have Jesse send it to me, and I'll forward it to you."

"Sounds good. I have to go, Rory. I'm kind of in the middle of something."

"I understand. I love you, Brock."

"I love you too, sweetheart. Always."

The call ends.

Okay.

I've made a commitment. I head back into the house and find Jesse on the phone in the kitchen. He gestures for me to be quiet.

"Sounds good. Thanks, guys. Rory and I both appreciate this." He ends the call.

"What was that?" I ask.

"It was a quick FaceTime chat with the band. They're all happy you're going to join us, and they're good with the room situation. You and I will share, and the three of them will share."

"Okay, good. I don't want the band to go to any more expense on my account. This is supposed to be a moneymaking deal after all, right?"

"God, I hope so." Jesse runs his fingers through his unruly dark hair. "We could all use some. But honestly, Ror, we're usually lucky to break even on these little gigs. The real value is in someone hearing us. Someone important."

"Which one is the venue where agents hang out?"

"The two outside Salt Lake City."

I raise my eyebrows.

"I know. Salt Lake. Weird. But it's true. I checked it all out."

"Okay. I will be at my best."

"You're a selling point for us, Rory. I'm really glad you're going. So is the rest of the band."

"I am too, Jesse. It'll be good to just make music for a week. To try not to think about . . . other things."

"I know. What did you and Callie end up doing with those photos?"

"We burned them."

He nods. "Let's hope that those were all Pat had."

"Yeah," I say. "Let's hope."

"You'd better get packed up. Take the sexiest clothes you've got." He shakes his head. "God, that feels like fifty shades of wrong to me, telling my sister to look sexy."

"Don't worry. I know the drill. Besides, you and the band need to look pretty hot too. How we look is nearly as important as how we sound."

"True enough." Jesse heads to his room.

I head to mine then and begin to pack.

Thigh-high boots studded with silver. Lacy skintight tank tops that show a lot of cleavage. Black leather pants and black jeans. And then my black and silver jewelry that I only wear when I'm performing with Jesse. I'm pawing through my closet when my fingers brush across soft satin.

I sigh.

One of my old cocktail dresses that I wore on auditions in New York. Several more hang in the back of my closet. Funny. I didn't even think about them when Brock broached the idea of a recital. I told him I would need a dress. In truth? I have several. Of course they're probably all out-of-date. I don't exactly keep up with runway fashion.

I pull out the dress. It's dark-red satin with a fitted bodice. Mom and Dad spent a mint on these dresses. Because of my large chest, I had to have all my dresses professionally tailored. Mom and Dad never complained about the expense. In fact, they gladly paid it, even though I came home from New York in tears each time.

This dress is gorgeous, as are the others. I close my eyes and try to recapture the feelings I used to have when I wore this dress. Being onstage, singing my heart out, knowing I looked beautiful in my perfectly fitted gown . . .

I open my eyes quickly.

This isn't me. Not anymore. I won't wear this or any of these other dresses when I sing at the recital Brock and I are planning.

I'll wear . . .

Well, I don't know what I'll wear—only that it won't be an old audition outfit. Maybe all those expensive dresses were bad luck. Bad juju.

I chuckle out loud. Right. A dress has bad luck. I don't believe it, and I never did. I just wasn't good enough.

Not good enough.

And that's okay.

I got over my failed opera career long ago.

I'm no longer an operatic mezzo.

But what am I, exactly? A teacher, for sure, but my first love is and always will be singing. I need to sing.

But if I'm not an opera singer, what am I?

I'm not a rocker, even though I enjoy my time with the band.

I fall somewhere in between.

I won't wear a cocktail dress for this recital. I won't be in spiky thigh-high boots either.

I'll have to find my own style. Maybe black leggings and a tunic. Or jeans and a camisole.

Maybe this recital will help me figure out exactly who I am now as a performer.

Because here's the truth—I don't want to be just a teacher anymore. I love teaching, and I'm good at it. I'll continue doing it, but I need to do something else. Something for *me*.

Something that doesn't just pay the bills, but something

that makes me—at the very core of my being—happy.

That's performing.

Going on this tour with Jesse and the band is just what I need. Maybe it's a good thing that Brock and I are separated for a few days.

Everything happened between us so quickly. It was like a lightning flash or a volcano erupting.

I love him. I'm sure of that, but how much of our need for each other is brought about by the situations we both find ourselves in?

Separation will be good.

We'll be able to see what's truly important between us.

I pack my bag quickly, and then I realize I'm going to have to call Dave again to have him watch the dogs.

Until—

Callie comes strolling into the room. "Hey."

I look up. "Callie, what are you doing here?"

"Donny and I decided to come home."

"I know that."

"I mean, we're going to stay here. Take care of the house while Mom is gone. Make sure the dogs are taken care of."

"You're a lifesaver." I give my sister a quick hug. "I was just about to call Dave."

"Why?"

"I decided to go on tour with Jesse and the band. I'll be gone for almost a week."

Callie raises her eyebrows. "Rory? Are you okay?"

"Yeah."

She clears her throat. "I mean... You and Brock..."

"Brock and I are fine. He's going to be in Wyoming for a few days with his dad, as you probably know, and I... Well, I just want to focus on something else for a few days. Get onstage and leave my troubles behind."

"I hear that one."

"You and Donny should come to one of our performances."

"I'd love it. Send us the schedule."

"Will do. I'm sending it to Brock too. I'm hoping he'll be able to make one of the shows once he and Joe are done."

"Maybe Donny and I can come to the same one."

"That would be a lot of fun."

"Man, I wish I could escape with you."

"Maybe you can."

"Are you kidding me? I actually have a workload now, since Donny's the only city attorney. I love the work, and I don't know what Donny's going to do when I start law school on the first of the year."

"He'll probably hire another city attorney."

"Except he doesn't want to. He wants to save that position for me."

"Is that what *you* want?"

"Truthfully?" Callie shrugs. "I don't know. I think I might want to hang out a shingle and start my own practice."

"You have to do what *you* want, Callie. There are plenty of other lawyers Donny can hire to work for the city."

"I know, but I feel bad. This isn't the life Donny envisioned for himself. He was on a partnership track in downtown Denver, and he came back here at his mother's request."

"Well, then... Maybe the two of you can open a firm."

"In Snow Creek? We wouldn't have enough business."

"Not in Snow Creek, Callie. In Grand Junction maybe. Or even in Denver."

"Except... Donny won't. You know how close he and Jade are. He'll stay here, as the Snow Creek city attorney. He'll do it for his mother because he promised her."

"Even if it doesn't make him happy?"

"It makes him happy to make her happy." Callie sighs. "But he's not challenged, Rory. He tells me all the time. And then he wants me to come work with him as the assistant city attorney, and then I say to him, 'Why? So we can *both* be bored?'"

"What does he say to that?"

"Usually nothing. And then he finally says that all he wants is the best for both of us."

"I think you're marrying a mama's boy, Cal."

Callie chuckles. "I always knew that."

"Tell him to hire someone," I say. "Be honest with him and tell him that you don't want to be a city attorney."

"I will. It's just that with everything else going on, I don't want to throw a wrench into his plans right now."

"I understand."

"So what do you think… You said you might be moving in with Brock?"

"Yeah, I will be. Sometime after the tour, probably. Brock may want to wait until more of his family issues are resolved."

"I doubt that."

"I just don't know. We haven't had a moment in the past couple of days to sit and talk together."

Callie nods. "I know. Donny and I feel the same way. At least we work together and can talk at lunch."

"I'm glad you haven't quite finished moving in with him. I'm glad you'll be staying here while Mom is gone."

"Me too. It was actually Donny's idea. He knew it would be a load off Mom's mind."

"You know?" I say. "The Steel boys are just damned good men."

Callie smiles. "They are."

# CHAPTER TEN

**Brock**

Brittany shoves her hands into the pockets of her jeans. "I shouldn't have told you about the atropine."

"You haven't told me anything about the atropine."

"Haven't I?" She shakes her head. "I swear I'm keeping so many secrets that I feel like I'm ready to burst."

"I'm happy to unburden you."

"God, I wish you could. But I'm as guilty as anyone else."

I step forward. "Why do you speak of guilt?"

"You know why, Brock."

"Let me be honest with you, Brittany. I totally understand that you feel some loyalty to your father. He's your father, after all. But why Pat Lamone?"

"You'll think it's stupid."

She's no doubt right. "Try me."

"Back in high school, I had a major crush on him. So I . . ."

"So you did his bidding."

"But you have to understand, Rory and Callie—"

I hold up a hand. "If I were you, I'd stop right there."

"Please just listen to me. Rory and Callie drugged Pat with something. Rory got him to admit that he spiked the punch that night at the bonfire. They were doing it all to get the family's reward."

"I already know all about that."

Her eyes widen. "So you know the Pike sisters aren't innocent in this matter."

"To the contrary, the Pike sisters were trying to *help* my family. They wanted to find out who poisoned Diana."

"They wanted your reward," Brittany says dryly.

"Maybe. Is there anything wrong with that?"

"Not when you're a gold digger."

Rage curls onto the back of my neck, but I'm determined to stay calm. "The Pikes are hardly gold diggers. They haven't taken any of the help our family has offered them since the fire."

"That's because they started that damned fire themselves."

Again the rage. "They did *not*."

"What if I gave you proof?"

"Then I would tell you your proof is manufactured."

"Pat—"

I hold my hand up to quiet her. "Pat cannot be trusted. If he has given you any proof, it's definitely manufactured. Let's be honest about Pat. He had a major crush on Rory in high school. That's common knowledge. So when Rory gave him the chance to"—I swallow back acid—"*be* with her, he jumped at it. So yes, Rory used him to get him to confess. But he was going to use her to get what he wanted as well."

Brittany says nothing, simply purses her lips into a line.

"So whatever"—air quote—"*proof* Pat has given you is fake."

"To be honest . . ."

"Yes?"

"Pat didn't give me any proof. He only told me that he *has* proof."

"Seriously?" I scoff. "You can't possibly be that naïve, Brittany."

"I'm not. Not usually. But Pat . . ."

"Old crushes die hard, I guess."

"They do. He's so good-looking. So much better than I could ever get."

Brittany is not unattractive. But she's no Rory Pike.

"He's a bastard, Brittany."

Brittany drops her gaze to the ground. "I know. But I'm in too deep now."

"My family can help you." Damn. I hate lying. Even to Brittany Sheraton.

"Your family would never help me. You didn't help my father when he needed it."

Right. As I suspected, this goes back to Uncle Bryce and Dad not offering Doc Sheraton the position he wanted with our family.

And I need to find out why.

"My father is a good man," I say, "and he had his reasons for what he did at the time. Just like I have my reasons for everything I do. Do you, Brittany? Do you have a good reason for everything you've done?"

She doesn't answer at first.

And just when I think she's not going to—

"I'm not a bad person, Brock."

"Aren't you?"

"I don't like everything we've done."

"Then undo it," I say. "Because you may feel like you're a good person in your heart, but that's not what you are in the eyes of others. In the eyes of others, you are your actions, not your thoughts."

"He's my father. I love him."

"I understand. But Brittany, what the hell has he gotten into?"

She opens her mouth when my phone buzzes—

Damn it! Of all the bad timing in the fucking free world.

It's Dad.

"Yeah?" I say into the phone a little more harshly than I mean to.

"Brock, come on back to the house now. Doc and I are working up a contract."

"But I—"

"Now," Dad says. "This is important."

Is it as important as the information I'm about to get out of Brittany? Of course I can't say this right in front of her.

"Brittany and I will be there in a moment," I say.

"Leave Brittany there," Dad says.

"But I—"

"Do as I say." Dad ends the call.

Okay. How am I supposed to tell Brittany I have to go back to the house without her? She'll come along. After all, it's her house.

I'm pretty good on my feet, but I'm stumped.

"I have to go," I say, "but this conversation isn't over."

"I've said all I can say."

"I don't believe that for a minute."

"It's not for you to believe or not. I know very little. But I do know . . ."

"You do know that whatever your dad is involved in is not good."

She doesn't reply.

I have my answer.

"Stay here," I say.

"Why?"

"Trust me."

I turn and walk back toward the house.

"Brock!"

I don't turn back.

"Brock, what is going on?"

"Damn." This time I turn around. "Please. For your own safety, do *not* follow me."

Once I reach the house, I don't bother knocking. I walk in through the back door. No dogs stop me.

"Dad?"

"In the study, Brock."

Study? I don't know where the study is. I walk through the short hallway and look in the first room. Clearly Brittany's bedroom.

The second room, and—

I drop my jaw, but I manage to hold back a gasp.

My father . . .

"What the hell are you doing, Dad?"

# CHAPTER ELEVEN

### Rory

Callie and I fix a late dinner—rather, I fix it because Callie is a menace in the kitchen—for the three of us. Mom always keeps a stocked pantry and refrigerator. The only difference is that it's stocked with less expensive foods than it normally is because we don't have much money coming in right now.

So ground chicken it is, fashioned into burgers, on slices of white bread with cheddar cheese, lettuce, and tomato. And potatoes—boiled, cut into cubes, and mixed with some chopped onion, mayonnaise, and chopped pickle. Poor man's potato salad.

I call Jesse in for dinner as Callie sets the table.

"Look at the two of you," Jesse says, smiling. "Feminists that you are."

"Are you kidding me?" I give him a good glare. "You're a worse cook than Callie. I'm glad to cook if it means we don't have to eat your slop."

"But you, Callie, lawyer-to-be, setting the table."

"Shut your trap," Callie says dryly. "You'll be cleaning up."

Jesse chuckles as he sits down. "Where's the ketchup?"

"In the fridge," I say. "Get it yourself."

My brother rises, still chuckling, and retrieves the ketchup.

"Ketchup on chicken burgers is disgusting anyway," Callie says.

"What do you suggest?" he asks.

"Mayonnaise, of course. With a little cumin added. Donny's aunt clued me in, and it's fabulous."

"That sounds amazing," I say. "I'll whip up a batch." I grab the mayo from the fridge, squirt some into a bowl, add a little cumin from Mom's spice rack, and mix it together. I set it on the table. "Here you go."

"Thanks," Jesse says, "but I'll take the ketchup."

I roll my eyes. "This is what I'm going to be putting up with for the next week?"

"Actually, on tour we can't afford ketchup." Jesse takes a bite of his burger.

I laugh. "Just as well. Ketchup, as a condiment, is overrated."

"Blasphemy," Jesse says through his second bite of burger.

"If Mom were here, she'd be all over you for talking with your mouth full," Callie says.

"Well, Mom's not here."

We chat about mundane things after that. We leave the elephant in the room alone. Until we hear otherwise, we've decided to assume Dad is okay. After dinner, we'll check in with him and Mom.

And you know what? Dinner is delicious.

Which is strange, since I haven't been able to eat or taste anything for a while.

But my father is healing well. And I'm going on a mini tour with Jesse and the band. Strange how that has made me happy.

Plus, I have Brock. I've found the love of my life, and he loves me back.

For some reason, all those things together make chicken burgers on white bread taste like a feast fit for royalty.

After dinner, Jesse cleans up, but only after trying to escape the kitchen and getting a stink eye from Callie.

Callie and I retire to the deck with some water, and we watch the dogs play.

"So when does Donny get here?" I ask.

"He's having dinner with his parents. He'll be over when he's done."

"How come you aren't having dinner with them?"

"Honestly?" She shrugs. "I begged to be let off. I played the *I'm worried about my father* card. I love Talon and Jade, but I didn't want to be peppered with questions about Dad."

I nod. "I get it."

"Besides, I figured they'd probably be talking about the Steel family troubles, and I'm interested, of course, but I don't want to be concerning myself with anything other than Dad right now."

"Yeah. I hear you. Brock is in Wyoming, finding out God knows what, and I haven't been able to bring myself to text him and check in. I care. I truly do, but I just . . ."

"You just want a break," Callie says. "It's okay to feel that way, Ror."

"Still, I feel pretty guilty about it."

"So do I, but just keep telling yourself that it's okay to need a break from all of it. Especially after what happened with Dad."

Jesse joins us then. "The kitchen is spotless, my ladies."

"You want some water?" Callie asks.

Jesse holds up a Fat Tire. "No thanks."

Callie rises. "You know what? I think I'll have a beer as well."

"Yeah, get me one." I absently glance at my abdomen. I'm

not pregnant, so I don't need to worry about drinking anymore. And a beer sounds pretty good.

Callie returns with two bottles, already opened. I take a sip of the sweet ale.

"Hello," I say to the bottle. "It's been a while."

Callie laughs. "Rory, you're such a card."

"What do you mean it's been a while?" Jesse asks.

"Nothing," I say.

He takes a pull from his beer. "We leave early tomorrow. We want to be on the road by eight."

"By eight? Why? We're going to Grand Junction. It's half an hour away."

"Actually . . . Our first gig is in Utah. We end the tour in Grand Junction."

"Thanks for telling me." I roll my eyes and take another sip of beer.

"Hey, you just decided to go two hours ago. After telling me you were in and then out and then in and then out and then in again. Don't even think about trying to weasel out again."

"I'm not weaseling out."

Donny's voice calls from the kitchen. "Callie?"

"We're out here on the deck," Callie replies.

Donny joins and eyes the beers. "That looks good."

"Sure you don't want me to mix you a margarita?" Jesse scowls.

Callie rises. "Oh, for God's sake. Will the two of you just get over yourselves?"

"I agree," I say. "This high school rivalry of yours is what, fifteen years old now?"

"Fourteen," Jesse says.

"Whatever," Callie says. "Jesse, Donny is my husband-to-be. And Donny? Jesse is my brother. So the two of you are going to have to get along for my sake. Because you both love me deeply and without question."

Neither of them responds.

This time I rise. "Are you both freaking kidding me? For God's sake, shake hands."

Neither of them move.

"Get off your ass, Jesse," Callie says. "Stand up and shake hands with my fiancé. And you"—she turns to Donny—"shake hands with my brother. Get over yourselves, because you're going to be family."

Jesse stands reluctantly. He takes a step toward Donny. Donny takes a step toward him. They're still ten feet away from each other.

I roll my eyes. "You guys are acting like a couple of chicks."

They both raise their eyebrows at me.

"Yeah, I'm serious. This is what teenage girls do. They hold grudges. Guys—especially adult guys—don't do that. They quarrel, and then they're drinking buddies the next day. So get over yourselves and act your age."

That gets them. They shake hands.

"Damn, Rory," Callie says. "You should've said that years ago."

"Listen." Jesse withdraws his hand. "It's no secret that I was angry when you got MVP senior year."

"It was a toss-up," Donny says. "I'm not sure I could've made the decision between the two of us myself."

"You got it because of your name, Steel."

"Maybe I did," Donny says. "I honestly don't know, Pike."

It is possible. Callie and I know that now. The rumors that the Steels own Snow Creek? They may very well be true, but I believe that Donny did not know that at the time. Nor Brock. Nor any of the Steel kids. I can't say this, however, because Jesse doesn't know about any of that yet.

"Yeah, well, it pissed me off," Jesse says.

"I don't blame you." Donny rubs his temple. "I'd feel the same way, no doubt."

"See?" Callie says. "The two of you *can* get along."

"I doubt we'll be best buds," Jesse says.

"Probably not," Donny agrees.

"You don't have to be," I say. "You just need to get along for Callie's sake. And you know what? Once you truly let the stupid high school crap go, you may end up finding you have more in common than not."

"A lawyer and a rocker?" Jesse says. "I doubt it."

"Two men who love Callie," I counter.

They seem to soften at my words. Will it last? Who knows?

"I'll let it go if you will, Pike," Donny says.

"All right, Steel."

"And your names are Jesse and Donny," Callie says. "This Pike and Steel shit has to stop. Besides, my name will be Steel soon."

"Now that's just crap," Donny says. "Guys call each other by their last names all the time."

"Not guys who are related."

Donny rolls his eyes. "Fine. *Jesse*."

"*Don*," Jesse replies.

"That's better." Callie takes a seat. "Now, which one of you men is going to get me another beer?"

# CHAPTER TWELVE

### Brock

"Dad," I say again, forcing my voice not to shake, "what the hell are you doing?"

My father stands over Doc Sheraton, who's seated behind his desk. He holds a gun to the back of Doc's head.

"Brock?" Doc Sheraton's voice cracks. "Would you please tell your father to put his gun down?"

"Not a chance," my father says through gritted teeth. "Brock? Start searching this office."

"Dad . . ."

"I had no choice, son. Now do as I say."

"You realize this is trespassing," I say.

"Are you going to call a cop?" Dad asks.

Oh my God. How am I in this situation? And what the hell has happened to my father?

"I'm going to tell you a story," Dad says. "And after I'm done, you will do as I ask, and you will search this office."

"I'm listening."

"Doc Sheraton and I were discussing the purchase of some guard dogs," Dad begins. "We were having a nice conversation, drinking Brittany's delicious lemonade, when Doc here happened to mention his biggest client."

"And . . ." I say.

"A corporate client, by the name of the Fleming Corporation."

My blood runs cold. I've heard that name before.

"Perhaps Doc had no way of knowing," Dad continues, "that our family has prior history with the Fleming Corporation."

"We do?"

"We're in no way involved with the company, of course, but the people behind Fleming have a huge history with our family. With Talon in particular. And probably with Dale and Donny as well."

My blood no longer runs cold. It has frozen into icicles in my veins.

Human trafficking. Uncle Talon. Dale and Donny.

"I'm not involved in anything untoward," Doc Sheraton says, his voice cracking again.

"I want to believe you, Mark. I do. But first, you're going to have to do as I say and pull up all the records on that computer. Otherwise, I *will* pull this trigger."

Dad's voice is low and menacing. My father's not a killer, but the ice in his voice? If I were on the other side of that gun, I would believe him.

"Joe," Doc Sheraton says.

"Be quiet. Just shut the fuck up, Doc. Do as I say, and no one will get hurt."

I stand, frozen.

Dad does not take his eyes off the nose of his gun pointed at Doc's head. He does not look at me. "Brock, begin looking. Anything out of the ordinary, take note."

Talk about being stuck between a rock and a hard place. I'm not a criminal. I don't believe in trespassing. On the other hand, if Doc is involved with the Fleming Corporation, whoever they may be at this point, we need to know.

*Don't turn your back on him.*

My mother's words. The conversation floats back into my head, haunting me.

*"I promise you that your father is the same man he always was. He's a good strong man, the love of my life, and he was a good father to you."*

*"I never said he wasn't."*

*"No, you haven't said that, but he made a choice. A choice he has to live with now. Don't turn your back on him."*

*"I won't."*

*"Good. Because there may come a time, before this is all over, that you want to. And I'm telling you now, Brock. If you do that, it will kill him."*

Did my mother know this was coming?

My father has always been a hothead. But never in my short life have I witnessed him point a gun at another human being.

So if he's doing this? He's been driven to it.

In the end, I trust this man. I trust him with my life. With the life of everyone I love.

I nod, and then I realize my father can't see me. "All right, Dad. If you think this is the right thing to do."

"I do, Brock. Thank you for trusting me."

My father's voice doesn't shake a bit. It's like he's turned to frost.

That itself scares me as much as the sight of him pointing a gun at another human being.

"Start typing, Doc."

Doc's hands are shaking. "I'm trying."

"Try harder," Dad says through clenched teeth.

I begin to look around the office. What am I looking for? I have no idea.

I'm hyperaware of my own piece strapped to my ankle. *Please,* I beg silently, *please, Dad, don't make me pull my gun out.*

I will if I have to. If somehow Doc overpowers my father, I will defend him.

I know this in the depths of my being. But I don't want to be that person. I don't want to be the person who holds a gun on someone else.

A file cabinet stands against the adjacent wall. I start there. I pull open the top drawer . . .

"It's locked," I say.

"Where's the key?" Dad nudges the gun into Doc's head.

Doc swallows. "Top drawer of the desk."

"Retrieve the key, Brock."

I don't want to go near that desk. It will entail going near Doc and my father with the damned gun.

My father will never hurt me, but Doc? I don't trust him. Plus, my father has a gun to his head. What better way to get my father in line?

Threaten his son.

But I don't back down. I was taught to be strong in the face of adversity, so I walk as calmly as I can behind the desk, taking care not to touch Doc or my father. I open the top drawer a few inches—any farther will disturb Doc and my father. With luck, I find a set of keys and grab it.

"Is this it?" I ask.

"Yes," Doc says, shaking.

I don't bother asking him which key is which. It's best that

I get the hell out from behind the desk. I'll try each one of them.

Finding the key to the filing cabinet is easy. It's smaller than the rest of them. I unlock the top drawer and open it.

It's full of file folders, obviously. Fleming Corporation. I don't see one that says Fleming Corporation. It's mostly household bills.

But I know better. If he is truly doing something bad, he could be hiding information anywhere. So I pull out file after file and breeze through them. Nothing so far.

Meanwhile Doc is tapping on his computer.

"I'd go faster if I were you," Dad says to him.

"Joe, I'm doing the best I can. My hands are shaking."

I close my ears to what is happening. But I remain alert. Totally alert to the gun strapped to my ankle. Because if my life—or my father's—is threatened, I will have to react quickly.

I pull out another file folder, keeping one eye on my father behind the desk. I leaf through it quickly. It's mostly public service bills, which makes sense since the file folder says *public service.*

I replace it in the file cabinet and take the next folder.

"Finally," Dad says.

I keep looking through the folders. More household expenditures.

What a waste of time.

"Brock..."

I look up at my father.

"Come here."

"What do you need?"

"Doc and I are going to go through these files on his computer," Dad says, no tremor anywhere in his voice. "I'm going to need you to hold the gun."

My heart drops to my stomach. “Dad . . .”

“Son, this is a necessary evil.”

“I’m busy,” I say.

“Brock . . .”

No. I can’t go there.

This is how it happens. You cross the line once, and then it gets easier to cross.

I can’t let that happen to me.

I can’t let that happen to my father.

He’s already crossed this line. “Dad, sit next to him and point the gun to his heart as you go through the documents. It’s more important that I stay where I am.”

My father doesn’t turn to look at me. His gaze is fixed on Doc Sheraton.

Just when I’m sure he’s not going reply at all—

“All right, Brock. We’ll do it your way. This time. Bring me a chair.”

I don’t like being involved with this at all, but I slide one of the other chairs behind the desk, and Dad sits down next to Doc Sheraton, who’s white as a ghost.

Doc Sheraton is frozen. He doesn’t move.

If it were me, I’d try to overpower Dad at this point, try to get the gun from him.

But that’s what I’ve been taught to do.

Doc Sheraton is a veterinarian. He doesn’t take lives. He saves them.

Except not always. Veterinarians put animals down all the time. Perhaps Doc has made peace with death.

God, what am I even thinking?

How have we come to this?

Doc *is* involved with something. Brittany all but admitted

it. And if that something is as heinous as I believe it may be, perhaps my father is right to aim a gun at Doc's head.

Or to his heart, as it is aimed now.

I return to my work in the file cabinet. The top drawer has proved to be fruitless. So I open the next drawer.

And right at the front of the folders is one that is marked *F Corp*.

"I should never have said what I said," Doc Sheraton says.

"But you did, Mark. You did, and now I'm pretty sure whatever you're doing is not good."

"Not good for . . ." Doc Sheraton stops.

"Not good for what?" Dad asks.

"I need to stop talking. You've got my nerves on edge."

"Indeed I do. But you're going to tell us everything you know eventually. You do know that, right?"

"I don't care about my own life," Doc says. "I haven't cared about it since Sheila died."

He must be bluffing. Everyone has a survival instinct. I grab the folder marked *F Corp* and run my fingers over the manila covering.

Inside may be the secrets we're looking for.

And part of me? Part of me does *not* want to open this file folder.

"Those," Dad says. "Those documents, Doc. Open them."

Doc's hands shake.

And then—

"Daddy, what are you doing in—" Brittany gasps. "Oh my God!"

# CHAPTER THIRTEEN

**Rory**

Donny returns to the deck with another round of Fat Tires, but Jesse shakes his head and excuses himself. With him gone, the tension decreases instantaneously.

"Sorry," I say. "Our brother can be rude as shit."

"Yeah," Donny says. "But he has reason to be upset."

"He *had* reason to be upset," Callie says. "It's been fourteen years."

"I know, but if what we're finding out about my family is true..." Donny shakes his head. "I was good. I was a damned good football player that year, but so was your brother. I wasn't lying when I told him I'm not sure I could've chosen between us either. And now? I may well have gotten it because of my name."

"Whatever the circumstances are," I say, "it's been over a decade. It's time for my brother to get over it. And for you as well."

Donny nods. "I want to be a member of your family. I'm *going* to be a member of your family, and I don't want any bad blood."

"If there's time, I'll try to work on Jesse a little more while we're gone," I say. "He'll see reason."

"He has to," Callie says. "You're also all but married to a Steel as well."

My cheeks warm. "I think that's putting the cart before the horse."

Donny smiles. "Under any other circumstances, I'd say you're right. But I've never seen Brock the way I've seen him since he's been with you. He's a different person. It's like he's allowed his emotions to come to the surface for the first time in his life."

My neck and the tops of my breasts join my cheeks in the warmth. "You think so?"

"I know so. Remember who you're talking to. I taught Brock everything he knows about women. The one thing that set him apart from Dave and me was that he truly knew how to suppress emotion. He never let it get involved. It was all physical for him. Until you."

"Why in the world would I be the one who reaches him?"

"The most beautiful woman in Snow Creek?" Callie says, her eyes rolling. "Gee, I have no idea."

"Second-most beautiful." Donny brings Callie's hand to his lips and kisses it.

Callie blushes.

I'm so happy for my sister. She deserves everything in the world, and she seems to have found it with Donny Steel. All those years when she thought herself ugly just because of some stupid comment Pat Lamone had made a million years ago.

I'm almost angrier about that than anything else he's done to us. How dare he put those thoughts into my sister's head? Callie is much more self-assured now.

"I'm going to check in with Brock." I rise. "So please excuse me. Then I should get to bed, since we're apparently leaving early in the morning."

"Good night, Ror," Callie says.

I walk into the kitchen, throw my beer bottles into the recycling bin, grab myself a glass of water, and then stride to my bedroom. I flop down on the bed and whip out my phone.

Nothing from Brock yet.

In fact, I haven't heard from him in a while. That's a bit strange. But he and his father are probably busy.

I text him quickly.

*Hey you. Turns out I'm leaving early in the morning to go to Utah. How's everything going in Wyoming? Love you.*

I close my eyes, stretch my arms over my head, and wait for him to reply.

# CHAPTER FOURTEEN

### Brock

"Brittany, leave," I say as calmly as I can.

Dad is still cold as ice. He hasn't moved the gun. Nothing fazes him.

And that scares me more than almost anything else.

"Leave," I say again.

"Daddy?" Brittany says through trembling lips.

Doc says nothing.

"Why are you doing this? Please don't hurt him."

"Go," I say. Then I turn to my father. "Dad?"

"Leave, Brittany." From Dad this time.

"Please don't hurt my father."

"No one will get hurt as long as everyone does as they're told," Dad says. "And that means you leave this room. Now."

Brittany glances at her father. Opens her mouth. Closes it. Makes a sobbing sound, and then leaves, closing the door behind her.

"Dad," I say. "I need to go after her. She's going to call the police."

Dad nods. "Go."

I head out the door, closing it behind me as well. Brittany stands in the hallway, holding her phone. I run toward her and smack it out of her hand. It clatters onto the hardwood floor.

"Don't," I say.

"Are you kidding me, Brock? Your father is holding a gun."

"For good reason," I say.

"What the hell kind of a good reason is there ever to hold a gun to another person's head?"

"Brittany, your father's in with something nefarious. And if you know anything about it, you need to tell me now."

"I need to tell the police."

"Listen, if your dad is doing what I think he is, you don't want to call the police. Sure, they can arrest my dad and haul him in for assault with a deadly weapon, but they're going to get your dad on something a lot worse."

"What could be worse?" Brittany asks, again her lips trembling.

"Homicide. Human trafficking. Child molestation."

Brittany's hand goes to her mouth. "My father would never."

"I hope you're right. For his sake. And yours."

"*I* did it," Brittany says. "I did it. I stole the tranquilizers and the syringes from my father's clinic, and I injected Callie and Rory. It was me. And I'm sorry."

"We've gone way beyond that," I say.

"The atropine. My dad, he asked me to get it out of the cabinet for him."

"You said Pat asked you for some."

"He did, but I refused. When my dad asked, of course I got it. He uses it all the time."

"Did he tell you what it was for?"

"Why would he? He just asked me to get it."

"If my suspicions are correct, it was used to poison my uncle. But that's not even the worst part."

"You said something about a baby."

"The atropine was left for the nurse in her baby's diaper."

Brittany falls to the floor. I'm still holding her phone. I help her up, walk her to the living room, and set her on the couch.

I have no love for Brittany Sheraton. She and Pat Lamone have made Rory's and Callie's lives hell. But at this point, I believe her. I believe she trusted Pat, and I believe she trusts her father.

"If you know anything more," I say, "now is the time to tell me."

"Pat and I sent the email."

"I figured as much. Does your father know that you sent it through his account?"

She shakes her head. "I deleted it as soon as I sent it."

"And the phone call to Rory?"

"That wasn't me."

"Was it Pat?"

"I honestly don't know, Brock."

I sigh. Now what? Truth be told, I'm happy as hell to be out of that study. If I had been forced to grab my gun . . .

It weighs heavy on my ankle.

I may be forced to use it.

This is never what I wanted.

How can I be worthy of Rory Pike if this is what I've come to?

All because of my damned family. Because of lies they told. Because of truths they withheld.

And my father?

Everything I knew about him to be true is now in question.

"Who shot my uncle, Brittany?"

"How would I know that?"

"Whoever shot him also tried to poison him in the hospital. We already know that your father asked you to get atropine from his clinic. Which means . . ."

She shakes her head vehemently. "No. My father is not a killer. He would never."

She seems sure.

Except she's no paragon of virtue herself.

The apple may not have fallen quite as far from the tree, but it has definitely fallen. Brittany Sheraton has already shown she's willing to cross a line.

"Seriously, Brittany. It's time to tell me everything you know. I can only help you if you tell me."

"You're not going to help me. You're in love with Rory."

"I am. And I hate what you've done to her. What you're still doing to her. But right now, I need to know everything you know. And if you tell me, and it helps my family, I can and I will protect you."

"I'm not a bad person." She swallows.

"In your heart you may not be. But I think we've already had this conversation."

She nods. "My dad started the guard-dog business about ten years ago. We needed the extra income, so he bought the property here in Wyoming."

"And exactly how did he buy property in Wyoming when he needed income? That doesn't make sense. How did he pay for the property?"

"I don't know. I was a kid then, Brock."

"Surely he got the money from somewhere."

"I don't know."

"That's about the time when my family took all our veterinary care in-house."

"Is it?"

"Yes. Why else would your father need money?"

"I was just a kid. So were you. How do you even know all of this?"

"I'm the one asking the questions," I tell her. "You were a kid. I'll accept that. Do you remember anything strange at that time?"

"Your father . . ."

"What about my father?"

"I remember one time my dad was in a really bad mood. I asked him what was wrong, and all he said was 'Jonah Steel is what's wrong.'"

"Are you sure? Those were his exact words?"

"Yeah. I remember it because it was right around the same time your family was offering a reward for information on who poisoned Diana."

Damn. "All right. This is important. Did your father say that before or after my family offered a reward?"

"I don't know, Brock. It was ten years ago."

"Yes, I know. It was ten years ago, and you were just a kid. You were crushing on Pat Lamone, though I have no idea why."

"Right. I think it was before."

"All right. Why do you think that?"

"Because . . . Pat seemed to have a grudge against the Steel family. He mentioned it to me, and this was before the bonfire. When he told me, I mentioned that my father also had a grudge against the Steel family."

Now we're getting somewhere.

My mind races. "Did Pat mention *why* he had a grudge against the Steel family?"

"Not at first. I mean, I found out later that he believes he might be a relative of yours."

"All right. Maybe that's why he held a grudge. Jealousy."

"Why shouldn't he be jealous? You guys have everything, and maybe he's entitled to some of it too."

"That's another discussion entirely," I say dryly. "For now, we're going to stay on the subject. I don't need to remind you that your father is with my father in the office, and you don't want to know how angry my father can get."

"Please don't let him hurt my father. He's all I have." She sinks her head into her hands.

I can't think about her father and my father right now. I can't think about the fact that my dad is holding another human being at gunpoint.

Instead, I need to use this time to gain as much information as I can.

"So you and Pat are really over?" I say.

"I don't know." Her voice is muffled as she's speaking into her hands. "I just don't know."

"What the hell is that supposed to mean, Brittany?"

"I just . . . My father . . ." She raises her head and meets my gaze. "What if he *is* into something bad? What if you're right? If I can't count on him *and* I don't have Pat, what do I have?"

"Look, I'm not here to help you work out your relationships. That's on you, not me. I'm here to protect my family. I'm here to find out what your father's up to and how it affects my family."

"I'm really sorry." She sniffles. "About the atropine and your uncle."

"You know what? I don't really care if you're sorry, Brittany. You need to own what you did. And so does your father."

"Well . . ." She gulps. "If I have to own what I do, then so do you. And so does *your* father."

She's not wrong. But my father knows how to take care of himself.

At least I hope he does.

I still can't get the image of him holding a gun to another man's head out of my mind. It's something I've never seen before—something I never imagined I'd see in my lifetime.

"So you really don't know what your father's been up to?"

"Why would I know anything like that?"

"You work for him, Brittany. You have access to his files."

"He doesn't show me everything."

"What do you know about the Fleming Corporation?"

She doesn't reply at first, but then— "I know we get payments from them. That's all I know."

"How often do these payments come?"

"Quarterly," she says.

"And what are their amounts?"

She swallows, and her face goes white.

"Brittany . . ."

My phone buzzes.

Jesus fuck. Really?

I pull it out of my pocket to find a text from Rory.

*Hey you. Turns out I'm leaving early in the morning to go to Utah. How's everything going in Wyoming? Love you.*

How's everything going in Wyoming? Man, is that ever a loaded question.

And now she's leaving . . . Going on tour with her brother as originally planned and then not planned and then planned again.

I need to allow her this. This brief respite. She deserves it. Hell, we all do, but at least I can give it to her.

I type a quick response.

*All is good here so far.*

God, I hate lying to her.

*You be safe on the road. I love you.*

I shove my back phone into my pocket.

Brittany is wringing her hands together, her thighs trembling.

"Can you help him? Can you help my father?"

"I don't think I can, Brittany. Not any more than you can help mine. But here's the thing… If your father is doing what I suspect he is? He's going away for a long time. The best way you can help him is to tell me what you know."

"How would that help him?"

"Maybe there are mitigating circumstances. Maybe you know something I don't. I'm sure you do, actually."

"I'll never betray my father."

"Won't you?"

"Of course not."

I pause a moment. "Would he do the same for you?"

"Of course he would. Everything he does is for me. I was left motherless as a small child. He raised me. I owe him everything."

"Which is why you've never questioned anything. Why you've never wondered where those large payments from

Fleming Corporation come from, and what they're for."

"I never said they were large . . ." she hedges.

"I can easily find that out."

"How exactly?"

"I have my ways."

I can hire the best hackers in the business and find out everything I want to know. Hell, we would've done it before now if we had thought for a second that Doc Sheraton was truly behind this.

"It would be easier, though, for you to tell me now. Easier on you *and* on your father."

"They're high. Around ten thousand dollars."

Okay, not a lot of help. Those may seem like high payments to Brittany, but I know for a fact that if Doc were truly engaging in anything related to human trafficking, the payments would be a lot higher.

"You look disappointed," she says.

"No, but I just had a thought. Fleming Corporation may pay in a different manner."

"What do you mean? Money comes to the bank."

"Money has many forms, Brittany. Does your father ever get paid in cash?"

"Well, sure. Some of the people in Snow Creek pay with cash. Some of them pay him in fresh eggs, beef. You know the drill in a small town."

"I'm not talking about his veterinary patients. I'm talking about other kinds of payments."

"You're asking about jewelry and stuff."

Give the girl a gold star. And since she knew to mention jewelry, I'm betting she knows more than she's letting on.

"Right."

"I honestly don't know."

I sigh. Okay. I've done about all I can. Either she truly doesn't know, or she's a damned good liar. I'd put money on the latter, but until I can figure out a way to get more intel out of her, I need to let her rest.

"Fine. We'll leave it at that—"

I stop talking when Doc Sheraton emerges from the hallway, my father still holding a gun to him.

# CHAPTER FIFTEEN

**Rory**

*All is good here so far.*

*You be safe on the road. I love you.*

I smile at Brock's texts, and then I reply.

*I will. Love you too.*

It's early yet, but I'm tired. I'm all packed, so it's best to just go to sleep. I'll have to get up early and shower if Jesse truly wants to be on the road by eight o'clock.

Road trip in a van with my brother and his bandmates.

Maybe I'll take my own car.

I really want to hear Brock's voice. He said everything was going okay, so maybe he'll be able to take a call.

I call him quickly, and after a few rings, I get a text from him.

*Will call you as soon as I can.*

Okay. Good enough. Maybe he's in the middle of an

important conversation. He said everything was okay, so I need to take him at his word, right? Still, I can't shake the feeling of worry that's permeating my gut.

Something's wrong.

Something's wrong, and he's not telling me.

I hover my finger over his name on my phone, ready to call him again.

But he won't answer. Already I know this.

Something is keeping him from answering me.

And deep in my gut, I know it's not good.

# CHAPTER SIXTEEN

**Brock**

"Brock," Dad says. "Brittany."

Brittany's entire body trembles, but she does not say anything.

I can't imagine my father pulling a gun on a young woman, but she's scared. For her father, of course, but also for herself.

She's twenty-seven years old, a year younger than Rory and three years older than I am. Yet still she depends on this man—her father—for so much.

"Dad..."

"Dr. Sheraton has agreed to cooperate with me," Dad says.

I nod. Although the word *agree* may be stretching it.

"I don't want my daughter involved in this," Doc says.

Dad gestures to Brittany with his free arm. "She's already involved."

"Everything, everything is my fault." Doc shakes his head. "Please. Let her go."

"You do know that your daughter poisoned two high school students ten years ago," I say.

"She was a kid then."

"So you *are* aware," I say. "Does it really matter that she was a kid? She's hardly innocent."

Brittany widens her eyes and looks at me. "Brock, please."

"I told you I would protect you if you cooperated, Brittany.

But if your father's going to cooperate, I no longer need you."

"No," Doc says. "You have to protect her."

"I don't have to do anything," I say. "She and her boyfriend have been tormenting the woman I love."

"Brock . . ." Dad shakes his head slightly at me.

"Are you kidding me, Dad? I get that we're uncovering something much bigger. But this woman is far from innocent. She—along with our supposed cousin, Pat Lamone—has been making Rory's and Callie's lives hell."

"We will deal with Lamone," Dad says, his voice still never wavering. "But right now, we have something much more important to flesh out."

I look outside. The sun is already setting.

"What are we going to do?" I ask.

"You and I are going to stay here tonight. One of us will be awake at all times. As soon as the sun rises in the morning, Doc is going to show us around his . . . property. And by that, I also mean the property he's leasing from us."

"I see."

"Brittany," Doc says. "You need to make us some dinner."

Brittany is still shivering on the couch.

"I'll make dinner," I say.

"Fine," Dad says. "The door will also remain locked. Brittany and Doc may sleep, of course, but one of us will be watching them at all times."

"You've made your point, Joe," Doc says. "I've already agreed. Brittany and I aren't going anywhere."

"Yes, so you said," Dad says. "I'm sure you'll pardon me if I don't quite trust you."

"You'll never understand why I've done any of this."

"You're right," Dad says. "I never will."

"I haven't hurt anyone."

"That's bullshit."

"I haven't. I only move . . . cargo."

"Right. If that's what helps you sleep at night, Mark." Dad shakes his head.

"Look, I've told you I would help you. I'll be honest with you, and I'll show you everything. But I don't even know who's behind all of this," he says. "No one gives me their name."

"But they give you a hell of a lot of cash, don't they?" Dad says.

Doc doesn't reply.

"Come on, Brittany." I pull her up off the couch. "You and I are going to make dinner."

"I'm not hungry." Her lips tremble.

"Me neither, but we've got to eat."

Brittany and I head into the kitchen, where I have a look around. The pantry is stocked with dry goods and canned goods, and there's a chest freezer in the hallway leading out to the back door. Inside are all kinds of frozen meat.

"You have any specialties?" I ask.

She shakes her head.

"All right, then. Hamburgers it is."

"We don't have any buns."

"Then bunless burgers it is." I point to the pantry. "Get out some potatoes and fry them. Find some cans of green beans or corn or something."

She meekly obeys me.

So this is what I'm reduced to. Cooking dinner with Brittany Sheraton, whom I can't stand, when I'd much rather be with Rory, going on tour with her and the band, sitting in the audience every night and cheering her on. And knowing that I'm the lucky one she comes home to at night.

I grab the burgers out of the freezer and defrost them in

the microwave. I don't want to go outside to grill them, so I find a frying pan.

Brittany slices the potatoes and fries them in a cast-iron skillet with some butter and olive oil. She adds salt and pepper.

"These will take a while," she says.

"Fine by me. You said you're not hungry anyway."

"I mean, you may want to wait to start the burgers."

I nod. She's right. I turn the heat off the burgers.

She also retrieved a can of corn.

"Anything for dessert?" I ask.

"There are some apples in the pantry."

"Perfect. Aunt Marj once showed me how to make a really quick microwave apple crisp using only apples, brown sugar, and oatmeal. It will come in handy right now. Do you have cinnamon?"

"I don't know. If we do, it would be in the pantry."

I check the pantry once more. No cinnamon, but some whole cloves. I could throw them in for flavoring, but how would I get them out? Brown sugar will be the only flavoring, then. Suits me.

I get to work slicing and peeling apples, while Brittany watches the potatoes.

The idea of staying in this home all night, taking turns with my father keeping watch, really sucks.

I hate it. I hate it because I should be home, helping Rory through this difficult time with her father. I was going to have their house professionally cleaned and stock their kitchen as a surprise. And now? I'm stuck here in Wyoming dealing with Doc and Brittany and God knows what else.

How did we come to this?

I suppose it doesn't matter. Doc Sheraton—and whoever he works for—has been using our property to move bodies.

Somehow, Dad and I are going to have to prove we knew nothing about it.

And the thing that scares me the most?

I'm not sure we can prove that.

I'm not sure of anything anymore.

# CHAPTER SEVENTEEN

**Rory**

Early to rise.

I chuckle softly. Compared to the time Brock gets up every day, it isn't early at all.

He never called me back.

Which has me worried, of course.

He said he'd call when he could, but I did get a text from him around midnight. It woke me up.

*Still can't call, but everything's fine. I love you.*

I texted him *I love you* back, and then I tried to get back to sleep without worrying.

It didn't work very well.

Who does he think he's fooling? If he can't call, then everything is definitely *not* all right.

So here I am, up, having gotten very little sleep and ready to go on the road with Jesse and the band.

I meet Jesse in the kitchen, and he's already got a pot of coffee brewed.

"Hey," I tell him. "I think I'll take my own car."

"Not necessary," he says. "I'm driving, so you can just ride with me. The rest of the guys will go in the van."

"Sounds good."

Perfect. I prefer not to drive when I don't know exactly where I'm going. I'll leave that to Jesse. Plus his car will be much more comfortable than a van filled with equipment in the back and only four actual seats. Being squeezed between Dragon and Jake Michaels for four hours in the back seat doesn't sound like a lot of fun.

"Have you checked in with Mom this morning?" I ask.

He nods. "Just got off the phone with her. Dad is doing really well."

"Thank God." Some weight lifts off my shoulders.

But not all.

I'm still worried about Brock.

"Do we have time for breakfast?" I ask.

"Yeah. What do you want?"

"You're going to make breakfast?"

"Sure. You seem to think I'm a worse cook than Callie. I'm going to prove you wrong."

Callie walks in then. "I heard that."

"What are you doing up so early?" I ask her.

"I want to see my sister and brother off, of course."

"It's Saturday morning," I say. "You can sleep in today."

"I'll go back to bed after you're gone," she says. "Donny's still asleep."

Jesse goes slightly rigid.

"Hey," I tell him. "You promised . . ."

"I can let my high school rivalry go," my brother says, "but that doesn't mean I like the idea of him in bed with my sister."

"They're going to get married," I say.

"Whatever . . . I'll believe it when I see her walk down the aisle."

"Hey." Callie waves her engagement ring in Jesse's face. "It *will* happen. We haven't set a date yet because of all the other stuff going on."

"The Pat Lamone stuff?" Jesse shakes his head. "I'm

happy to take care of that for you, sis."

Callie doesn't reply.

She's talking about the stuff going on with Donny's family, of course, and Jesse doesn't know about that.

"You want some breakfast, Cal?" Jesse asks.

"Sure. Maybe a slice of toast or something."

Jesse nods and throws a few slices of bread in the toaster. Then he starts cracking eggs into a cast-iron skillet.

"Do we have bacon?" I ask.

"Looks like we're out," Jesse says. "Cal, you're going to have to go to the grocery store."

"Donny and I can go later today."

Jesse's neck twitches at the mention of Donny's name again.

But at least he keeps his mouth shut this time.

★ ★ ★

Jesse and I have been on the road for about an hour, saying little to nothing, when he finally turns to me at a stoplight.

"I need you to level with me about something."

"What?"

"Something's going on with the Steel family," he says. "I need you to tell me what it is."

"I don't know what you're talking about." I look down at my lap.

"Look, it's palpable whenever you and Callie are in the same room. Like this morning, when she mentioned the stuff going on and why they haven't set a wedding date. Something's happening, and I want to know what."

"I . . . can't."

"So you *do* know, then."

"I know I can't speak of it. It's not my story to tell. It's Donny's. And Brock's. But it's not truly about them. It's more about their parents and grandparents. Their families. Callie and I only know about it because we're in relationships with two of them."

"Is this going to affect your performance?"

"*That's* what you're concerned about?"

The light turns green. Jesse starts the car forward and returns his gaze to the road. "I'm concerned about you and Callie. My sisters. It's bad enough you've got this whole Pat Lamone debacle going on. But now you're involved in the Steel troubles as well."

"We're not exactly involved."

"Maybe not, but something's going on. And if it's affecting you and Callie, I'd like to help if I can."

"You? Mortal enemy of Donny Steel?"

"Look, I was serious last night. I'm going to let that go. I can't help it if I still get a little pissed every time I look at the guy."

"You're going to be looking at the guy a lot more in the future. Like, at every family gathering. And between us and the Steels, that's a *lot* of family gatherings."

"I know that. And if he makes Callie happy, then I'm happy for her. I'm trying, Ror. I'm really trying."

Jesse's gaze is fixed on the road ahead of him, but his facial features are still a little tense and rigid. He's going to have to try a lot harder than he is.

"You can't tense up every time his name is mentioned," I say.

His features relax. A bit. "Like I said, I'm trying."

I draw in a breath. I wish I could confide in my big brother, but I can't. "All right. Yes, the Steel family is going through some stuff right now. But as I've said, I'm not at liberty to tell you what."

"Are *you* in any danger?"

"From the Steels' problems? No. Why would I be?"

"Because the Steels are a powerful family, Rory. They always have been."

"They're a powerful family only because they're so financially independent," I say. "They're not into anything bad."

But I wonder. Is that true? I know without a doubt that Brock and Donny aren't, but what about the rest of them? Talon Steel was just shot. Why?

"I hope you're right, sis."

"I am," I say with more confidence than I feel. "At the very least, I know Donny and Brock are okay. They're good men, Jesse."

"I think you're probably right. My problem with Donny all these years has less to do with him as a person than it has to do with his family's power. He truly was an excellent football player, and I have to agree with him. If I'd had to make the choice between the two of us, I'm not sure it would've been an easy one."

"Thank you for saying that. I know Callie will appreciate it. As do I."

"I have no beef with Brock," Jesse continues, "other than that he's very young. And he's a known playboy."

"So was Donny."

"But he's a lot older. He's my age."

I'm not sure what to say. I've had the same doubts about Brock myself, but I know he loves me. I know it in the depths of my soul. I don't have one sliver of doubt.

"I don't know how to convince you, Jess," I say. "All I can

say is that I just know. We are in love. Have you ever been in love?"

"One or two times," he says. "But so have you, Ror."

"You're right. And I don't know how to tell you this in any other way or in words that will make any sense, but this time is different. With Brock, it's different."

"I guess I have to take your word for it."

"Take my word because it's all I can give you. It's true. It's something different from what I felt with Raine or anyone else. Male or female."

"Okay, Ror. I'll leave it alone."

"Thanks."

"But I'm still worried. Not about Donny and Brock and their love for you and Callie, but about their family as a whole. About what they may be into."

I don't reply. Because in truth? I'm worried myself. The fact that Brock hasn't been able to call me in twenty-four hours? Big red flag.

Part of me thinks I should be home and not on the road. After all, Dad is still in the hospital, and then there's this thing with Brock. But I've already been in and out of this gig more times than I can count, and I won't let Jesse down this time. Besides, in the end, don't I have to be true to myself? Don't I have the right to do something that makes *me* happy?

Sitting home alone, worrying about Dad… Worrying about Brock… That won't make me happy. It will only make me miserable.

But going on the road with Jesse and the band? Sure, those other things are still in the back of my mind, but performing makes me happy. It gives me a high that nothing else does.

It's not the same high I get from making love with Brock, but it's close.

And since Brock isn't around? I'll get my high from performing.

# CHAPTER EIGHTEEN

**Brock**

I'm fucking exhausted.

I was supposed to get some sleep during Dad's couple hours of watch, but I didn't. How the hell am I supposed to sleep when I'm in a strange home, sleeping on the floor, with my father holding a gun?

I got to hold the gun while Dad was supposedly sleeping. That was fun.

Turns out, he didn't really sleep either.

We both downed two or three cups of strong coffee this morning, which I made. I used double the amount of the expensive Kona coffee Doc had in the kitchen.

Expensive Kona coffee.

Not a Kona blend—pure Kona, from Hawaii.

That shit's not cheap.

It's little things like this that we have to be aware of. The Kona coffee. The gold signet ring Doc is wearing on his right hand.

I never noticed it before, but when the hell had I ever looked at his hands?

We're in the car now, Doc's four-wheel drive, driving through his property and onto ours. No paved roads, but this path has been driven enough times that two distinct tracks are visible.

Brittany is with us, of course. We couldn't leave her home and let her call the cops.

As we drive, two barns appear in the distance.

On *our* property.

"Did we have those built, Dad?" I ask.

Dad shakes his head in the front seat, his gun still pointing at Doc, who's driving.

"Great," I say under my breath.

I already know what was being kept in an old barn on our property back in Colorado.

"Let me guess," I say. "Those two barns coincide with the GPS coordinates left for Donny in that safe-deposit box."

"They appear to," Dad says, his voice still steady.

My father's something else. He's running on no sleep, and still, he's steady as a fucking rock.

I'm thankful for that, as I'm scared out of my mind.

The barns come nearer, and the four-wheel drive jerks and jostles as we drive through and over rocks and weeds.

Finally, Doc brings the truck to a stop. "Here we are."

"What exactly am I going to find inside those barns?" Dad asks.

"Honestly? I can't tell you."

"Take an educated guess," I say.

Doc sighs. "The east barn houses live freight. The west . . . Not alive."

I swallow. "Not alive meaning dead, right?"

No reply.

"Say it," I grit out. "Say the word, Doc."

"Dead. Yes," Doc says.

"You're going to insist on calling human beings freight?" Dad asks.

I suppress a shudder. I always knew, deep down, that we

were talking about human beings, but this is the first time Dad has actually said the words to Doc Sheraton.

"I don't do anything," Doc says. "I just provide the shelter. And the guard dogs."

Interesting. Dale, Donny, and I were right about the dogs. When we determined that whoever commandeered the barn on our own property was using working dogs, we figured we could find the culprit that way—by figuring out who supplied the dogs.

"On *my* property," Dad says.

"That I lease," Doc retorts.

"Yeah, and an important provision of that lease states that you will not carry out any illegal activity on my property."

"I built two barns," Doc says. "That's all I did."

"Well, you'd better hope these damned barns are empty," Dad says. "Because if they're not? You're in a heap of trouble."

He's in a heap of trouble anyway, but I understand what Dad is doing. He's trying to make Doc a little more comfortable. You know, as comfortable as someone can be with a gun pointed at him.

"We may not find anything," I say. "There aren't any other vehicles around."

"The cargo is usually flown on a small plane," Doc says.

"And no one would think anything of a small plane over farmland," I say.

"That's right, son." From Dad.

"Why in the hell would these people be using *our* property?" I ask. "It just doesn't make any sense."

Dad doesn't reply.

Does it make sense to him? Didn't our family take down that human trafficking ring all those years ago? Back when they rescued Dale and Donny and countless others?

Damn.

Maybe that's it.

Maybe these traffickers, still after all these years, hold a grudge against our family for bringing them down.

Which means . . .

Not all of them were captured.

Some of them escaped, and . . .

Nausea claws up my throat.

Horrendous, horrific things are happening on our property.

How long must this go back? At least sixty years. That's when Patty Watson died, and her bones were found on our property. And what about those red fingernails? Those red—

Oh. My. God.

Brittany is still wringing her hands, and only now do I notice that she's wearing bright-red nail polish.

It's probably just nail polish. Not plastic fingernails.

I grab one of her hands, yanking it away from the other.

"What do you think you're doing?" she demands.

"Lovely nails, Brittany," I say.

"Since when do you give a shit about a woman's nails?"

"Since"—I slide the tip of my finger underneath one of the fingernails, yank harshly, and the nail pops off—"now."

She pulls her hand away. "What the hell? That hurts."

I hold the red nail between my thumb and forefinger. "So you wear fake nails. The plastic ones that you glue on."

"So what?"

"Doc Sheraton," I say, "do you want to tell your daughter about the importance of these fake fingernails?"

Doc shrugs. "I don't know what you're talking about."

"You didn't tell him, Dad?"

"No. Not yet. I guess I didn't have any reason to. Until now."

"Tell me what?"

"A couple of plastic fingernails, identical to the ones your daughter appears to be wearing, were found in the barn on my property on the western slope. Close to the Wyoming border."

"So what? Lots of women wear those nails."

"Actually," I say, "lots of women *don't* wear those nails."

"How the hell would you know?" This from Dad.

"Rory told me. She used to go out with a cosmetologist, remember?"

It's a lie. Rory and I have never once discussed women's fingernails. She'd probably freak if I asked about fake nails. I honestly have no idea how common plastic fingernails are.

But the explanation seems to be enough for Dad.

"You want to explain this, Doc?" he says.

"Brittany has nothing to do with any of this. I've already told you that."

"Someone sure wants us to think she does," I say. "Any idea who that might be?"

Doc gulps audibly. "Oh my God . . ."

"Start talking," Dad says, his finger on the trigger.

We're still sitting in Doc's four-wheel-drive pickup. The two barns loom ahead of us. I'm still sick, knowing what's inside them.

Or at least what *has* been inside them.

"We still have those nails," I tell Dad. "We can get fingerprints."

"They're not mine," Brittany says. "I swear it. I've never even been to your property on the border."

"But someone wants us to think you have."

Doc shakes his head. "They're going to frame us, aren't they? Brittany and I are going to go down for all of this."

"What?" Brittany gasps.

"My God..." Doc Sheraton grasps his head in his hands. "This is all your fault, Steel."

Dad's jaw tenses. He's been icy so far, but now he's pissed. "Why? Because I didn't give you that job all those years ago?"

"You ruined me," Doc says. "What was I supposed to do? I had a daughter to support."

"You're supposed to make an honest living," I say.

"As a veterinarian in a one-horse town like Snow Creek? Without the biggest ranch in my corner?" Doc rubs his temples. "What do you *think* happened, Steel? None of the other ranches trusted me after that. I ended up taking care of dogs and cats, the occasional horse."

"Yeah," Brittany says. "That's why Dad started training guard dogs."

"If you haven't figured this out already, Brittany," I say, "your dad is doing a lot more than just training guard dogs."

Again I regard the plastic fingernail I'm still holding. I can have the others run for prints, as Dale, Donny, and I were all gloved when we found them. My fingerprints, however, will be on this one. Not that it matters.

"It's time," Dad says. "We'll begin in the east barn."

The east barn.

The one where they keep live cargo.

God... What might we find inside?

But we have to look. If people are in there—people being held against their will—we need to know. We need to rescue them.

I gulp down my nausea. What if it's kids? Little boys like Dale and Donny were? Like Uncle Talon was?

Or little girls?

God. I'm going to puke.

But I need to stay strong. Like my father. I'm no iceman, for sure, but I need to appear as though I am.

"Brock?" Dad says.

"Yeah?"

"Get out your gun."

Fuck. "Dad . . ."

"I need to stay out here with Doc and Brittany. I need you to go into that barn."

"By myself?"

"You're armed. You'll be fine."

"I don't think so," I say. "We'll take them with us. All four of us will go together. Besides, shouldn't they be forced to see what's going on in there?"

"All right," Dad says. "You're right. If anyone is in there guarding, they will most likely be armed."

"What about the dogs?"

"Either Doc or I can get the dogs to behave," Dad says. "Something I got out of him last night. He teaches all his dogs a command that only he knows."

"Good. Then we're all going." I brace myself.

I'm twenty-four years old. I haven't even been alive a quarter century.

And I'm about to walk into this horrific setting, gun drawn.

God help me.

# CHAPTER NINETEEN

**Rory**

After crossing the Utah border, we stop to fill our gas tanks and hit the bathrooms.

As usual, there is a line for the women's room. My bladder is about to burst, so once Jesse and the others leave the men's room, I scramble in.

And oh my God . . .

What I find in there is enough to make me swear off men forever, if I weren't so in love with Brock.

Gas station bathrooms aren't the best anyway, but I may as well be in a latrine in the woods. I have to hold my nose the entire time I'm in there, and then I wash my hands vigorously, wishing I could take a shower in hand sanitizer.

I leave the room, my eyebrows raised.

I meet Jesse and the rest of the guys outside. "You people are pigs."

"What the hell was that for?" Jesse asks.

"Instead of waiting in line to go into the women's restroom, I decided to give yours a try." I pinch two fingers over my nose. "I can still smell the stench. I'll never make that mistake again."

"For God's sake," Dragon drawls.

"Seriously, what's with the smell? I felt like I was in a Porta-Potty."

"Don't blame us if they don't clean the bathrooms," Jake says.

"I have *never* been in a women's room that smells like that."

"You weren't in *this* women's room either. For all you know, it could be just as nasty."

I wrinkle my nose. "I doubt that."

"Well, we'll never know, will we?" Dragon says in his dry tone.

"Shit," I say. "I forgot to get myself a Diet Coke."

"Got you covered, sis." Jesse tosses me a bottle.

"Thanks." I open it, holding it away from my body just in case Jesse's throw caused it to fizz up. It releases a little bit of pressure, but all the contents stay in the bottle.

I down about half of it.

"I wouldn't drink it that fast," Jake says. "We'll have to stop again, and you might be forced to go into a disgusting men's room."

"Never again," I say.

"Let's get back on the road," Cage says. "My turn to drive."

Jesse and I get back into his car, and soon enough, we're back on the road.

I check my phone.

Nothing new from Brock.

What in the world is going on in Wyoming?

Since we've been together, we've never gone this long without talking. Except for that first time, when we had our date on a Monday evening and then didn't get together again until the weekend. But that was when the relationship was brand-new. It wasn't even a relationship.

Should I text him?

I'm at a loss because what if he's in some strange situation and can't be bothered?

Of course, if that's the case, he would've turned the ringer on his phone off, so if I text him, no one will be the wiser.

Unless—

He's been put into a situation quickly and wasn't able to turn his ringer off.

Oh my God . . .

Gruesome images invade my mind. What if, what if, what if?

This isn't leading to anything good.

"You okay?" Jesse asks.

I clear my throat. "Why are you asking me that?"

"Because you're holding your phone with the grip of death."

"Just keep your eyes on the road."

"It might help you to tell me," he says.

"You just want to know what's going on with the Steels. And if I'm honest? None of us really knows."

"It's pretty clear you haven't talked to Brock since you got up this morning. We've been together most of that time, and I would've known."

"He's busy in Wyoming with his dad. Business."

"Right. Okay. But you're leaving for a week-long tour. Wouldn't he want to talk to you?"

You'd think. In fact, I know he would. Which is why . . .

"I'm a little bit worried." I bite my lip.

"Rory, what the fuck is going on with the Steels?"

# CHAPTER TWENTY

## Brock

My heart is hammering, and it's beating so fast I'm not sure I'll survive this. Tachycardia, I think it's called, when your heart goes ballistic and starts racing like this. I heard the term when I was with Rory at the hospital.

This can't be good for my body, can it? My heart beating so wildly I can actually see my chest moving?

I breathe in. Out. In again.

Normally that calms me, but not this time.

I have my gun out now, trained on the barn door. Dad's is still on Doc Sheraton.

Brittany is holding on to my other hand.

Her palm is cold and clammy.

She's frightened. Is she being aboveboard with me? Does she truly not know what's going on here? But those fingernails… And her history with Rory and Callie…

She's far from innocent.

But is she innocent in *this* instance? Regarding these barns? Is Doc? They both claim to be, but something doesn't sit right.

Not at all.

The door hovers in front of me, and with each step, it doesn't seem to be getting any closer.

Until it nearly hits my face.

I crack it open.

Inside, dogs are growling.

"There's at least one dog in here," I say.

"Cochise!" Doc Sheraton yells.

Two Dobermans lope out of the barn, no longer growling.

They're big and strong dogs, obviously well-fed, which means someone comes here regularly.

"Down."

The dogs obey Dr. Sheraton.

"That's your secret command?" I say. "Cochise?"

"Yeah. I suppose I'll have to change it now that you know it."

"It's brilliant, actually," I reply. "It's not like anyone would come up with that on their own."

Dad nods to me. "Go on in, son."

Does it have to be me? I suppose so, because I don't want to be the one holding a gun on Doc Sheraton. For now, at least, no one can get me on assault with a deadly weapon. All I've done is point my weapon at a barn door.

No sounds come from the barn.

I want to be relieved, but that doesn't mean much. Whoever is in there could be caged or otherwise imprisoned. I wish I had a flashlight. There are no windows in this building. None at all, and it's dark as hell.

I walk in.

I inhale.

Yep, dog shit. Of course, if the dogs are forced to stay in here, they're going to crap. Just like they did in the barn on our Colorado property.

"Anyone in here?" I call out.

No answer.

I walk slowly forward to let my eyes adjust.

I still can't see a lot, but some blankets and buckets sit on one side of the large barn. No beds or anything, but a few heaters with propane tanks attached.

We're nearing December. Do they really bring people here when it's freezing? The heaters won't do much. Maybe that's why no one's here. Maybe this is their offseason.

God . . .

I walk the perimeter of the barn, watching out for dog shit, though the crap seems to be concentrated in the front corner of the barn.

Do they really just leave the dogs in here?

If that isn't animal cruelty, I don't know what is. At least the hounds appear to be fed and otherwise healthy.

Still walking the perimeter, I stumble over something in my path.

I look down.

A bone.

A big bone.

Not too unusual. Dogs like bones.

I don't want to touch the thing, but—

I gasp.

This doesn't look like a beef bone. It looks . . .

It looks a lot like a human femur.

I swallow, but I can't hold back the retch.

I puke.

I don't want to be a wuss, but between the smell of dog shit, the knowledge of what goes on here, and now a human femur?

I'm not going to berate myself for doing what any normal human being would do.

"Dad?" I say.

"What is it, son?"

"We're going to need flashlights. And Doc? You need to answer some hard questions."

I pick up the femur, walk across the barn, and out the door.

Brittany gasps. "A bone?"

"Doc," I say, "you're a veterinarian. Tell me. What the hell kind of bone is this?"

He doesn't reply.

I walk forward and hold the femur in front of Doc's face. "I run a beef ranch. I'm well-versed in bovine anatomy and physiology. This is not a beef bone."

"Son," Dad says, his voice catching slightly, "that's a human bone."

"Yep," I say. "I have a feeling I know why these dogs are so strong and well-fed."

This time I'm able to hold back my heaves. Good thing I emptied my stomach in the barn.

"Christ, Doc," Dad says. "How could you?"

Doc shakes his head. "I built the barns. That's all I fucking did. I built the barns."

"Your name is on the lease of this property," I say. "You're responsible for what goes on here."

Doc struggles to stay on his feet. "I . . ."

I look over to the Dobermans. They're well trained. Still lying down, still obeying Doc, but they're very interested in the bone I'm holding.

"Are these dogs really locked inside that barn all the time?" I ask.

"I don't know," Doc says. "All I did was build the barns."

Dad rubs his forehead. "And supply the dogs."

"For a price."

"You're a vet," I say. "You're supposed to love animals. These animals are kept locked inside here. They shit inside the barn. They feed on human remains."

"We don't know that," Doc says.

I wave the bone in his face, and both of the dogs' ears perk up.

"This is a fucking human femur. I found bones on our property, too. You say you know nothing. Maybe it's true. I don't fucking know, and I don't fucking care. But someone is using our property to do this, trying to take us down, and I swear to God, if we go down, you're coming with us."

Dad clears his throat. "No one's going down, Brock."

I pace, still holding the femur. "How can we not? Look at this? Live cargo. Dead cargo. Dogs feasting on human remains. This is evil, Dad. It's so evil."

"Evil is holding my father at gunpoint," Brittany says.

The back of my neck heats. Man, I'd love to clock this woman into next week. Yeah, I know the rule, and I won't break it, but damn . . .

"I should've never gotten involved in this." Doc shakes his head, pushes his hair back from his forehead.

"I've got news for you," Dad says. "My family is *not* going down for this. But someone is. So you're going to help us figure out who it is and who is behind all of this, or I will make sure it's *you* who goes down."

Doc falls to the ground and sobs. He actually sobs.

Brittany runs to him. "Daddy? Please, Daddy. Make this all go away. You can do it, can't you? Just like before?"

*Just like before?*

What is she talking about?

I open my mouth to pose the question when she looks up at me.

"Brock, I'm so sorry. I'm so sorry about what I did to Rory and Callie all those years ago. I'm so, so sorry. And the atropine? All I did was get it out of the medicine cabinet in the clinic. I didn't know they were going to try to poison your uncle."

"Doc," Dad says. "Do you realize they're making it look like you're the one who's doing all of this? You're a patsy. They're framing you. How the hell did you get involved with these degenerates?"

"I had no choice."

"Bullshit," I say. "There's always a fucking choice."

"And don't pawn it off on Bryce and me either." Dad scowls. "You want to know why we didn't give you that job all those years ago? Because I don't trust you, Doc, and it seems my trust issues were well-founded."

"I never did anything to you," Doc says.

"You didn't have to. I go with my gut, and rarely does it let me down. Clearly it didn't this time."

"What about your gut told you I wasn't trustworthy?" Doc asks.

"If I could put it into words, then it wouldn't be my gut."

"Stop it!" Brittany yells. "My father's a good man. If he did anything, it was only to ensure his and my survival."

"You know," I say, "if a small-town vet can't make a living in a small town, he could move to a larger town where there's more of a need for veterinarians."

Doc says nothing, just continues sobbing like a child.

"You may think you haven't done anything," Dad says, "but your fingerprints—and your daughter's—are all over this. These people you're working with are not novices. They know how to cover their tracks, but clearly you don't. And you know what? They will take advantage of that. You can bank on it. They're ready to frame you, to let you take every fall. You and your daughter. You see, these people don't care that she's a young woman. They *deal* in young women. They deal in children."

"I didn't know," Doc pleads. "You've got to believe me. I didn't know."

"Sell it to someone else," Dad says. "My son and I aren't buying. Not today."

"I have to agree with my father," I say. "How could you not know something bad was going on? On property that you have a leasehold on? That we own? You didn't think it was strange that they asked you to build the barns to hold"—air quotes—"*freight*?"

No reply.

"And they need your dogs to guard them? What do they pay you for all this?"

"They think we've got money somewhere, Daddy," Brittany says.

Doc says nothing.

"I'd be willing to bet your father has a lot of money stowed somewhere. It's probably not in cash. My guess is it's in jewels or gold or something, probably buried somewhere on your property."

Doc's cheeks redden, though they're already pretty ruddy from his sobbing.

"So my son is right," Dad says.

Doc doesn't reply.

Brittany inches toward her father. "Daddy . . ."

"Please. Leave my daughter out of this."

"Your daughter's already in this," I say. "She supplied the

atropine that was used to try to poison my uncle."

Dad goes rigid, sets his jaw.

Just the mention of Uncle Talon . . .

"Dad, you okay?"

"Not even slightly." He cocks his gun, points it straight at Doc's head.

"Dad"—I will my voice not to tremble—"you're not a murderer. Don't be that guy."

Dad puts his gun down. "You're right, son. I'm not that guy. I'm not my old man. At least not today." He trains the gun back on Doc. "Get up. It's time to look in the other barn."

# CHAPTER TWENTY-ONE

**Rory**

How I wish I could confide in my brother. My big brother, who has always been my protector. He was four when I was born, and it was only the two of us for the first two years of my life. I don't remember any of that, of course.

Callie and I are the closest of all my siblings, only two years apart. Maddie didn't come along until five years after Callie, so we have Jesse on one end and Maddie on the other, and then sandwiched in between, only two years difference in age, are Callie and me.

Callie, who is so different from me in almost every way, is my closest sibling.

But my brother… He and I are close as well, but in a different way. We're close because we share the same interests. Music, most of all. We're both creators, performers. But we also have sports. Jesse was a star athlete in high school, and though I was never as good as he was, I did start for softball and girls' basketball.

Callie didn't play any sports, and neither did Maddie.

Even though I'm closest to Callie, I have the most in common with Jesse.

If only…

"Ror?" he prods.

"Do I have your complete confidence?" I ask.

"That goes without saying."

"Does it? Because when Callie and I told you about Pat Lamone and the high school crap, your first inclination was to go pummel him."

"Yeah, and I'm still leaning toward that."

"You're very protective of us," I say. "I appreciate that. I do. But I can't have you going after the Steels."

"Have the Steels done anything to you?"

"Of course not."

"Then why would I go after them, Rory? Pat Lamone hurt you and Callie. It's my job, as your big brother, to make sure he pays for that."

"No, it's not your job. Callie would say it's the job of the justice system."

"Callie's not here."

"Jesse, I know you're a big strong man, and I know at heart you're still the athlete you were all those years ago. Plus you're a rocker. You're full of testosterone and endorphins all the time from being onstage. But you're also thirty-two years old. Thirty-two-year-old men don't go around beating other guys up."

"Have I done it?"

"No. But only because Callie and I begged you not to."

He sighs. "Look. I talk a good game, but I'm not that guy, Ror. Even if I want to be when it comes to my sisters."

I smile then. "You're a good big brother, Jess. You always have been. Except for that one time."

"What are you talking about?"

"Remember that time when I begged you and the guys to let me go sledding with you? And you didn't make sure I stayed warm enough?" I laugh. "Mom had your ass that day."

"I haven't thought about that in ages." He laughs. "As I recall, though, you didn't mind at all."

"Are you kidding me? I got to go with the big boys. Plus, you guys all took turns pulling me on the sled. It was a dream."

"Well, I should've taken better care of you that day."

"You were eleven," I say. "You didn't know any better."

"An eleven-year-old boy should know better. Hell, eleven-year-olds babysit."

"Eleven-year-old *girls* babysit. Not too many eleven-year-old boys do. There's truth in the fact that girls mature faster than boys."

"Well, whatever," Jesse shrugs, his gaze fixed on the road. "I will always protect you, Rory. You, Callie, Maddie. All of you."

"I know that, and I appreciate it. But protecting me doesn't mean beating Pat Lamone into a pulp, no matter how much I'd love you to do it."

Jesse laughs. "So the truth comes out."

"Are you kidding me? The guy's a troll. I'd love nothing more than to see him beaten to a pulp. Just not by my brother's hand."

"The guy's an asshole."

"You're telling me."

"But I didn't start this conversation to talk about Pat Lamone," Jesse says.

"I know you didn't. So do I have your confidence?" I turn and regard him, his gaze still fixed. "Because, Jesse, I have to talk to someone about this. I'm in love with Brock, and Donny is engaged to Callie. Pretty soon our families will be joined. And . . . I'm worried. So worried."

"I know you are. I'm your brother. If I can ease some of

that burden on you, I want to do it."

My brother is an amazing person, and he gets me in a way Callie doesn't. He understands my emotional side. I do want to confide in him.

Except...

"Brock's and my relationship is still tenuous. We're in love, but it all happened so fast, which is unlike me. And certainly unlike Brock."

"It happened fast for Donny and Callie too. When I asked her about that, she told me that the Steels have a habit of falling hard and falling fast."

"Brock told me the same."

"But the Pikes? We don't have that habit. More the opposite."

"Says the guy who hasn't had a relationship in years. How would you know?"

"You've had a couple, sis, and I don't remember any of them happening this fast."

"They didn't, but they did happen. I'm not afraid of my emotions like you are."

"Who says I'm afraid of my emotions?"

"You let all your emotions out onstage, Jesse. You're a rocker, and you're incredibly good-looking, and you always have women falling all over you. Including Steel women. Yet you haven't dated in... how long?"

"Maybe I don't want to."

Is my brother speaking the truth? He doesn't actually want a relationship?

"I have a lot of belief in Dragonlock," he goes on. "We're good. We're damned good. For one reason or another, we haven't gotten the attention of an agent, but I believe that someday we will. I believe that I was meant for something greater than playing local bars. I've spent the last several years of my life working toward a goal. I don't have time for a relationship."

"Wow."

"Does that surprise you? I've never taken any interest in the ranch or the winery. Sure, I was a star football player in high school and college, but I was never good enough for the pros. I always knew that. Music has always been my dream, just like it was yours. As for a relationship? Someday, for sure. I love kids, and I want them. But right now my focus is the band."

How did I not know this? Years ago, when I gave up my opera performance dreams, my brother was still working toward his own musical dream. He's amazing.

"Then I'll help you, Jess. I'll help you put this band on the map."

"Seriously?"

I sigh. "I love playing with you guys. Singing, leaving all my inhibitions behind. Singing opera was always so controlled. But singing rock? It's freeing, Jess. Maybe it's time I leave opera behind for good."

"Rory . . ."

"It's not a rash decision. It's not even a decision. Opera turned its back on me long before I turned my back on it." I punch his arm but not hard enough to startle him. "Oh, and nice redirection, by the way."

"What?"

"I believe we were talking about you not dating recently."

"I explained that." He shakes his head. "And actually, sis, we started by talking about what's going on with the Steels."

"Honestly, I don't know a lot of what's going on with them.

Very little, in fact. But if you promise to keep this between you and me, I'll tell you what I know."

"I promise, Rory. I won't go after anyone, and I won't mention it to Callie."

"Good, because she and Donny are engaged. She's much closer to being a Steel family member than I am."

"Pinky swear," he says.

"Don't joke, Jesse."

"Who's joking? I promise, Rory. I promise."

I clear my throat. "It appears the rumors may be true. The Steels may very well own Snow Creek."

His eyebrows rise. "What does that mean, exactly?"

"That's just it. We don't know. This is all news to Donny and Brock as well. But apparently the Steels have liens on almost all the town's property."

"On ours?"

"That's the weird thing. They don't. Mom and Dad own our property free and clear."

"Of course," he says. "Our property isn't technically in Snow Creek."

"Right. It's unincorporated county property. But most of the properties in town? They have liens, held by the Steels."

"Okay . . ."

"And there's more . . ."

He clears his throat. "That's what I was afraid of."

# CHAPTER TWENTY-TWO

## Brock

We trudge to the other barn, my stomach and bowels churning.

Again, it's up to me to open the door.

God, what might I find in here? Bodies? That horrible sweet stench?

I brace myself, holding my nose. And I open the door.

No dogs this time.

Odd, because if there *are* dead bodies in here, surely whoever put them there would want them guarded.

*You have to do it,* I tell myself. *You have to inhale with your nose because you have to know if that horrible pungent odor is here.*

I inhale.

"Oh God," I say out loud.

Again, the syrupy smell of decaying human flesh.

Again, no windows, and I almost don't want my eyes to adjust.

But they do.

And I find . . .

Nothing.

A sigh of relief whooshes out of me like a gust of wind.

No bodies piled anywhere.

Only a few tarps stacked and folded in the corner.

Again, I walk the perimeter of the place, and I come

across dog shit once more. Which means . . . They do indeed keep guard dogs here when there is *cargo* stored here.

But that's it.

No bones this time, and thankfully, no bodies.

But the bodies have been here.

My nose tells me that.

I draw in a deep breath—through my mouth of course—and walk back outside.

"What did you find?" Dad asks, still training his gun on Doc Sheraton.

"Tarps," I say, "and nothing else. Except . . ."

"Except what?"

I draw another deep breath, this time of fresh air tinged with dog shit. "The odor is there, Dad. The one we told you about. Dead flesh."

"Jesus Christ." Dad shakes his head.

"No," Doc says. "Please, no."

"I know the odor," I say. "I've smelled it before, and Donny and Dale told me what it is."

"How would they know?" Brittany asks.

I say nothing. None of her damned business anyway.

"Answer my daughter's question, please," Doc says. "I don't understand any of this."

"The only thing you need to know," Dad says, "is that we know the fucking smell. As for *how* we know it? That's none of your concern."

"Yes, it is," Brittany says. "If you know what dead bodies smell like, what does that say about the two of you?"

"Shut her up, Doc," Dad says.

"Wait a minute," I interrupt. "We know because Dale and Donny, before they were adopted by the Steels, came in contact with decaying human flesh. It's not a pretty story, Brittany, and that's all you're going to get of it. But trust me. That is the odor I smelled. Judging by the fact that your fingernails have been left at our property, where we also smelled decaying human flesh, I'd say you're done talking."

Brittany gulps, and she says nothing more.

"My God," Doc says.

"Don't give me that." From Dad. "You had to know something nefarious was going on. I will never believe that you didn't. I might believe that *she* didn't." He nods to Brittany.

Brittany.

Unlike my father, I'm *not* convinced of her innocence. Something's off with her for sure.

"I didn't, Mr. Steel," she says. "I swear."

"You're not innocent, though," Dad says. "You knew something was going on when your father asked you to get that atropine."

"But I didn't—"

"Save it," I tell her. "Whether you knew or not is irrelevant. They're framing you. They've got a plan all in place."

"My son is right. They're not going down, but you are. So your only chance to *not* go down is to help us."

"And what do we get in return?" Doc asks.

Dad laughs. It is a sarcastic, caustic laugh. "What do *you* get? You get to live."

Doc gulps.

Brittany gulps.

I gulp.

"Dad..."

"I'm not a killer," Dad says. "I've never shot another human being in my life, but I've come close. And I'm pretty damned close now."

"Please, no!" Brittany shrieks.

Doc says nothing. Just stands, and I give him credit for his fortitude. He may have been crying like a baby on the ground earlier, but so far he hasn't lost control of his bladder.

"Where are the riches?" Dad asks.

"There aren't—"

"Are you still playing that tune?" Dad shakes his head. "It is so old and tired, and so am I, and my patience is wearing thin. How do they pay you, Sheraton?"

Brittany's eyes are wide. But something's wrong. She's feigning surprise. She's . . . something. Ever since I noticed those nails, I've just had an itch at the back of my neck. Yesterday, when she and I went to the kennels, I was convinced she was innocent.

Now? I'm pretty sure she's just a good actress . . . and her skills are fading.

She knows more than she's letting on. How much more? And how might it relate to Pat Lamone? That's what I need to find out.

"Fine," Doc finally says. "There's a safe. Buried underneath the kennels."

"Good idea," Dad says. "No one's going to go looking under a kennel full of guard dogs."

"Right."

"Back to the car, then," Dad says. "And then to the kennels."

★ ★ ★

It's nearly lunchtime by the time we take care of moving all the dogs to one side of the kennel so Doc Sheraton can access his safe buried underneath the building.

The floor is made of concrete but covered in an indoor-outdoor carpet-type material. Once we move all the dogs out, Doc takes a box cutter and removes the carpet from the area in question.

And there it is. Instead of concrete, a flat wooden board covers an area of about nine square feet.

Doc Sheraton removes the wooden board and reveals the safe below.

"Open it," Dad says.

"Give me a minute." Doc's hands shake.

"You have two seconds," Dad says.

Drops of sweat trickle down Doc's cheeks.

Brittany is shivering as well. "Daddy?"

Doc doesn't answer. His hands continue to shake as he works the combination, and I, with my perfect vision, watch closely.

Twenty-four.

Forty-seven.

Three.

I have no idea if the numbers are significant at all, but they're embedded in my brain now. I won't forget that combination.

Doc opens the safe, and—

"This is it."

"Take it all out," Dad says.

The dogs bark from the other side of the kennel. A wall separates us, but it's not soundproof for sure. I love animals, but right now, the constant barrage of noise is making my head pound.

Still, I'm going to save them. I've been thinking about how I'll do it since I found out about the electric shock collars yesterday. I wish I could take them all home with me, but between Sammy and Zach, I'm not sure we can handle more dogs. Maybe one or two, but not the twenty or so in this kennel.

And that's not counting the ones in the outside runs or the litter of pups.

I'll call the Humane Society, I guess. Or the local animal control.

The thing is, though, I don't want them ending up at a kill shelter. I want them to go to nice homes. Or, if they're truly good guard dogs, I want them to do their jobs, but for people who will take care of them and treat them well.

Just another thing on my to-do list . . .

Doc pulls out a velvet bag. "These are diamonds."

Dad is still holding the gun. "Take a look inside, Brock."

I grab the bag from Doc Sheraton, open the drawstring, and pour three gemstones into my palm. "They look like diamonds, but I'm no expert."

"They're diamonds," Doc says. "I had them checked out."

"And no one asked you where the hell you got them?"

"People who appraise gemstones don't ask questions," he says. "They do their job, and they're paid."

"How much did you pay?" I lift my eyebrows. "Or maybe you just gave them one of these diamonds as payment instead?"

Doc doesn't reply.

Which means I have my answer.

Doc pulls out the next bag. He hands it to me this time. "Emeralds."

I return the diamonds back to the first bag, open the second, and pour them into my hand.

The green stones sparkle in the artificial fluorescent lighting streaming from the ceiling of the kennel.

"I don't know if you'll believe this," Doc says, "but my gemstone expert says these are even more valuable than the diamonds."

"Why would they say that?" Dad asks.

"Because these emeralds are flawless, and flawless emeralds are much harder to come by than flawless diamonds."

"What else is in there?" Dad says.

"Two more bags," Doc says.

He pulls another out and hands it to me. Again, I pull a little drawstring on the black velvet bag, open it, and pour three gemstones into my hand.

These are yellow. I don't know much about gems, but these stones look curiously similar to the yellow diamond in Aunt Marjorie's engagement ring.

"Dad? These are yellow."

Dad's jaw goes rigid, but his stance remains steady, the gun still trained on Doc.

"Yellow diamonds," Doc says.

"For sure?" Dad says, between gritted teeth.

"Yes. I had them checked out. They're worth more than clear diamonds, if they're flawless, like these are."

"Dad . . . Are you thinking what I'm thinking?"

Dad doesn't reply, which means we'll talk later.

"This is the last bag." Doc pulls it out of the safe and hands it to me.

This one feels different. It's heavier. I open it, pour the contents into my palm, and—

I drop my jaw.

This one is a ring. Not loose gemstones but a ring.

An orange stone in the middle, surrounded by white sparkling stones, and set in some kind of white metal.

I've seen it before.

So has Dad.

In Uncle Talon's safe . . . and on Callie's finger.

"All right," Dad grits out. "Which one of you wants to start explaining how you have a ring that once belonged to my mother?"

# CHAPTER TWENTY-THREE

### Rory

I don't immediately tell Jesse anything more.

Finally—

"This century, Ror?"

"Apparently the Steels own a lot of property that they don't use, here and in Wyoming."

"Not surprising, since they apparently do own the town of Snow Creek. I imagine they own a lot more than that."

"Jesse, having liens on properties isn't the same thing as owning them."

"You sound like Callie."

"You're a smart man. You don't have to be a law student to know that."

He huffs. "Yes, I know that, Rory, but a lien is still a lien. Whoever owns the property can't do anything with it until the lien has either been paid or until he gets the lienholder's approval."

"Which is another weird thing," I say. "Property changes hands in Snow Creek all the time, so obviously the Steels don't hinder that. I mean, Raine just sold her salon to Willow White, and it has a lien."

"Who holds the lien?" Jesse asks.

"The Steels, Jess. Haven't you been paying attention?"

"That's not what I mean. Which Steel?"

"No." I shake my head. "It's something called the Steel Trust."

"I don't know much about trusts," my brother says.

"I don't either. But it's an ownership. Or rather, a lien hold."

"Maybe we do need Callie," Jesse says. "I mean, you and I know what a lien is, but how can they hold liens on all the property, yet the property changes hands all the time?"

"There's one property in town that they don't hold a lien on. Well, a couple. Ava's bakery, for one."

"She owns that outright?"

"Yeah."

"That makes sense." He snickers. "Seeing as she's a Steel and all."

I clear my throat. I'm not sure how much more I can tell him. I mean, I trust my brother, but the rest of it is just so . . .

"You going to elaborate?" he says.

"It's all so . . . unreal, Jesse."

"What is, exactly?"

"The Steels. Brock and Donny are innocent."

"Wait, wait, wait . . . What the hell is going on, Rory?"

"Pull over," I say. "I'm going to be sick."

Jesse jerks the car and stops on the side of the road. I scramble out of the passenger side, doubled over.

I don't throw up. I don't even heave.

But my stomach is cramped up.

Jesse rubs my shoulders. "What the hell's going on, Rory?" he says again.

I collapse into a heap on the ground. Cars whizz by us, and the November breeze tousles my hair.

"Jesse, the band. They're behind us. They're going to stop when they see us on the side of the road."

"You're right." Jesse rises and helps me up. "Let's go."

We scramble back into the car, and Jesse gets on the road, his gaze fixed ahead of him.

"This stuff going on," I say. "It's stuff I don't understand and stuff I don't want to understand. I honestly think the Steel family is innocent. They're good people. But someone has been using their property for . . ."

"For what?" Jesse says, his jaw tensed.

"For . . . illegal activities. Really disgusting illegal activities."

"How much more do you know?"

"Not much. Not anything that can be proved yet, anyway."

Jesse curls his fists around the steering wheel, his knuckles white. "Rory, I want you to stay away from whatever the hell is going on."

"But Brock—"

"I don't give a flying fuck about Brock," Jesse says. "I give a fuck about you. You and Callie."

"Callie is engaged to Donny."

"Engagements can be broken."

God. Now I really am going to puke.

"They're in love. This is the best thing that's ever happened to Callie, and Donny has nothing to do with any of the other stuff."

"Do you think I care? You think I want either of you involved in anything?" His knuckles whiten around the steering wheel. "Hell, I don't even know *what* it is. But the way you're talking, the way you're clenching your hands together, the way all the color is drained out of your face, Rory. It's bad. It's fucking bad."

What can I say? He's right.

It's bad.

It's worse than bad. It goes so far beyond bad I can't even describe it.

Jesse checks his GPS. "This is the town, coming up. We're going to get checked into the hotel and then get some lunch."

"Like I could eat," I say.

"Yeah, I'm not too hungry either."

"But the band, Jesse. We have to act normal for the band."

"How the hell have you been acting normal all this time?" Jesse asks me.

"I haven't known about this other stuff for very long. But the whole Pat Lamone thing has been hanging over my head for a while. Haven't you noticed that Callie and I haven't eaten much lately?"

"I don't notice how much a person eats," Jesse says.

"Because you're too busy guzzling food yourself."

"You want to go there, Rory? You want to insult me right now?"

I sigh. "No, I don't want to go there. I'm sorry. But sometimes Callie and I just have to find something to laugh about. Because if we don't, we won't be able to exist."

"God, everything you guys have been dealing with, and then Dad's heart attack on top of it all."

"No kidding. But at least he's going to be okay."

"I know." Jesse rakes his fingers through his long hair. "Thank God."

We pull into the small town of Furbish, Utah. Jesse roams through the streets until he stops at a small motel.

"This is it."

"The Sundown Inn?" I say. "Sounds kind of... creepy."

"It has good reviews on Yelp. If it turns out to be creepy, take it up with Jake. He's the one who books our stays."

"I'm sure it's fine."

"Not that it matters," Jesse says. "We'll only be sleeping here."

"Yeah."

Except that doesn't help me at all. There are probably holes in the walls where peeping toms check out women.

And I'm a peeping tom's wet dream.

Jesse pulls into a parking spot, and we scramble out of the car. I look around. The van should be arriving any minute.

Sure enough, five minutes later, the van rumbles into the parking lot.

Cage is driving, and he brings it to a halt. He and the two others exit the van.

"You check us in yet, Jesse?" Cage asks.

"Nope. We just got here ourselves. Let's do it."

Jesse and Cage go into the office to check us in while I stand next to Jesse's car, my hands shoved in my jeans pockets, leaning against it for support.

Time to put on my game face.

# CHAPTER TWENTY-FOUR

**Brock**

"Explain what?" Doc asks. "This is how I've been paid. They were very clear that I needed to keep the same lifestyle I always had. Not to look like I'd come into money. So I only sold one of the jewels, and Brittany and I have been living on that plus my income."

"This ring," I say. "We've seen it before."

"You have?" Doc raises his eyebrows.

"On Callie Pike's finger, Doc," I say. "Like my dad said, it belonged to my grandmother. How the hell did you get it?"

Doc swipes his hand across his forehead. "My God, Jonah, could you please take the gun off me for one second? I've cooperated fully. I've told you all I know, and I've shown you how I've been paid. What else can I do for you?"

"This gun's not going anywhere," Dad says, his voice even lower than normal.

"Then I'm at a loss." Doc wipes at his forehead again. "I don't have anything else to tell you. Anything else to show you."

My mind races. We have the original ring—which Donny had appraised and traced to our grandmother—and we have the duplicate that Donny had crafted for Callie. So where the hell did *this* one come from? That ring was one of a kind. Yet we somehow have three of them?

I hold the ring up to the light. I'm no jeweler, but it's flawless and brilliant.

"We need to have this looked at," I say.

"Yeah, we need to have *all* of this stuff looked at," Dad agrees.

I try to read the engraving on the inside of the band, but I don't see anything. But that could be because I don't have a jeweler's loupe and there isn't any good lighting inside the kennel.

I don't even know what I'm looking for other than *LW*. Maybe a mark on the metal for gold or something?

"You won't mind, Doc," Dad says, "if we confiscate all this stuff and have it checked out?"

"How can I mind? You've got a fucking gun to my head, Joe."

Dad, who's been icy cold this entire time, finally cracks a smile. Albeit a small smile.

"When you're right, you're right."

I've never seen my father like this.

He's usually hot with emotion. Red Joe, as Donny and Dale say.

But today? His rage—which I would normally expect to see during something like this—is absent.

It's been replaced with . . .

An icy cold exterior.

And frankly? It's frightening.

Especially after what he'd told me about his own father and how he'd resorted to tactics not unlike what Dad is doing now.

Perhaps it's true that the apple doesn't fall far from the tree.

But I make a vow, here and now, that once we get through all this? Once we put it all to rest for good? I will never, ever hold a gun to another human being unless it's to defend my family or myself.

Perhaps Dad feels that's what he's doing. And in some ways, he's probably right.

But this new side of him that I see? I don't like it. I don't like it at all.

*Don't turn your back on him.*

My mother's words echo in my mind.

I won't turn my back on my father, but we *will* have a talk after all this. Because if he continues with these tactics? I don't know how I can stay loyal to him.

But then I look before me at the jewels we've uncovered. I consider the barns on our property.

Without Dad's tactics, we would've still found the barns. It's our property, after all, and we would've thoroughly searched it.

But the jewels? Would we have thought to look underneath the kennels?

Probably not.

I place the ring back in the black velvet bag and draw the string.

And only then do I notice something.

Brittany.

Brittany, who doesn't seem disturbed by any of this.

I've known something was off with her—that she's hiding something—but I never thought she could actually *be* a part of this. Those red fingernails . . .

Brittany breached her ethics—if indeed she ever had any—ten years ago, when she stole the tranquilizing drug from her father's clinic and injected it into Rory and Callie, letting

Pat take those incriminating photographs.

Once you cross the line . . .

Not that I'd know. I've never crossed that line. But wasn't it Dad who told me that once you cross the line, it becomes easier and easier to keep crossing lines?

Which means two things.

First, it will now be easier for Dad to hold a gun on someone else. Great.

And second . . . Brittany has probably been crossing lines since she drugged Rory and Callie ten years ago. Maybe before then, even.

She's a good actress. I'll give her that.

And as I move my gaze between her and her father, something dawns on me. Doc's features are extended. His jaw is dropped. He has no issue making eye contact with me or Dad. Perhaps it's because there's a gun pointed at him, and he needs to be alert at all times.

Or maybe . . .

Maybe he has no idea how the rings got switched.

Doc thinks this is the ring that he was paid with.

Brittany, on the other hand . . .

Oh. My. God.

She knew all the time. She knew what her father was doing.

"It's you," I say.

Brittany doesn't meet my gaze. She tries, for sure, but she's looking past me.

"What do you mean?" Doc says. "I've told you all along she has nothing to do with this."

"Maybe not, but she knows. Don't you, Brittany? You know a lot more than you're letting on. You know a lot more than your father thinks you do, don't you?"

She shakes her head vehemently. "They're lying, Daddy. I swear to God, they're lying."

"What I'm trying to figure out"—I rake my gaze over her in an attempt to further interpret her body language, her stance, her facial expression—"is whether you were trying to *help* your father or *hinder* him."

"Brittany..." From Doc.

"He doesn't know what he's talking about, Daddy."

"Don't I?" I hold up the pouch containing the ring. "This is *not* the ring your father was given for payment, is it?"

"How should I know?" she gasps out.

"You. You're the one who left these things in the safe-deposit box in Donny's name."

"I don't know what you're talking about." This time she gulps.

I glare at her. "How did you get in? How did you get a safe-deposit box open in Donny's name? And how the hell did you get into Uncle Talon's house and leave that key for Donny in his medicine cabinet?"

My father's eyebrows rise. Yet he still holds the gun trained on Doc. Man, nothing fazes him. Where is Red Joe?

"Sheraton," Dad says, "tell your daughter to start talking. My son has a gun as well, and he can put it right to her head."

Man, I don't want to do that. I don't want to hold my gun to another human being. Especially not a woman.

And especially not if...

If Brittany left all those things for Donny, she's the reason we know anything about this.

She's the reason...

"I know you're not trying to protect us," I say to her. "It's

Lamone, isn't it? He truly *is* our relative, and it's him you're trying to protect."

She doesn't reply.

"Who the hell is that woman in the hospital, Brittany? Sabrina Smith?"

"I told you," Brittany says, trembling. "She's Pat's grandmother."

"All right. Does that mean she was once married to William Elijah Steel?"

Dad is beginning to redden, and I see the rage building up in him. And man, I want him to put down that gun. I want him to put down that gun so badly. Red Joe shouldn't be holding a gun on anyone.

"I don't know anything about William Steel," Brittany says.

"Don't you? If you left all that stuff for Donny, then *you* are the reason we know about this horrible stuff going on at our property."

"I don't—"

"Save it." This from Dad.

His voice sounds like it's powering straight up from hell.

"You will level with us now, Brittany. Or I swear to God, I will send a bullet through your father's skull."

She collapses in a heap of sobs.

Part of me wants to comfort her. Part of me wants to grab the gun out of my father's hand and shoot her.

And man, I really don't like that thought, but I can't deny its existence.

But *is* she the enemy? If not for her, we'd still be ignorant about what's happening on our property. Is she protecting her father? Or is she protecting Pat Lamone?

She's not protecting us.

"Stop your whining," Dad says in his hellish voice. "And start talking because I'm not kidding. I'll shoot your damned father. I don't give a rat's ass whether he lives or dies."

Brittany sniffles. "All right, all right. Please just don't hurt my daddy."

"Talk," I say.

"He needs to take the gun off my father."

"I will *not*," Dad says.

"He can't, Brittany. How else do we know that you'll talk?"

"I promise, I promise. I'll talk. But not until you take the gun off him."

"This may be new to you," Dad says, "but normally the person holding the gun makes the demands. You don't. So start talking now, or I *will* end your father's life."

Brittany gulps back her sobs and suppresses a shiver. "My dad never told me what he was doing, but I figured it out."

"How?" Doc demands.

"I'm not stupid, Daddy. I have access to all your computers. You know this."

"But why would you go through my stuff?"

"Because I wanted to know what was going on. I saw you going out to the kennels that night. And then, all of a sudden, all our bills were paid. I figured it out."

"So you knew . . ."

She shakes her head. "I didn't know exactly what you were doing. I just knew it wasn't on the up-and-up. So I followed you."

"How could you follow me to the barns? There aren't any roads to get there."

"I hid in the back of your truck one night after you thought I'd gone to bed."

Doc's head falls into his hands. "Damn..." He looks up. "The safe. How did you know the combination?"

"That wasn't difficult to figure out. I tried several combinations of numbers I knew were important to you."

*Twenty-four.*

*Forty-seven.*

*Three.*

How are those numbers important? Does it even matter?

Brittany gulps. "It's not too late, Daddy. Maybe the Steels will strike a deal with you. Maybe they'll let you off the hook if you help them."

"Don't bet on it," Dad says.

"I'd help you if I could, Joe," Doc says. "These people don't exactly deal in the daylight."

"I'm betting," I muse, "that if I take this ring to a gemstone specialist, I'll find out that it's a complete fake, won't I, Brittany?"

"Yes." She gulps. "I found the original, and I took it to a jeweler in Grand Junction. He duplicated it. This is sterling silver covered in white gold plate and cubic zirconia in the right color."

"How did you know it belonged to us?" I ask.

Brittany gulps again. "I didn't. But when I found out how much the original was worth, I knew that if I left it for one of you along with the GPS coordinates, you would pay attention."

"What got our attention more than that was the fact that you were able to get into the house. Uncle Talon's house."

"That was simple enough," Brittany says. "I did it myself. Once Talon was shot, I went over to offer my condolences, and only Darla, the housekeeper, was home. She let me come in, and I asked to use the bathroom. It was simple enough after that to place it in Donny's cabinet."

"Why Donny?" I ask.

"Because I knew he was home, and I knew he would find it. And I had a reason—offering sympathy for the shooting—for getting into the house. It was the simplest way."

"And how did you open the safe-deposit box in Denver?" I ask.

"Pat helped with that."

"Of course. Pat."

"You're saying Pat Lamone knows all about this?" my father asks.

"Yes. He knows. And he has every right to know. He's one of you, after all."

"I wouldn't take that to the bank," Dad says.

"He can prove it," Brittany says.

"And how do you think he can do that?" I ask.

"Well, there's DNA."

"Which may not be conclusive from half siblings three generations ago," Dad says.

"He has records. He's a grandson of William Elijah Steel."

"So you have heard of him," I can't help saying snidely.

"Then maybe you can shed some light on something," Dad says. "Who the hell is William Elijah Steel's mother?"

"I don't know. Why would I know that?"

Dad says nothing more.

He doesn't want to give much away, but I know he's thinking of the birth certificate we found in Murphy's place, under the floorboards. The birth certificate for William Elijah Steel that shows George Steel as his father, with the area for his mother left blank.

Which in itself is very strange.

According to Donny and Dale, our family has a reputation for doctoring documents.

"Daddy," Brittany says, "can you ever forgive me?"

"Of course. You're my daughter."

"I was just trying to protect you. I knew you were into something bad. And I was trying to protect Pat. He's a Steel, after all, and if the Steels go down for this . . . then what is left for Pat?"

"You know"—my mind whirls with ideas—"on the face of it, this all sounds altruistic. But do you want to know what I think?"

"What do you think, son?" Dad says.

"I think you *want* the Steels to go down, Brittany. I think you and Pat both do, because if he truly *is* one of us? With all of us out of the way, our undivided fortune would be *his*."

# CHAPTER TWENTY-FIVE

## Rory

I'm an actress. I'm a vocalist first, but I'm also an actress. Still, putting on my game face is more difficult than I imagined.

I still haven't heard from Brock, and he never leaves my mind. He's big and strong and is with his father. He can surely take care of himself, but he's not bulletproof.

No one is.

In the last several weeks, I've seen my father—my healthy, robust father—taken down by a heart attack. I've additionally seen Talon Steel—also healthy and robust—felled by a bullet.

They made it through, most likely because of their overall strength and health, but both instances reiterated to me how fragile life truly is.

And Brock... Brock is so young. Only twenty-four. We just found each other. We can't lose each other. Not yet.

Not ever.

Jesse hands me a key card. "Here you go, sis."

We unload our bags from the car and set them in our sparsely furnished room.

This is not the Carlton, for sure.

Two double beds are covered in threadbare rust-colored cotton, a nightstand between them, and a small bathroom with only one sink, a toilet, and a shower. The walls are covered in tacky flowered wallpaper straight out of the seventies. I inhale. A little musty, but clean.

That's it. No chairs, no desk, only an old TV. And I mean *old*. Not a flat-screen TV.

Well, as Jesse said, all we'll do here is sleep.

We shove our bags inside and then meet the rest of the band back down at the cars.

"Lunch," Cage says, "and then we go over to the venue, check it out, have a rehearsal. Sound check."

"Sounds good. And we're on at what, eight o'clock?" Jesse asks.

"Yep," Cage says. "Eight o'clock sharp. Two sets. A break in between."

"Is this one of the venues where agents hang out?" I ask.

"It is," Cage says.

I nod. "Don't you find it odd that agents come to a small town outside Salt Lake City?"

"On its face, yeah," Cage says. "But the guys who own these two places used to work in LA, so they've got connections."

"Okay. Makes sense."

Cage smiles. "It's on you, cuz. You need to look the part tonight."

"Since when do I ever *not* look the part?"

"I hate to be the bearer of this news to you, you being my sister and all," Jesse says, "but T and A sells. We may have all the talent in the world, but you're going to be the one selling this performance."

I roll my eyes. He's no doubt right, but it still irks me.

"All right," Jake says. "Everybody in the van. Let's go have some lunch."

"If you guys don't mind, I think I'll skip lunch."

"Sis," Jesse says, his eyes serious. "I understand, but we've got a performance tonight, and there could be an agent in the audience. You need to be at your best, which means you need to eat."

I sigh. He's right, of course. "Can't I just order something in?"

"Does this look like the Four Seasons to you?" Jesse asks.

I sigh again. A couple of nights in a suite at the Carlton paid for by Brock, and I've become spoiled. I'm not that person.

"All right, all right. Where are we going?"

"I've got a hankering for tacos," Jake says.

"Tacos sound great." From Cage.

Dragon stays silent. He's not a big talker, so that's not surprising.

"Tacos are fine," I say.

"Tacos it is, then," Jesse says. "Let's go."

★ ★ ★

I managed to force down one taco, a few chips and salsa, and a draft beer. Normally I don't drink alcohol this close to a performance, but the beer helped me relax a little.

But only a little. I've texted Brock a few times since we got here, and he has not replied.

What is going on in Wyoming? I'm here, in Utah, and he's in Wyoming. We're so far away from each other.

I don't like it. I don't like it at all.

After lunch, we arrive at the venue, and the manager greets us.

"Hey, Dragonlock. It's great to have you here." He holds out his hand, and Jesse takes it. "I'm Guy Landon. I'm the general manager here. Let me show you what we've got set up for you."

"Lead the way," Jesse says.

"Who are you?" Guy eyes me.

"She's my sister, Rory. She sings lead with me."

"You will be a draw for sure," Guy says.

I'm used to this. Used to being judged solely on my looks. It's annoying, but I deal.

I paste on a smile. "We're very happy to be here."

"We're thrilled to have you guys," Guy says. "We're expecting quite a crowd tonight."

"We've heard that agents sometimes come to hear your shows," I say.

I figure he'll talk to me as much as to anyone else. Probably more so.

"Yes, they do. I have it on good authority that one of the major talent agents from LA will be here tonight. Someone from the Rossi Group."

Jesse's, Jake's, and Cage's eyes all widen.

Dragon looks bored, as usual.

Classic Dragon.

"That's wonderful," I say. "Thank you for this opportunity." Cue dazzling smile.

"There's no guarantee," Guy says. "Like I said, I have it on good authority. I don't want you to get your hopes up, but both Crybaby and Potato Soup got their start here."

This time I widen my eyes. "I love Crybaby."

I don't listen to a lot of rock, but Crybaby is a new band with a female lead who has a background in opera like I do. Her voice is fabulous. The keyboardist is quite a talent as well. The only thing I don't like about them is their name. Crybaby? Really?

"Yeah, they're hot right now, aren't they?" He pats himself on the back—literally. "And they can thank old Guy here for getting them on the map. In fact, it was someone from the Rossi Group who signed them after they performed here."

"Well," I say. "That's amazing. I love their music."

Guy eyes me again. "I've got to say, Delia Forest has nothing on you, honey."

Jesse's jaw goes rigid. So does Cage's. Delia Forest, the vocalist I admire, may not be runway material, but her voice is something powerful, and she's attractive in her own way.

*Oh? You haven't heard me sing yet. How would you know she's got nothing on me?*

The words hover near the back of my throat, but I make sure they stay there. I'd like to smack Guy upside his head for his comment.

Instead, I cue the dazzling smile once more. We want Guy on our side.

"And Potato Soup?" Guy continues. "They haven't made it quite as big, but they're on their way up."

"I haven't actually heard of them," I say. I resist the urge to make fun of their band name.

"Like I said, they're on their way up. I think they're supposed to open for Emerald Phoenix on their next tour."

"We'll have to check them out," Jake says.

"Yeah, do. They're pretty darn good."

We follow Guy to the stage area, and Jesse, Cage, and Jake talk to him about sound and other stuff that I know nothing about.

Opera is never electronically amplified, so I know nothing about sound. It's all acoustics. I leave this to the guys when we perform. They know what they're doing.

Dragon hangs back with me.

"Hey, Rory," he says in his low voice.

"Dragon."

"I've been thinking about you."

"Oh?"

"Yeah . . . About how we almost . . ."

Right. Thank God I averted that big mistake.

"I was in a bad place, Dragon. I'm better now."

"Hey, you don't need to be in a bad place. We can have some fun anyway."

"I'm flattered, but . . ."

"I know. Brock Steel."

"Good news travels fast."

"Not that fast. Just from your brother."

"Yeah. It surprised the hell out of me, but I'm happy."

"Good. I'm happy for you."

I suppress a chuckle. Wasn't he just hitting on me?

"What's going on with you, Dragon?"

"Not much."

"You ever think about settling down?"

"With whom?"

"I don't know. With anyone. You've got that dark rocker thing going. Women are always all over you."

"I seem to attract only women who are too young for me."

My sister Maddie's face pops into my mind. Maddie and the awesome foursome all seem to be completely enamored with Dragon. That dark demeanor is irresistible to them. Hell, I almost fell for it recently.

But man, Dragon has an edge to him. Nobody really knows his story. No one except Jesse, and his lips are sealed.

I get it. Whatever Jesse knows, it's not his story to tell. But damn . . . I just went way out of my comfort zone today to let him in on a little bit of the Steel story.

That's different, of course. I'm involved with Brock, so Jesse is concerned.

No one I know is involved with Dragon, so there's no need for me to be concerned.

"I'm sure Jesse has told you to stay away from our sister."

"Yeah, he hasn't minced any words on that."

"She's young. Impressionable. Only twenty-one."

"I know. Your brother has made that clear. She's hot, though."

"She's my sister, Dragon."

"Hell, you're all hot. You, Callie, and Maddie. But you . . ." He licks his lips.

"Sorry. Taken."

"My loss." He shoves his hands in his pockets. "I'm going to join the guys."

"Okay."

He ambles off, and I can't help a glance at his ass. It looks pretty darn good in his jeans. He's built, for sure. Tattoos cover both his arms. I have no idea of any of their meaning. Long jet-black hair seems contrary to his hazel eyes. Does he color his hair? Somehow I can't see Dragon doing that. His eyes are the kind that seem golden amber sometimes and nearly emerald green at other times. They're almost mystical.

There is definitely *something* about Dragon Locke. Something dark and sexy and powerful.

And I almost fell for it.

If not for that drunken phone call from Brock . . .

I shudder to think of it. I'm so glad I didn't stray. I'm so glad I remained true to Brock, even though, at that time, we had no commitment between us.

"Hey!" Jesse yells. "Let's unpack and get ready to rehearse."

# CHAPTER TWENTY-SIX

### Brock

Brittany is silent.

Doc is silent.

Dad is silent.

Does this mean I've stumbled onto something?

My mind continues to whirl. "I'm also thinking that whoever is behind all of this—whoever hired your father, Brittany—figured out that you were trying to communicate with us. I'd be willing to bet that's why they planted those red fingernails—which I'm pretty sure will have your fingerprints on them—at the site in Colorado."

"No." Brittany shakes her head.

"You need to remember something." I gesture to the safe. "Something you obviously didn't give any thought to. People who can pay small-town veterinarians in jewels are not your run-of-the-mill average people. Everything they do is meticulously planned. They're intelligent people. They may not be ethical people. Hell, they may be absolute psychopaths. But they're not stupid, Brittany."

"Are you saying my daughter is stupid?" Doc asks.

"Shut up." Dad keeps a steady hold on his gun.

I roll my eyes. Brittany's not stupid, but I won't give her the satisfaction of saying that aloud. But these psychos are smarter than she is. "I'm just saying these people know what they're doing. They've thought through every contingency."

"Daddy..."

"Not a word, Doc." From Dad.

"You think he can save you? If you'd stayed out of it, maybe. Maybe they would've considered you an innocent bystander. But you didn't stay out of it, Brittany. You decided you could take on criminally unhinged human traffickers. People who pay your father in priceless gemstones. People who have the kind of money to make you disappear."

"My son is right," Dad says to Brittany. "You're damned lucky they didn't take *you*."

"But I..." she chokes out.

"You really have no idea what you're dealing with, do you?" I say. "Did you know what was going on in those barns? Did you know what these people were doing? What your father has been helping them with?"

She shakes her head vehemently. "No... I just thought maybe they were robbing people. Stealing."

"And using our property to do it?" I ask.

"Well... yeah."

"To implicate us?"

She nods. "That's what I thought."

"And do you really think any law enforcement officer in the world would believe that we—the Steels—are thieves?"

She stays silent.

"We have enough money to support our family for generations to come if none of us lifts another finger. And you think law enforcement would believe that we are engaging in common theft?"

"Yes. Maybe. I don't know. Maybe I wasn't thinking. But I didn't know. I swear I didn't. Human trafficking? Who does that?"

"You're right on one point," Dad says. "You weren't thinking."

"If you were that concerned," I say, "why not just come to one of us?"

No reply.

Not that I expected one. I already know the answer. She wasn't trying to help us. She was trying to help Pat.

"I think we're done here," Dad says. He finally puts his gun down.

A huge sigh whooshes out of Doc Sheraton.

Brittany crumples to the ground.

"We can't just leave them here," I say. "They'll do… I don't know what they'll do, but it won't be good."

"We don't have a choice, son," Dad says. "We can't stay here any longer. We need to stop what they put in motion, and we can't do it here in bumfuck Wyoming."

My father is, of course, right. He usually is.

Except when he pulls out guns and holds them to people's heads.

Then again… Would we have gotten where we are now without him doing that? It may have been wrong on every level, but we finally got some answers.

"Then what? What do we do?"

"First thing is we hire somebody to bulldoze those two barns to the ground."

"You mean after…"

"Yes. After we've had them combed for evidence."

"So we're not going to alert the authorities?" I ask.

"Absolutely not. You were right when you told Brittany that the authorities would never believe her. They won't believe us either, son. This stuff is on our property, and somehow it got on our property without any of us knowing. That's on us, and we have to do better."

He has a point. We are good people. We were raised to be good people. Honest people. But by virtue of who we are, we have our enemies.

Whether it's because of jealousy, or in Doc's case, because we didn't give him a position he wanted. Or myriad other reasons related to our good fortune.

"When will all this start?" I ask.

Dad is fiddling with his phone. "It's already started. I've alerted our teams, and they'll be investigating all the GPS coordinates as well as the rest of our land. Now that we know how to call Doc's dogs off, there shouldn't be a problem."

"What about the dogs that are here?"

"Humane Society," Dad says.

"Those dogs are my property, Joe," Doc grits out. "You can't just take them."

"Watch me." Dad shakes his head at Doc. "I made the right call all those years ago, Mark. I don't like the way you treat these animals."

"I use top techniques for guard-dog training."

"I still don't like it. The Humane Society will be here tomorrow."

"Dad . . ." The Humane Society is far from my first choice, but I can't take the dogs myself. I would if I could.

"These are good dogs," Dad says. "Well trained, even if we don't like Doc's methods. They'll find homes. Or jobs. I know what you're thinking, son. I am too. I don't want these animals to lose their lives."

I nod, thinking of Sammy and Zach.

Already I've come to think of Zach as my dog as well.

I've always loved animals. You can't grow up on a ranch and not love animals.

Doc clears his throat. "What about us?"

"Do what you want at this point," Dad says. "We won't try to stop you."

"What does that even mean?" Doc asks.

"It means you're being watched. Do what you want. Whatever it is that you want. But I have a feeling you're going to be an upstanding citizen from now on."

"What about her?" I gesture to Brittany.

"Same thing." Dad looks at Brittany. "You want to cause any more trouble? Stir anything more up? Go for it. But we know what you're up to now, and you *will* be watched. Every second of every day you will be watched."

"That's illegal," she says.

Dad laughs. A wonderful Jonah Steel guffaw. The iceman has finally melted. My father is back.

"Do you really think you're the person who should lecture us on what is illegal and what is not?"

That shuts her up.

"Stay here," Dad says, "or return to Snow Creek. It's up to you. But every move you make will be documented, so tread carefully. Oh, and Brock and I will be taking the jewels with us. We will have them appraised and their ownership traced." He grabs the last velvet bag, shoves it into his pocket, and turns to me. "Brock, let's get the fuck out of here."

# CHAPTER TWENTY-SEVEN

## Rory

After an awesome rehearsal, we take a break at three p.m. Time for rest, and then a light dinner, before the show.

My phone dings with a text.

"Thank God," I say out loud.

It's from Brock.

*Hey, sweetheart. Dad and I are on the road back to Colorado. Where will you be tonight?*

*Thank God you're okay! I've been so worried.*

I quickly add the address of our venue.

*I can't believe I won't see you for a week.*

*I know. I miss you. I'm just so glad you're all right. What happened?*

*I'll call you later. Once Dad and I get back and I'm alone.*

*Okay. I love you.*

*I love you too.*

I breathe a sigh of profound relief.

All this time, even during a rehearsal that went well, I had something holding me back.

No longer.

Brock is safe.

We'll be okay.

★ ★ ★

Perspiration slides over my face.

But it's good perspiration. The perspiration from a hard evening's work.

We killed it tonight. The house was packed, and we were on fire.

Jesse and I were so in sync with our vocals, and the whole band was with us the whole time. All the way.

Two encores.

They clamored for a third, but we never do a third encore. Maybe we should rethink that position.

When I mention it to Jesse, though, he says, "Nope. That's our band's motto. Always leave them wanting more."

"Then why not stop after one encore? Or don't do any encores at all?"

"Because we love our audience. We have to give them something."

My brother's such a rocker. Tonight, more than any other time performing with his band, I really felt a part of things.

I've never considered myself an actual member of this band. I don't perform with them all the time.

But for the first time, I wonder…

What would it be like to be a permanent member of the band?

I'm sure they'd have me, but am I ready to give up the rest of my life? Teaching? My holiday concert? I've already been going through programming in my head. I just haven't had the time to jot it down.

"Was the guy from Rossi here?" I ask.

"I'm not sure," Jesse says.

We're packing up our instruments, when—

"You guys rocked it," Guy says, walking to the stage. "The agent from Rossi is here and wants to meet you."

My heart skips. "That's amazing."

"Absolutely," Jesse says. "Where is he?"

"It's a she, and she wants to talk to you at her table."

"Maybe we could go somewhere quieter," Cage says. "It's still pretty noisy in here."

Guy nods. "Let me ask her. Maybe she'll come backstage."

"That'd be great."

We continue packing up, and once we're about done, Guy returns.

"Hey, guys. This is Selena Campbell from the Rossi Group."

Selena Campbell is dressed in black jeans and a bronze halter top, plus spiked platform heels. She doesn't look like an agent, or at least not how I assume an agent would look. She looks more like a *Playboy* centerfold.

"Jesse Pike." Jesse holds out his hand. "This is my sister, Rory. And my cousin, Cage Ramsey, our lead guitarist. Jake

Michaels on keyboard, and Dragon Locke on the drums."

"Dragon Locke?" Selena raises her eyebrows.

"Yes, ma'am," Dragon says.

"So they named the band after you?"

"They did."

"It's just a really cool name, don't you think?" Cage says.

"I do. You guys were terrific, especially you." She eyes me.

I've seen that look before.

Jesse won't recognize it. Neither will the guys.

This woman is attracted to me.

She's beautiful, no doubt, with blond hair, blue eyes, and a killer body. But I'm not the least bit interested in anyone except Brock.

And I hope . . .

I hope she's truly interested in the band and not just me.

"Thank you very much," I reply.

"Have you ever thought of going solo?"

Jesse's jaw drops.

Shit. Now they're going to be pissed at me.

"In rock? No, I haven't. My background is in classical singing and musical theater."

"Musical theater . . . You do have an amazing voice for that as well. I could totally see you as Mimi in *Rent*. Or maybe Maureen."

Both roles I know well. But I don't volunteer this. Besides, opera singers as a rule don't care for *Rent*, as it's a poor rip-off of *La Bohème*, which doesn't even have a mezzo role for me.

"Could we speak privately?" Selena asks me.

"I suppose so." I glance toward Jesse.

His lips are pursed a little, but he gives me a slight nod. I move to a quiet corner with Selena.

"I'm horny as hell for you," she says, "and for your brother."

I inch backward. Not what I was expecting.

"You're very attractive, but I'm in a relationship. As for my brother? You'll have to ask him."

She smiles, her gaze landing on my breasts. "I don't think you're getting my drift."

"What other drift is there?"

"Rory . . . I'm interested in a . . . threesome."

I can't imagine what my face looks like. I know only the feeling of disgust that rolls through me at the thought. A threesome with my brother? Seeing each other naked? Even if we don't touch each other, it would be way too weird.

It's a pretty sick thought.

"Ms. Campbell . . ."

"Selena."

"Whatever. Are you interested in our band at all?"

"You guys were terrific. I'm not lying. But I think you have potential for a solo career."

"I tried a solo career. I didn't make it."

"When was this?"

"Seven years ago. I tried for an opera career."

"You were too young."

"I was twenty-one."

"Yes, and for your voice type—which I assume is a dramatic mezzo, based on what I heard tonight—that's too young."

"Well, that's in my past."

"It doesn't have to be . . ."

"Look. If you're interested in me as a solo artist, we can talk some other time. Tonight is all about the band."

"The band is terrific, but I'll be honest with you, Rory. I'm not looking to sign any new acts right now. Solo artists *or* bands."

Then why the hell is she here?

Easy enough question to answer. She likes going to bed with rockers. She wants to hit the sack. Specifically with my brother and me. Simultaneously.

Right. So not happening.

"Then I'm sorry for wasting your time." I turn.

She grabs my arm. "Can't you talk to your brother?"

"You really think I'm interested in having a threesome with my brother?"

"Why not? I've had similar escapades before, and it's hot."

"You've gone to bed"—I clear my throat—"with a brother and sister?"

"I have. Not everyone's as uptight as you seem to be."

I stop myself from dropping my jaw to the floor. This is rock and roll, I guess. Sex, drugs, and rock and roll, as they say—though I don't exactly know who *they* are. This would never happen in the opera world.

"Right. I'm uptight because I don't want to get naked with my brother." I shake my head. "If that's uptight in your book, then I guess I'm uptight." I whisk away.

That left an acidic taste in my mouth.

"Let me guess," Cage says when I return. "She wants you and not the rest of us."

"Not exactly . . ."

"What the hell was that all about?" Jesse asks.

"Unfortunately, she's not signing any new bands *or* solo acts right now."

"Really? Even after that stuff she said to you?"

"Really."

"Then what did she want to talk to you about?" Jake asks.

Jesse rolls his eyes. "She has the hots for my sister."

I inhale. How exactly do I say this? "You're partially right."

"What the hell is that supposed to mean?" my brother asks.

"Trust me. You do *not* want to know."

"Yeah . . . I kind of do."

"You really don't."

"I really do."

Cage, Jake, and Dragon are listening, their ears perked up.

"Hey, guys," I say to them, "she's not signing anyone, but if you're horny . . . Give it a shot. She's ripe for the picking."

Then I turn to Jesse. "Are you sure you want to know?"

"Yeah."

"She wanted a threesome, Jess. With *both* of us."

I don't see a look of pure disgusted shock on my brother's face often, but I see it now.

"That's not only revolting," he says, "it's degrading to both of us. Who the hell would do that?"

"Right?" I shudder. "At least she was honest. She's not signing anyone right now, which means she was only here to get laid. She could've easily made us think she'd sign us if we did the deed."

"Looks like Cage and Jake may satisfy her need for a threesome." He gestures.

Selena still stands in the corner. Jake and Cage are smiling, Cage with one hand on her shoulder, and Jake with his arm around her.

"I hope they have more sense," I say.

Jesse laughs. "Don't bet on it."

My phone buzzes in my back pocket.

I catch my breath when I see that it's Brock.

*You rocked it tonight.*

*Thank you,* I start to write, when—

He's here?

"I've got to go, Jesse." I leave backstage and race into the main room.

Brock sits at the bar, a bottle of Fat Tire in front of him.

"Brock!" I run toward him and launch myself into his arms, nearly knocking him off his stool. "What are you doing here?"

"Seems I was free tonight."

"You can't even know how happy I am to see you."

"I think I know." He kisses my lips hard.

He tastes like Fat Tire and like Brock himself—all spicy and masculine.

Jesse comes out and saunters up to us. "Brock."

"Hi, Jesse. You guys were awesome tonight."

"Too bad the agent in the audience didn't think so."

"She thought so," I say. "She's just not signing anyone right now."

"Then why the hell is she here?" Brock asks.

Jesse and I burst into laughter.

# CHAPTER TWENTY-EIGHT

### Brock

Maybe the two of them are high on their performance. But they're giggling like a couple of schoolgirls.

"Have the two of you been drinking?" I ask when they finally stop laughing.

"Nope. We wouldn't drink before a performance." Jesse signals to the bartender. "But I sure as hell need one now."

"What's so funny?"

"It's not funny so much as disgusting," Rory says. "The agent is a woman, and she asked me quite bluntly to have a threesome with her and Jesse."

I wrinkle my nose. "She does know you're brother and sister, right?"

"Oh, she knows."

"That's disgusting."

"Yes. Extremely disgusting."

Though an image comes back to me from my college frat days... The time Dave and I had a threesome with a woman. We were totally focused on her, obviously. The two of us had no desire to touch each other in any way. First of all, we're cousins, and second of all, we're both very straight males.

I wouldn't do it again because it was too weird seeing my cousin naked.

But a brother and a sister? That's repulsive.

"Yeah, I set her straight pretty quickly." Rory grabs my Fat Tire and takes a drink from it. "Too bad the band isn't getting an agent out of this, though."

"We don't need an agent who sleeps around," Jesse says.

Rory chuckles. "LA agents probably all sleep around."

"You're probably right." I take another drink of my beer.

The bartender takes Jesse's drink order.

He looks at Rory. "You want anything?"

Rory smiles at me. "Do I want anything, Brock?"

My groin tightens. "No, you don't. Let's get the hell out of here."

★ ★ ★

So much races through my mind. Everything we found in Wyoming. My father and how he acted. I can't figure out if I admire him or hate him for it.

But all of that?

I push it to the back of my mind because I have Rory.

She laughs when I drive up to the Sundown Motel. "This motel? Really?"

"Hey, you told me this is where you were staying."

"It is. I just figured that . . . you know . . ."

"That Brock Steel would put you up in the most lavish Waldorf-Astoria type place in bumfuck Utah? I got news for you, sweetheart. It doesn't exist."

"Hey, I'm not the one with champagne tastes."

"I'm a rancher. A rancher who drinks beer. I don't have champagne tastes either. I'm not Dale or Uncle Ryan."

"Honestly," Rory says, "the place has a bed. That's really all we need, right?"

"God," I groan.

I've already checked in, so I grab her hand, haul her to the room, get us both inside—

Then I crush my mouth onto hers.

Her lips are already parted, and I dive in with my tongue. I'm hungry for her. Aching for her. Especially after the freaking day I've had.

Not to mention the night.

I haven't slept in nearly twenty-four hours.

Sleep can wait.

Nothing is more important right now than being with Rory.

She meets my tongue with her own, and we kiss harshly, passionately. One of those kisses we're famous for—all lips, teeth, and tongues.

She's dressed provocatively, having just come from a concert with the rock band, and those thigh-high boots are making me insane.

I'm going to remove them one by one. Peel those tight jeans and tight tank off her glistening body.

Right now, though, I can't take my mouth from hers.

Can't stop the kiss long enough to do any of those other things.

It's not my decision, though. Rory breaks the kiss and then gasps in a breath of air.

Her lips are swollen already—red and puffy from the kiss.

God, she's beautiful. So beautiful and sexy and—

"You look hot," she says.

Do I? I don't know what a hot guy looks like. We got home from Wyoming, and I took a shower. A long hot shower to wash the filth of the past twenty-four hours off me.

I'm wearing cowboy boots, Levi's, and a blue-and-white striped button-down.

Hardly hot in my book, but what do I know?

"Baby, you *define* hot," I say.

Her spiked thigh-high boots... Her skinny black jeans... Her tight black tank with *Dragonlock* written in silver sequins.

Her hair is down, floating over her shoulders, and she's wearing makeup.

Rory doesn't need makeup, but I understand its necessity under the lights.

Her eyes are heavily lined in black with gray and bronze shadowing. What Diana and Brianna call a smokey eye. Again, nothing Rory needs, but it works right now with the clothes she's wearing.

The clothes she soon will *not* be wearing.

"I'm going to undress you," I say. "And I'm going to take my time. Even though I want you naked right now, my cock embedded inside you. But this... You're a fucking work of art right now, Rory. You're fulfilling all my lurid sex fantasies of fucking a hot girl rocker. I'm going to peel those boots off your legs."

I push her gently until she's sitting on the edge of the bed. Then I kneel before her.

God, those boots. I almost want to lick the sleek black leather as if it's a part of her.

I resist the urge and instead slowly unzip the boot, beginning midway up her thigh and moving downward, all the way down to her sexy ankle.

I peel the black-and-silver boot off Rory's foot.

Damn. The leather again. I grew up on a ranch. I should be used to the smell of leather. But this... Rory's boot... I inhale its earthy scent. This isn't the scent from the ranch, though. It's the leather of the boot mixed with Rory's aroma.

Her natural perfume, which smells like roses and musk and sweet cinnamon spice.

I set her boot down and remove the other.

Then her socks, and her pretty feet come into view.

Yes, this woman even has pretty feet. Perfectly formed, with perfectly square toenails painted red.

That's new.

Usually they're light pink.

I kiss her big toe. "Red?"

"Seemed appropriate."

"Appropriate for what?"

"Appropriate for my sexy boyfriend to surprise me in Utah."

I smile. "You knew?"

"Of course not. I just missed you, and in the back of my mind I hoped."

"Being away from you was like being without air," I say.

"For me too."

"You had plenty of air, sweetheart. You sang like a freaking nightingale tonight. You are amazing."

"Maybe on some level I knew you were in the audience."

"You didn't see me?"

"Not until I got your text. But don't take that personally. I get really into the performance. The audience doesn't really exist."

"Not at all?"

"Okay," she says. "I didn't explain that very well. I perform *for* the audience. It's all for the audience. But the lights are usually so bright that it's difficult to see them, and I wasn't looking for anyone in particular tonight."

"Not even the agent?"

"Especially not the agent. If I think I'm auditioning, I get nervous. So I put agents out of my mind."

"Do you?"

"Brock, I have to. When I was auditioning for agents and companies in New York, I didn't have any luck. I can't let that cloud my mind during a performance."

"I understand." I kiss her toe again.

Time to get back to the task at hand. I move to her jeans, unsnap them, unzip them, and then I slide them over her hips, down her legs. I set them next to the boots.

Cotton panties. No lace, no silk. And still the hottest thing ever. I suppress every urge I have to rip the rest of her clothes off and plunge inside her.

But I want to make this last.

She and I both deserve some slow lovemaking after the days we've both had.

"White cotton panties tonight," I say. "You really weren't expecting me."

"Only hoping," she says again.

"You make white cotton panties look like the laciest lingerie." I peel them from her hips, bringing them slowly over her legs.

I smell her already without even inhaling.

She's wet for me. Wet and sweet and pungent.

I could spread her legs right now. Free my cock and be inside her in a matter of seconds.

And though my entire body is telling me to do just that, I hold the desires at bay.

She's not wearing a bra. Already I can tell. Her hard nipples are protruding through the black stretchy tank. One pokes out through the *a* of *Dragonlock*, the other through the second *o*.

I can't help myself. I flick my fingers over both.

She gasps.

"Feel good, sweetheart?"

"You have no idea how much I want you right now," she says.

"I think I might have some idea."

"Then get inside me, damn it. Fill me. I need you."

"Damn, baby." An animalistic growl emanates from my chest. "I want to go slow with you."

"Fuck slow," she says.

That's all I need to hear.

Within another minute, my cock is free and I'm inside her, pumping.

Every ridge, all so familiar.

The perfect cast for my cock.

My God, has anything ever felt so good?

All the other women I've been with—and there are a lot of them—have disappeared.

I'm a virgin again. Every time with Rory is like the first time.

Her period's due in a day or two, and we already know she's not pregnant. I should be wearing a condom, but chances of pregnancy at this time in her cycle are low.

And I don't even care.

Maybe she will get pregnant.

Maybe—

"Oh my God!"

I release into her. I release into her with such force, it's like I'm dumping my entire soul into her body.

For a brief time, I'm actually soulless, letting her house the most intimate part of me.

All that I am is inside Rory Pike.

And I don't want it back.

I want to be with her. Always.

I lose myself in this woman. But it's not a bad thing. I'm still me—I'm just a better me with her.

I still have the ring my mother gave me, but I didn't bring it with me.

If I had?

I'd be down to my knees right now asking Rory to be my wife.

The pulsing of my dick finally slows, but I don't want to leave the beauty of being inside her.

But she deserves more than this. More than a quickie from her horny boyfriend.

I had such good intentions . . .

I pull out, and then I slowly remove her tank top, letting her gorgeous breasts fall free.

Her nipples are hard, and they beckon. I take one between my lips, the other between my fingers, and I begin my feast.

She sighs against me. "Feels so good . . ."

"Tastes good, sweetheart," I say against her flesh. "Your nipples taste like cherries."

I'm not even lying. There's a sweetness about Rory's flesh that's indescribable. Everything about her is perfect, delicious, formed by the angels in heaven.

"God, I love you," I say between sucking her nipples.

"I love you too, Brock."

Her hands go into my hair, and she pulls on it, driving me crazy.

I could suck her nipples all night, but I haven't taken care of her. She needs her orgasm. So I drop her nipple and flip her onto her stomach.

"Get on your knees," I command.

She obeys me quickly, which turns me on even more.

Her gorgeous ass is a feast before me. I slide my tongue between her cheeks, and she shudders.

"Every part of you is beautiful," I say. "From the top of your head, your gorgeous hair, your beautiful brown eyes, your full red lips. Your luscious breasts, your flat tummy, your beautiful pussy, and your long shapely legs. Your red toenails on your beautiful feet. And this ass . . . This ass, Rory Pike. You have no idea what I want to do with it."

"I have some idea," she says, her voice shaking a bit.

She's not ready. It's okay. I know this. I didn't come prepared anyway. I don't have any lube with me.

But I can give her the rimming of a lifetime.

I flatten my tongue, massage it against her asshole.

She trembles beneath me.

I won't be able to get her to come this way, but—

I plunge two fingers into her wet pussy.

I find the spongy G-spot, scissor my fingers over it.

A total recipe for orgasm.

Then, with my other hand, I find her clit, slide my fingers over it as I lick her sweet ass.

Her ass tastes as sweet as the rest of her, like cherry pie a la mode. Is it all in my mind? Who the hell cares? It is what it is, and I could lick her forever.

But I don't allow myself to get caught up in the act. I work her clit and G-spot as I lick her, and soon—

"Brock! My God!"

Her vagina quivers around my fingers. And damn, her ass tastes even sweeter with her orgasm. I ease up a bit, let her come down, and then I go crazy on her once more.

"God, yes!"

"You taste so good," I say against her ass.

Then I continue.

I pull another orgasm out of her, and I probe my tongue into her asshole.

I don't dare use a finger yet, but my God...

The things I dream about...

When she comes down from her fourth climax, I climb back on top of her, shove myself into her pussy from behind, doggy style. It's amazing how different the act feels with each position.

My dick is so sensitive, having come only moments before.

I'll last longer this time, and I plan to.

# CHAPTER TWENTY-NINE

## Rory

The ache. The emptiness. How Brock eases all my worries with one simple thrust of his hard cock.

He's fucking me hard, fast, and even now, after so many climaxes… Even now I want more of him.

I want his tongue between my legs, between my ass cheeks.

I want his tongue between my lips, licking my nipples, licking every part of my body.

I want his mouth everywhere.

I want my mouth everywhere on him.

I vow that once he comes again, I will have my turn on top.

And there is not an inch of him that my tongue will not touch.

Thrust, thrust, thrust…

He empties into me, and he's so deep within me, that I swear his dick is touching my heart.

Never have I felt the way—not with another man or another woman—that I feel with Brock Steel.

He stays inside me for a few moments, and I relish the feeling of his strong muscular body on top of mine, his chest to my back.

I straighten my legs, flatten onto the mattress, and his body completely covers mine.

Perfect. So perfect.

We rest for a while this way.

Until finally, I lift my hips, nudging him.

He rolls over to his side and then onto his back, his arm strewn across his forehead.

His body is covered in a light sheen of perspiration, only it doesn't look like sweat. It looks like a glistening, almost ethereal, light.

"My God, sweetheart . . ."

"You just lie there," I say. "Lie there, because I'm not finished with you."

"You're going to have your way with me?" He chuckles.

"Oh, yes. I am totally going to have my way with you." I climb on top of him, kiss his lips, let my tongue tangle with his for a few moments. It's a soft kiss. Not a necessary kiss but an enjoyable one. A postcoital kiss.

I've got four orgasms under my belt, and he's got two.

Now I just want to savor his body. To taste every inch of him.

I kiss his forehead, his cheeks, the strong outline of his jaw. He's salty, from the sweat, but also spicy and musky. The flavor of Brock Steel.

He groans. "Feels good, sweetie."

Sweetie. A new endearment. Usually from Brock it's sweetheart, sometimes baby. Sweetie. I like it. It warms me inside.

I gaze over his entire body, the perfect specimen of masculinity.

His cock lies semiflaccid against his belly. I wonder if I can coax another orgasm out of him.

He's gotten four out of me so far, but as a bisexual woman,

I know better than anyone the differences between men and women.

I know all the hot-button spots for both sexes.

"You just lie there," I say. "Let me do what I want to do."

He closes his eyes, groans once more.

I slide my lips over his neck, over his bronze shoulders. His flesh is warm, hard, so enticing.

And again, the saltiness of his sweat stings my lips. But in a totally good way.

I glide down his chest, using my lips and my fingers to touch as much of him as I can. When I reach his nipples, they're already erect, waiting for me.

I lick one, tease it with my tongue.

He groans.

Yes, nipple stimulation. It's not just for women.

I suck his nipple between my lips and then bite it gently.

Another groan from him, and it emanates through his whole body and into mine.

I tease his other nipple with my fingers, and then I move to it with my teeth and tongue.

At the same time, I run my free hand up and down his flank. The pure warm muscle.

The perfection.

Once I'm done with his nipples, I rain kisses over his taut chest and abdomen, sliding my tongue through each line of muscle of his six pack.

Until I get to—the dark triangle of curls, and his cock...

Which is no longer semiflaccid.

He's hard again. Hard and beautiful, and I ache to suck it between my lips.

But not before I've kissed every part of his body.

I avoid his cock, but I kiss all around it, inhaling the musky scent of his bush. Then I move to his thighs, kiss them, knead them with my hands.

Down to his knees I go, and then I decide to tease him a little.

I turn my body around, so that while I'm kissing his legs, heading toward his feet, he gets a full view of my ass and pussy.

"Not fair, sweetheart."

I chuckle softly. Then I kiss his calves, all the way down to his toes.

I kiss each toe, suck on each one gently, and then I can't help myself.

I wiggle my ass.

Another groan from Brock.

"Turn over," I say.

He obeys quickly, and I massage the instep of his feet.

Another groan. "Man, that feels good."

I continue the foot massage for a few more minutes, but I don't want him to get too used to it. I have other things to do.

I turn around then because he can no longer see my ass anyway.

I continue my upward path, kissing the backs of his calves, up to his knees, which I massage. He chuckles.

"Ticklish?"

"Only the backs of my knees."

I kiss him there again. "Good to know."

I slide up his thighs, kissing them, licking them, massaging them . . .

And then I get to his perfect bronze ass.

I'm experienced with both men and women, but not with the ass.

I've never licked an asshole, not a man's or a woman's. It's not that I have anything against it. My sexual activities just never seemed to include it.

But boy... It sure felt good when Brock licked my ass.

Will it feel good to him?

No time to find out like the present.

I massage his ass cheeks gently, peck tiny kisses over them, and then spread them slightly and swipe my tongue over his asshole.

He quivers. "Damn, baby."

Is this a new sensation for him as well? Clearly he's licked a lot of asses, but has he ever had his own licked?

I'll have to ask him later.

Right now, I'm enjoying the quivering it's inducing.

I flatten my tongue, nudge it against his asshole. Then I roll it and swipe upward, all the way through the crease of his ass cheeks.

I force my tongue into a point next, and I go back to his hole and probe it slightly.

More quivering.

*Good. Nicely done, Rory.*

"Fuck, Rory. I want you," he says into his pillow.

But I'm not done yet. I'm not done worshiping this ass. I'm not done worshiping the rest of his body.

I play with his ass for a few more minutes, and then I finally move upward, massaging his back muscles and kissing him as I go. When I get to his shoulders, I straddle him, and I massage him, this time kneading a little more forcefully.

He groans.

He's so tense.

And I realize...

He hasn't yet told me what went on in Wyoming.

I'll ask him later.

Right now? My job is to make him feel good. To relax these tense muscles.

So I continue the massage. I'm good at massages. Raine is not a massage therapist, but she knows a lot about the discipline, and she taught me. I know where all the muscle groups are, and I know how to release tension in some of the upper back.

I do so now.

Trigger points. Compression. Then the long strokes of Swedish massage.

Ten minutes pass and then fifteen.

And when Brock's groans finally stop . . .

I realize he's fallen asleep.

I lean down, kiss the side of his neck.

"I love you," I whisper. "Relax now. Sleep. We'll talk in the morning. I love you."

# CHAPTER THIRTY

**Brock**

I jerk awake, and for a moment, I'm not sure where I am.

My dreams were hounded by all kinds of images.

Dead bodies.

Children huddled in corners.

And through it all . . . Doc and Brittany Sheraton.

But I find solace.

I find solace in the woman next to me, softly snoring, her brown hair fanned out on her pillow.

Rory. The love of my life. Rory Pike.

How lucky I am to have found her at such a young age.

Sure, I was looking forward to womanizing for the next ten years, but now I can't even imagine that fate.

She's so beautiful. So perfect.

I don't deserve her.

My family doesn't deserve her.

God, my family . . .

How did we let all of this happen?

Donny, Dale, Brad, Dave, Henry, and I . . . We should've seen what was happening.

We should have figured this all out before now, and we should have stopped it.

*Don't blame yourself.*

I hear the words in my mother's gentle voice.

The words are correct. None of this is our fault. We weren't told the truth of our past, so we had no reason to be looking for anything nefarious in the present.

Rory wakes up, stretches, smiles at me. "Good morning."

"Hey." I push her hair out of her eyes. "You're not supposed to be awake yet. I was going to wake you up with..." I lift my eyebrows.

"I'll enjoy it more if I'm awake."

"Spread your legs, sweetheart." I remove the covers from her and begin my morning feast.

She tastes amazing as always, sweet and tart and musky and perfect all at the same time. Once I pull two orgasms out of her, I climb on top of her and shove my dick inside.

Quick and dirty. That's what morning sex is all about. And God, I love it.

I'm in heaven inside her. She truly has heaven between her legs.

I kiss her lips, her neck, the tops of her breasts, and before I know it—

"God, Rory!"

I'm releasing inside her, emptying myself—heart, soul, and body—into her.

I stay inside her for a few moments, and then I turn to my side.

"Mmm," she says. "Such a nice way to wake up."

"We can wake up that way every morning, sweetheart, as soon as you move in with me."

"I'm going to. When we get back from this tour."

"Good. That's good."

Except...

Should I let her move in with me?

Will she be safe there?

Brittany Sheraton got into the main house to leave that stuff for Donny.

Uncle Bryce is supposedly finding a new security company for us, but when will that actually happen?

Rory crawls into my arms.

"Your muscles were so tense last night, Brock."

I don't reply. No big surprise there given my last thirty-six hours.

"Do you want to talk?" she asks.

Do I? I don't want any secrets from Rory, but I sure as hell don't want to put her in danger either.

"It's so much," I say.

"It's up to you. You can tell me or not. It's okay either way."

I rub at my hairline. "It's just..."

"It's okay," she says again.

"I saw a side of my father yesterday. A side I didn't like very much."

She tenses against me. "Oh?"

"Yeah. My father is a strong man, and he can hold his emotions at bay, except when he gets really angry."

"Oh my God. He doesn't..."

"No, of course not. He's never hurt me or my brother or my mother. But he's put his fist through more than one wall."

"I see."

"Dale and Donny coined the term Red Joe. Sometimes he lets his rage get to him. I'm used to it. I know he'll never hurt anyone he loves. I know he'll never hurt anyone, period. At least... I thought I knew that."

"What happened, Brock?"

"In Wyoming, we confronted Doc and Brittany. But there was only one way, in my father's eyes, to get the information he felt we needed."

"Okay..." Rory's voice shakes slightly.

"No one was hurt, Rory. But... my father was different. He pulled a gun on Doc Sheraton."

Rory tenses, moves away from me.

"Hey..."

"I'm okay," she says. "I'm fine."

"Are you? Because it's okay if you're not. I sure as hell wasn't when I witnessed it."

"Yeah. But... Did you get what you needed?"

"We did. Doc Sheraton is doing some nasty stuff on the property that he leases from us."

"And Brittany?"

"Brittany..." I shake my head. "I never would've pegged her for being as smart as she actually is."

"She was smart enough to figure out how to tranquilize Callie and me all those years ago."

"True, but she had been watching her father tranquilize animals for years. It probably wasn't that difficult to figure out the dosage for two teenaged girls." I sigh. "She's a good actress, Rory. But something didn't feel right to me. I almost doubted my instinct, but in the end, I was right."

Rory sits up in bed then. "You're going to have to start at the beginning, Brock, because I'm not following any of this."

"Right."

"It's okay if you can't tell me."

I cup her cheek, thumb her soft flesh. "I don't want to keep secrets from you, Rory. You're my future. I can't have secrets from you. I swear to God I'll never keep secrets from our children either. I mean, when they're young, we'll decide together what to tell them, but no way are they going to grow up like I did, having no idea of their family history."

"I agree with you. And I'm so sorry you've had to go through all of this."

"Sweetheart, we're both going through stuff."

"My father is going to be fine, and as for the rest, it's high school crap. Just stupid high school drama that is rearing its ugly head ten years later."

"And I'm thinking your high school drama is related to my family crap as well. But that's something we'll have to put together."

"I agree. I think it's related. I think Pat targeted Diana specifically, and it wasn't because he knew you'd put up some reward that he could falsely claim. It was because he held a grudge against the Steel family."

"I understand. He thinks he's entitled to have been a Steel this whole time. And maybe he is . . ." I shake my head. "I just don't fucking know, Rory. But let me tell you what went down in Wyoming."

I steel myself as I explain to her everything that happened.

She listens. She tries not to react, and as a trained actress, she's pretty good at it. She still drops her jaw more than once during my story.

"I would've thought the same thing," she says. "I never would have pegged Brittany for having as big a part in all of it."

"She could turn on tears like a fucking water faucet," I say. "I was nearly convinced until we found the ring."

"Wow. What is it with that ring?" Rory asks.

"I don't know. The original apparently belonged to my grandmother, but it's not her initials that are engraved inside.

They're the initials of her mother, or her brother. It doesn't make sense. There's a mystery there, and we need to solve it."

"In the meantime, how are you going to deal with the human traffickers?"

"My father's having all the GPS coordinates combed for evidence, and then we're going to destroy everything there."

"So let me get this straight. Brittany is being set up with the red fingernails, and someone wants your family to think she was at those places."

"Yeah, and at this point? I'm not sure she wasn't."

Rory shakes her head. "Brittany can't be trusted. Clearly she's a bad person. But is she a killer? A trafficker? No way."

"At this point, I trust Doc more than I trust her."

"Really?"

"Yeah. I mean, look at the evidence. Ten years ago, my family didn't give Doc a full-time job on the ranch. His income suffered, so he started the guard-dog business. It wasn't until after that that he got involved with the traffickers. But Brittany?" I shake my head. "She was already tranquilizing you and Callie right around that time. She thought nothing of hijacking her father's medicine cabinet and his email accounts. In essence, she stole from his business. Whatever went wrong with her went wrong a long time ago."

"It was probably Pat's influence."

"Maybe. And she was just a kid back then. Seventeen years old. But Pat Lamone? Do you really think he had that kind of control over a teenage girl?"

"High school is rough, Brock. When you're not born a Steel, it kind of sucks."

"Did it suck for you?"

She blushes then. "No. I was lucky. I was born beautiful."

"And I was born a Steel."

"So you get it."

I nod. "I do. But you know what? There are plenty of other people—the vast majority in fact—for whom high school is a shitty time, and they don't resort to crime."

She nods. "I know. You're right. Take Callie for instance. She's a beautiful girl, but she allowed one remark by Pat Lamone to color her entire high school career. She thought she was an ugly duckling. She felt invisible."

"But she didn't engage in any criminal activity," I say.

"So you really think," Rory continues, "that Brittany, even though she attempted to give you the information via that safe-deposit box in Donny's name, is actually *not* on your side."

"I feel it very strongly. She didn't do it for us. She did it for Pat."

"You may be right. I don't know her well enough. I have no desire to know her."

"I don't blame you. I wish none of us knew her. I look back, and I think… Even if my father had given Doc the job with our ranch, Brittany was still a bad seed. Even before that."

"You'll get no argument from me."

"I wish I could stay," I say, "and continue the tour with you. But I can't. I have to go back home. I have to see this thing through with my family."

She softens then. Crawls into my arms. "I understand."

"Thank you." I kiss the top of her head. "You mean everything to me, Rory. Everything. At least while you're on tour, I know you're safe."

# CHAPTER THIRTY-ONE

### Rory

Brock joins the band and me for breakfast at a local diner and then picks up the tab, which everyone appreciates.

Even Jesse is coming around on the Steels. In fairness, it was never Brock he had a problem with.

Once Brock is on the road back to Colorado, we finish packing the van and head to our next venue.

My mood is a mess. I'm worried about Brock and about what his family has to go through right now. I'm pissed off about the whole agent thing. I mean, Selena Campbell had no intention of signing us. She only wanted to bed the band. Which she did, according to Jesse. Apparently Cage and Jake gave her that threesome she wanted.

That only pisses me off more.

But I'm all in. I can't let Jesse down, so I will continue with this tour. Maybe we'll find someone at the next venue.

Or maybe we won't.

Maybe the idea is just to play our hearts out, to sing and be heard, to enjoy ourselves and provide enjoyment for the audience.

And that's never a bad thing.

# CHAPTER THIRTY-TWO

## **Brock**

I'm home by lunchtime, and after saying hi to Sammy, I head straight over to the main house.

My father's not home.

"He went into the office early this morning," Mom says.

"Okay. I'll see him there." I give her a kiss on the cheek.

Then I drive to the office—or rather, the office building on Steel property where we conduct our business.

Today I'd much rather be out with the livestock, doing hard labor with my hands.

I know everything about our beef business, and sometimes… Sometimes I wish I could just do nothing but the kind of work that keeps me outdoors interacting with the animals, with the land.

But that isn't my life today.

I head up to my father's office, pass his assistant and his secretary, and knock on his door.

"Busy," he says.

I open the door anyway. "It's me, Dad."

"I said I'm busy, Brock."

Bryce sits in the office with Dad, the two of them poring over some kind of ledger.

"Sorry. This can't wait." I close the door and lock it.

"Brock . . ." He's using his *I'm your father* voice.

"Nope. I'm not going anywhere, Dad. Uncle Bryce, I'm glad you're here as well."

"We're busy here," Uncle Bryce says.

"Save it. I'm sure my father's told you what we found yesterday."

"Son . . ."

"No." I walk closer to them, and I don't sit. I like standing while the two of them are sitting.

I'm no longer afraid of my father. I was never afraid of him, really, but I did respect his authority over my life.

I still do, to a certain extent.

But it's time for him to explain himself.

"I couldn't talk to you on the ride home yesterday," I say. "I was still too . . . freaked. But now I need some answers."

"Joe—" From Uncle Bryce.

Dad lifts a hand to stop him. "It's all right, Bryce. The boy is entitled to some answers."

I roll my eyes. "Boy? I'm a grown man, Dad, and I'm entitled to more than answers. But if answers are all I'm going to get today, I'll settle for them." I still don't take a seat.

"What do you want to know?" Uncle Bryce asks.

"This is a conversation between me and my father."

"Bryce can stay. He and I don't have any secrets."

"Fine. Have it your way."

"Sit down," Dad says.

"I'll stand, thanks." I meet my father's gaze.

I see so much of myself in him. He's basically an older version of me, except there are parts of him that I don't ever want to be.

"You frightened me yesterday, Dad. You weren't yourself."

"No," he admits. "I was my fucking old man. I'm not proud of it."

"It's not just that," I continue. "I've always known what to expect with you, Dad. You're a good man, an honest man, but you have your limitations. Your inability to control your anger is one. I've learned to deal with that. We all have, Mom included. We know you won't hurt any of us. But we know you *will* hurt inanimate objects. Walls, for example."

"And?" Dad raises his eyebrows.

Does he really not know where I'm going with this?

"You weren't like that yesterday. You should have been as angry as anything, but you were so . . . in control. In control of everything you did, and that included holding a gun to a person's head for nearly twelve hours straight. I'd bet you could've passed a lie detector test during that time. I've never seen you like that. You were pure ice, Dad."

Uncle Bryce takes note. Looks at my father. "Joe?"

Dad sighs. "I'm not an iceman, Brock. I've only known one iceman in my life."

"Really? Because didn't you always teach me that I shouldn't be judged by my thoughts but my actions?"

"I did."

"Your actions during the past thirty-six hours showed you to be an iceman. As icy a man I've ever seen in my lifetime."

"You're only twenty-four," Dad says. "And I hope you never have to see what you witnessed in Wyoming again."

"Yeah, that makes two of us," I say. "You need to explain yourself."

"I'm not an iceman."

"You're defined by your actions, Dad. Didn't I just say that?"

"Your father's not an iceman," Uncle Bryce says. "A true

iceman is icy all the time. A true iceman can make you believe anything. He can make you believe that he's the most devoted and kind father in the world, all the while doing unthinkable things that you know nothing about."

Uncle Bryce's blue eyes are stern, yet sad. He's speaking from experience.

"What Bryce isn't saying," Dad says, "is that he knew a true iceman. So did I. He was a father figure to both of us."

"Tom Simpson," I murmur.

"That's right. Uncle Bryce's father. Tom Simpson. That man led a double life."

"Still," I say, "I didn't like what I saw, Dad. It was frightening."

"I was on edge the entire time," Dad says. "I surprised even myself."

"Why? Why did you resort to such tactics?"

"What else would you have had me do?" Dad stands, coming face-to-face with me. "We had to find the information. We had to find out what Doc knew. And we did."

I don't respond, because in truth, I'm not sure how to. Silence reigns for a few unending moments, until I finally speak.

"I don't think Doc is a bad man at heart."

"Neither do I," Dad says, "or at least I didn't. But tell me, Brock. Would a good man at heart be doing what he's doing?"

"So you don't believe him? That he didn't know what was going on?"

"No, I do not believe him. He's not that stupid, Brock."

"For a hot minute, I was thinking Brittany was the truly bad person and that Doc was just... trying to make a living, you know?"

"We don't like to think the worst of Doc," Uncle Bryce offers. "But honestly, your father and I have never quite trusted him. Otherwise we would've given him the veterinarian job ten years ago."

"So you say. What was it about Doc that you didn't trust?"

"I could say it was a feeling," Dad says, "and that's certainly part of it. But we had reason to believe that his wife, Brittany's mother, was murdered."

My heart. My stomach. "Reason to believe?"

"Nothing we could prove, just information that came from our sources. It's nothing we ever investigated, but it was enough to make us look elsewhere when it was time to bring our veterinary care in-house."

"No," I say. "I don't need one more fucked-up thing inside my head right now."

"Like I said," Dad continues. "It's nothing we can prove. It's mostly hearsay. And it's nothing we ever looked further into. So it's not anything you need to concern yourself with."

"It sure as hell is. If Doc Sheraton is a murderer, it changes everything about what happened in Wyoming."

"Our information doesn't indicate that," Uncle Bryce says. "There's no reason to suspect that Doc himself was the murderer."

"Then what is the reason to hold it against Doc?"

Uncle Bryce clears his throat. "Our sources showed that he suppressed evidence. Evidence of who the real murderer was."

"Why would he do that?"

Dad and Uncle Bryce exchange glances.

"Don't even think about keeping this from me."

"Take a guess," Dad says. "Based on what we've just found

out in the past forty-eight hours, take a wild guess."

"Not Brittany?" My skin goes cold. "She was just a kid."

"A kid who we think has some kind of personality disorder. She's on medication. She has been since she was a little girl."

"Operative word being *little*. How does a little girl murder a grown woman?" But then I stop. "Doc's medication."

"Give the boy a silver dollar," Uncle Bryce says.

"Damn it, if either of you refer to me as a boy once more—"

"Calm down, son. We don't mean anything by it. We know you're a grown man. But we've also known you since you were in diapers, so you'll always be a boy to us. You'll feel the same way when you have kids."

"This just adds one more piece we don't need to this puzzle."

"You don't need to give it any more thought," Dad says. "It can't be proved, and it doesn't have anything to do with what's going on now."

"Are you kidding me? A child who was capable of murder?"

"That's just it," Dad says. "Children *can't* be capable of murder. They don't have the brain function yet to have the thought process. So even if we could prove it, nothing would happen to Brittany anyway."

He's right, of course.

But my opinion of Brittany Sheraton just lowered, and I didn't think that was possible.

All this time, I was concerned about Doc.

And Doc is certainly guilty.

But Doc is not a psychopath.

His daughter is.

All this time, Rory and I thought that Pat Lamone talked Brittany into tranquilizing the two of them. Maybe it was the other way around. Maybe it was all Brittany's idea. She's an accomplished liar and actress, no doubt.

Talk about an iceman.

"Uncle Bryce . . ."

"Yeah?"

"Some of the gemstones we found—"

Uncle Bryce gestures for me to stop. "I've already looked at them. I'm no jeweler, but they do look familiar. They look exactly like the ones my mother inherited from her aunt. The ones that my father kept from my mother."

"So what do we do about that? What does that tell us?"

"It tells us," Dad says, "that the human trafficking ring we thought we broke up twenty-five years ago? The Feds didn't get all of them. It also tells us that Tom Simpson was using those yellow diamonds, which never belonged to him, as payment, and some of them are still around."

"But again," Uncle Bryce says, "this is still a theory until I can determine that those yellow diamonds did in fact belong to my mother."

"How do you determine that?"

"It shouldn't be too difficult," Uncle Bryce says. "When your father and I found those diamonds hidden in my father's cabin twenty-five years ago, we had them checked out. The gemstone expert determined they all came from the same source."

"Okay, I get it. So if the ones Doc had came from that same source—"

"Right. Still an assumption, but in our eyes, we'll pretty much know."

Finally I sit down.

And boy, am I weary.

Not tired weary, but emotionally weary.

I finally got a decent night's sleep last night, with Rory at my side. But although my body is physically rested, my mind is not.

"So what now?" I ask.

"We set a trap," Uncle Bryce says. "And we bring these fuckers to justice once and for all."

My uncle's words make me want to shudder, but oddly, a feeling of calm settles over me.

Set a trap.

Bring the fuckers to justice.

*Yes, please.*

Because once that happens, I'll be free of this.

Free to marry Rory Pike.

Free to just be . . . *me.*

# CHAPTER THIRTY-THREE

**Rory**

I haven't heard from Brock since he left this morning, and now the band and I are getting ready for our next performance. After this one, we head back to Colorado and Grand Junction for a few gigs there.

Tonight is our last chance to catch the eye of an agent—the Grand Junction venues, while they're great little gigs and we play there a lot, don't attract agents at all.

Selena Campbell from Rossi turned out to be a bust. She was only interested in getting laid by a rocker—which Cage and Jake were happy to help her with.

Jesse gathers us for a moment of silence before the performance.

"There are supposed to be a few agents in the audience tonight," he says, "but of course the manager can't guarantee anything."

"Of course not," I say dryly.

"But we'll do what we always do," Jesse says. "We'll give it our all because we're not playing for an agent or anyone specific. We're playing for the audience, and we're playing for ourselves."

"That's right," I agree. "We're here to entertain. Not solicit."

"Agreed," Cage says.

Dragon and Jake murmur their agreement as well, and then we have a moment of silence.

Jesse started the moment of silence when the band first got together all those years ago. I have no idea what the other members of the band do during this moment. It's a private moment that we never speak about. I'm pretty sure Jesse says a quick prayer. We weren't brought up to be overly religious, but we were taught to believe in a higher power and to be grateful for our food, clothing, shelter. For our intelligence, talents, and most of all, our family.

I say a quick prayer too.

But it's not a prayer for success.

It's simply a prayer for the strength and power to do our best.

Back when I was auditioning in New York, I used to plead with God, or the universe, or whatever—my religious views changed weekly—for success. I begged to become an operatic superstar.

Those prayers were never answered.

I finally came to peace with it, so now? I simply ask whatever powers are out there to be with me so that I can do my best.

Once our moment of silence is over, we take the stage.

We're on fire tonight. Really on fire.

We leave last night's concert in the dust.

If there are any agents in the audience? They'd be foolish not to sign this band.

Jesse and I—our voices harmonize perfectly. The rest of the band is on it as well. I have two degrees in music, and I did not hear one missed note all night. That's almost unheard of. For any performer.

After our two encores, we leave the stage.

This particular venue has a crew to help us pack up—a nice perk. Even if we don't have an agent who sees us and signs us, we were a hit, and we'll be asked back.

I'm sweating profusely, so I tell the guys I'm going to head to the bar for some water.

"You guys rocked," a handsome bartender says. "How have we never booked you before now?"

"We don't play Utah very often," I tell him. "Mostly Colorado and California when we can."

"We need to have you back. The house was packed. Standing room only. Didn't you see?"

"Honestly? I love the audience. I'm singing for them, but I'm kind of inside my own head. Not worrying about who's watching. Sometimes I can't see them anyway because of the lighting."

"Really? That's surprising. You totally played the audience. You're sex personified up there."

I open my mouth to say . . . I don't know what, when—

"I agree. Sex personified."

I turn to the man sitting next to me. He wasn't there when I sat down.

Talk about sex personified . . .

Of course he's nothing compared to Brock Steel, but he's hot. He's wearing a suit, which is odd, for a rock concert, and his blond hair is cut short. His face is chiseled and handsome.

"I'm Sequoia McAllister." He holds out his hand. "With the Lane Agency out of LA."

An agent? Named Sequoia? Interesting.

"That's a very unique name," I say.

"I come from a long line of hippies," he says. "My mother's

name is Rainbow. She doesn't know what to do with a clean-cut guy like me."

I laugh. "Interesting. I'm Rory Pike."

"Oh, I know who you are."

"Which agency did you say you're from?"

"The Lane Agency." He pulls a card out of his wallet and hands it to me.

I take a look at it, run my fingers over the raised lettering. Sequoia McAllister. Junior Agent.

"Can I get you a drink?" he asks me.

"I'm just having water right now. I need to rehydrate."

"Great. A water for the lady, please," he tells the bartender. "And I'll have a Scotch. Macallan. Neat."

I don't know a lot about Scotch, but I do know that Macallan is one of the better ones. Jesse likes to drink Scotch on occasion.

"Coming right up," the barkeep says.

"So tell me, Rory. Are you looking for representation?"

"The band is—"

He quiets me with a gesture. "I'm not talking about the band. I'm talking about you."

I widen my eyes. "I'm part of the band."

"Sweetheart—" he says.

I don't like that he calls me sweetheart. That's Brock's name for me.

"*You* are the draw. Watching you up there is like watching magic."

"Well . . . thank you, but I'm a member of a band, and all of us are equally talented."

"You're right. You're all amazing. Your brother especially. His voice is almost as good as yours."

"So you see, we're a package deal."

"But you don't have to be. I can make you into a star, Rory. With your voice and those looks . . . The sky is the limit."

My heart begins pounding.

Part of me likes this offer. I've always wanted to be a star.

But I never wanted to get there on my looks.

Still . . . He's complimenting my talent as well.

But Jesse is my brother. Cage is my cousin. And Jake and Dragon? They're not family in the genetic sense, but they're still family. They've been with the band since the beginning all those years ago.

So yeah, we're all like family, and the one unwritten rule for the Pikes is you don't cross your family.

"Listen," I say. "I'm flattered. Truly. But I'm a member of the band. We're a unit."

"You drive a hard bargain. And I'll admit, your band is amazing." He lightly touches my forearm. "Tell you what. Why don't we go back to my hotel room and discuss our options?"

I discreetly move my arm away from him. "Okay. I'll go get my brother."

He lowers his gaze to my breasts. "I thought you and I could discuss things alone."

*Yeah, I know what you're after.*

Are all agents sleazebags?

"My brother is the de facto leader of the band. He'll want to be involved. He handles all our contracts."

Sequoia smiles. "You do drive a hard bargain, Ms. Pike. But you're worth it. That's fine. Go find your brother, and we'll chat."

I hop off my barstool, giddy with excitement. Maybe I misread his signals and he's interested after all.

"Thank you so much, Mr. McAllister. You won't regret this." I race through the bar and backstage to find Jesse.

He's looking at his phone.

"Jesse, you have to come with me," I say.

"Okay. What's up?"

"There's an agent from the Lane Agency in LA at the bar. He's interested in talking to us."

"Really?" Jesse nearly jumps out of his skin. "Lead the way, sis."

We head back to the bar, but—

"He was just here. Maybe he went to the bathroom." I gesture to the bartender, who's placing my water in front of me. "Hey, the guy who was just here, who ordered me this drink. Where did he go?"

"I don't know." He slides the Scotch Sequoia ordered in front of Jesse. "But he left without starting a tab."

"He ordered that Scotch," I tell Jesse. "Macallan, neat. He must've gone out to take a phone call or something."

"Cool." Jesse eyes the Scotch. "You know what? I'll have the same."

The barkeep nods and gets to work.

I down half of my water and then turn to Jesse. "It was strange, really. He was interested in talking to me about a solo career, but I told him I wasn't interested."

"Are you nuts? Of course you're interested."

"Not anymore, Jesse. Not that way. Not if it means forsaking you and the band."

"Rory, we always knew you were the commodity."

"But that's not true. We were on fire tonight. Sequoia even—"

"Sequoia?"

"Yeah, that's his name." I show Jesse the business card.

Jesse glances at it. "Damn. Sequoia."

"Yeah. Anyway, he said we were all amazing. That he was surprised to learn that we haven't been signed before now."

"Well, let's talk. Except that he's not here."

"Don't worry. He'll be back. He said he was serious."

So we wait.

Ten minutes pass.

Another ten.

After half an hour, I realize I've been played.

"I'm sorry," I say to Jesse.

"No worries, sis. He was probably trying to get you into bed."

I clamp my hand to my forehead. "What is up with these agents? They're agents, for God's sake. They can get laid whenever they want to."

"Maybe they can't."

"Are you kidding? That woman last night was beautiful, and this guy, Sequoia? He wasn't someone most women would kick out of bed."

"It's a power thing," Jesse says. "I've seen it before."

The bartender comes back with our check. "Hey, is your friend coming back?"

"Doubtful," I say. "And he's not a friend."

"Shit. I guess this comes out of my check, then."

I take the Scotch. "No, don't do that to yourself. We'll cover it."

I take a drink.

Tastes like dirt.

Kind of the way I feel right now.

I excuse myself to go to the bathroom.

And who's standing by the ladies' room, seemingly out of nowhere?

Sequoia McAllister himself. He smiles when he sees me.

"You're a pig," I say dryly.

"What are you talking about?"

"My brother and I have been sitting at the bar for half an hour waiting for you to come back."

"I'm sorry. I got a phone call that couldn't wait."

"A phone call that lasted half an hour? And that left you standing here by the women's restroom?"

"I've been authorized to make you an offer," he says.

"Oh? Let me be the first to tell you, I don't think we're interested."

Though I do want to hear what he has to say. On the off chance that he's on the up-and-up . . .

"My offer is this. I'll be happy to sign your band. You guys are great."

"Okay. What's the catch?"

A lazy—make that sleazy—smile spreads across his face. "You're a smart woman, Rory Pike. Why don't you tell *me* what the catch is?"

"I'm pretty sure it has to do with you and me in a bedroom."

"Like I said"—he curls his lips into a churlish grin—"you're a smart woman, Rory Pike."

I shake my head and let out a sigh. "And like I said . . . You're a pig."

"Clearly you're not naïve. You know how this industry works."

"I'm not for sale. Not at any price."

"Not even for stardom? For your brother? For your family? For that fire that devastated you and your property?"

"How did you know—" I shake my head again. "You weren't back here on a phone call, were you? You were back here searching for information on my family."

"Like I said, you're a—"

"Smart woman," we say in unison.

I shift my weight to one foot. "What is it with you? You seem to think we have potential."

"You have a lot of potential. You guys rocked it."

"So why not sign us, then? Make a lot of money for us and for yourself?"

"I could totally do that. I'm that good."

"Then why do I have to be in the equation?"

"Because I like you."

"You don't even know me. You just think I'm hot."

"Smart woman," we say in unison again.

"But seriously, why?"

"Because," he says, "I can."

I shake my head again, rolling my eyes. "It's a power thing with you. With most men. I've even seen it with women—just last night, in fact. She was at least upfront about it. She had no intention of signing us. She just wanted to fuck some rockers."

He laughs. "Selena was here?"

"Not here. At our venue last night. I take it you know her."

"Everyone knows Selena."

"Great."

"Listen, I *do* believe in you and the band. Spend the night with me, Rory, and I guarantee great things will happen for you."

Damn.

And the funny thing is? If not for Brock Steel, I would probably do this. It's no sweat off my back to have sex with an attractive man, even if he is a snake. Of course I'd have to see the papers—with his John Hancock on them—first.

After all, I'm a smart woman.

But I'd do it. I'd do it for my family. For Jesse.

"I need to see the papers first," I say.

"Of course."

"And I need to see your signature on them."

"Absolutely."

I force a smile then. "Fine. Then let's go."

# CHAPTER THIRTY-FOUR

## Brock

After spending the day in Dad's office with Uncle Bryce and him poring through all kinds of documents, we decided to hire a hacker.

The people moving bodies in and out of our property can't be hacked. We knew that before we went in.

We hired someone to hack into Brittany Sheraton's medical files.

Also into Doc Sheraton's medical files.

Now I'm sitting in Dad's office at home along with Uncle Bryce, and our hacker, Jeff Grayhawk, is on speakerphone.

"What's the good news, Jeff?" Dad asks.

"Your hunches were right, Joe. Brittany Sheraton is responsible for the death of her mother."

The blood in my veins runs cold.

"She was a kid," I say.

"Kids can be . . . a mess," Jeff says. "I've seen it before."

"So Doc has always known this, and he's kept it hidden," Uncle Bryce says.

"Seems that way." Jeff's voice.

"I can't believe she's a murderer." I shake my head.

"Technically she's not," Jeff says. "A child that age can't technically be a murderer."

"Semantics," I say.

"Her medical history is full of mental health treatment. She doesn't seem to know right from wrong. She was diagnosed with antisocial personality disorder shortly after the death of her mother."

"Can't it be treated?" I ask.

"I'm no doctor or psychologist," Jeff says, "but her records show that she's been hard to treat. Apparently she doesn't always give accurate accounts of her thoughts and feelings, which is part of the disorder."

"But she's been on medication."

"She has, but apparently there are no medications specifically approved to treat her disorder. She's been put on antidepressants to treat anxiety and depression, which sometimes are associated with the disorder."

"Can we bring Mom in on this?" I ask. "She'll know exactly what we're dealing with."

Dad sighs. "Yeah. Go ahead and get her, Brock. I hate to burden her with this, but she is an expert. Can you stay on the line, Jeff?"

"Absolutely."

I leave the office, my heart pounding. I find Mom in her own office, working on her book. I check my watch. It's nine p.m. already.

"Hey, Mom."

"Hi, honey. What are you doing over here so late?"

"I'm talking to Dad and Uncle Bryce in his office. And we need you."

"Oh?"

I clear my throat. "Yeah. We need your . . . expert opinion."

Mom rises and widens her eyes. "Regarding what?"

"I'd better let Dad explain. Can you come?"

"Of course."

We walk together to Dad's office, and then we enter without knocking.

"Jonah?" Mom says.

"Sit down, baby."

"Okay."

Mom sits next to Uncle Bryce, and I sit on her other side, facing Dad at his desk.

"I've got Jeff Grayhawk on the phone. He's our computer hacker."

"Hacker? What are you hacking?" Mom asks.

"It's a long story, sweetie, but we need your expert opinion."

"What the hell are you guys into?" Mom asks.

"*We're* not into anything," I tell Mom.

"Like I said, it's a long story, Melanie," Dad says. "And I'll tell you everything, but right now, Jeff's on the line and we need the basics. Can you explain the treatment for antisocial personality disorder?"

"That's a loaded question," she says. "It might be easier to explain the existence of God."

"We know it's a tough diagnosis." This from Uncle Bryce. "We're trying to figure out how Brittany Sheraton is involved in what's going on right now."

"Brittany Sheraton? Doc's daughter? I thought you said Doc—"

"He is. He's involved," Dad says, "but his daughter . . . Jeff hacked into her medical files—"

"Jonah Steel!"

"Melanie, please spare me the ethics discussion. I know it's not right. But Brock and I found out a lot of things about Brittany Sheraton while we were in Wyoming, and we had no choice."

Mom shakes her head. "It's so easy to say you have no choice."

"Mom," I say. "Please, trust me. I'm your son. This is important."

She softens a bit then. Her children are her Achilles' heels. "So you think Brittany has antisocial personality disorder?"

"We don't think," Dad says. "We know. Jeff, tell my wife what the records say."

What little color was left in Mom's pretty face drains as Jeff repeats what he already told us.

"So you see why we need your help," Dad says.

"I specialize in childhood trauma." Mom sighs. "How did I never see this in Brittany?"

"You never had any dealings with Brittany, Mom. She's older than Brad and I are. There was no way you even knew her."

"You're right, I suppose. Still, any psychiatrist, especially one who specializes in childhood trauma . . ."

"We didn't bring you in here to make you feel bad about yourself, baby," Dad says. "We brought you in here for your expertise. We need to know about this disorder."

"Personality disorders are very hard to treat," Mom says. "There are no medications—not for the disorder specifically. Medications can treat some of the symptoms associated with the disorders, like depression, anxiety, aggression—"

"Aggression?" Dad asks.

"Yeah. Some antipsychotics can be helpful with chronic aggression. Clozapine and risperidone are a couple."

"Is she on either of those, Jeff?" Dad asks.

"Nope," Jeff says. "Her records are only showing Zoloft."

"That's an antidepressant," Mom says, "but it's prescribed more for anxiety than depression."

"So nothing is treating her aggression." Dad rubs his jaw.

"She may not have any aggression," Mom says. "Aggression doesn't have to be part of antisocial personality disorder."

"I'm pretty sure she has aggression," I say. "After what she did to Rory and Callie."

Again, Mom does not look surprised. Dad has no doubt filled her in.

"Then again," I continue, "that could've been Pat's idea all along. But something tells me . . ."

"I'm with you, son. Pat Lamone is obviously a bad guy, but as far as we know, he doesn't have any mental disorders."

"As far as we know," I repeat.

Mom sighs. "Give me the records. I don't like it, but if you want my professional opinion, I need to see all the records."

"I've already sent them over to Joe," Jeff says.

"Fine. He can forward them to me."

"They're encrypted," Jeff says. "I'll send you the encryption software in a separate file."

Mom nods. "Sounds good."

"I'm sorry we had to drag you into this, baby," Dad says.

"Don't be. For better or worse, right?"

"That's why I love you." Dad smiles.

"We've had some worse, but we've had a lot of better too, Jonah. I'll help you figure this out."

"Thank you, my love."

"If you don't need me for anything else," Mom says. "I'll pull up these files on my own computer and figure it out from there."

"Thanks, babe."

Mom leaves the room.

"Anything else, Jeff?" Dad asks.

"Only one thing. But it's a doozy."

# CHAPTER THIRTY-FIVE

**Rory**

My phone dings.

A text.

From Brock.

*Sorry I haven't been in communication all day. Dealing with... Well, you know. I hope the show went great. I love you.*

I stare at his words.

Here I am, standing by the women's room. With another man.

I have no intention of sleeping with him. I was thinking maybe I could get him to sign the documents, and then somehow get out of here without...

But... no.

I don't want representation that way.

I certainly don't want representation from this guy, who's only willing to give it to me under these conditions.

For a moment, I allowed the idea of helping my family get ahead of everything else, including my self-respect.

No longer.

And as always, Brock helps me see the reality of the situation. His timing was perfect.

*Show was great. I love you too.*

Then I turn to Sequoia. "Change of plans. I won't be coming to your room tonight."

He strokes his jawline. "That's too bad. I could make your band the biggest thing this year."

I scoff. "This year is almost over."

"You think that matters? When the Lane Agency talks, the world listens."

"The Lane Agency might be interested to know of your tactics," I say.

"Do you think my tactics are any different from anyone else's?"

"Perhaps I'm naïve, but I'd like to think there are still a few agents out there who are ethical."

Sequoia chuckles. "You'd be sorely disappointed."

"Then I guess Dragonlock won't be finding representation anytime soon." I tear up the card he gave me and throw it at his feet. "See you around."

I return to the bar where Jesse still sits, along with the rest of the band now.

"I ran into Sequoia when I went to the bathroom," I say. "Turns out he's not interested after all."

"Shocking," Jesse says, rolling his eyes, "after making us wait half an hour."

I raise my glass of Scotch. "You know what? Who needs an agent anyway?"

"Well... We do, sis, if we want to get anywhere."

He's not wrong. I'm just so tired of it all. Two agents in two nights, both of whom thought we were great but also wanted something more in return.

"I guess we go back to Grand Junction tomorrow," I say.

"There won't be any agents there," Jesse says.

"But you know what will be there? Audiences. People. People who come to hear us play, Jess. People who love us. Who we can entertain. And at the end of the day, isn't that our only objective?"

"Sis, I get as much out of entertaining as you do, but right now we need cash."

I sigh and nod. "I know."

And I feel the worst about not taking Sequoia up on his offer.

But I can't betray Brock. I love him so much, and I want a future with him. If I went to another man's room, even with no intention of sleeping with him, how could he forgive me? He might not be able to.

And I wouldn't blame him.

I wish he were here.

But he has his family issues, and I'm glad to be away from it all for a week.

"I half expected Brock Steel to show up again tonight," Cage says.

"Not tonight," I say.

"So I guess you're rooming with me then, sis," Jesse says.

"I guess so. Try not to snore too loud, would you?"

"I don't snore. You snore."

We're back to normal now. Brother and sister giving each other shit. Feels good.

I don't miss Sequoia McAllister for a minute.

I do miss Brock, though.

I miss him so much.

# CHAPTER THIRTY-SIX

**Brock**

My blood runs the coldest it ever has.

*A doozy?*

I haven't checked in with Rory all day, so I text her quickly.

*Sorry I haven't been in communication. Dealing with... Well, you know. I hope the show went great. I love you.*

She texts me back.

*Show was great. I love you too.*

Part of me wishes I had driven to Utah again, but by the time Dad, Uncle Bryce, and I were done at the office, I couldn't have made it in time for the show.

If only I were there with Rory, in a hotel room making love, instead of here, waiting to hear what the *doozy* is.

"Don't keep us in suspense," Dad says.

Jeff clears his throat through the speakerphone. "She's been in therapy on and off since she and Doc moved to Snow Creek. But there have been times when she stopped going."

"And..." Dad prods.

"According to all the information you gave me and from other stuff I could find, those times all coincide with times she's been involved with Pat Lamone."

"So are you thinking that Pat tells her not to go to therapy?" Dad asks.

"I can't begin to know if that's the case. But it does seem suspect, don't you think?"

"I think we all know that Pat is far from innocent here," I say.

"I had that thought as well," Jeff says, "so I went ahead and hacked his medical records."

"Good man," Dad says. "What did you find?"

"Nothing," Jeff says. "I found absolutely nothing."

"No medical records?"

"No nothing."

"What exactly are you saying, Jeff?" From Uncle Bryce.

"I'm saying that Pat Lamone doesn't exist."

One by one, our jaws drop. First Dad's. Then Uncle Bryce's. Then mine. In a freaking row.

"That makes no sense," Dad finally says. "He came to our people, presumably with a birth certificate. He's claiming to be related to our family."

"And he has a grandmother in the hospital," I offer. "Sabrina Smith, who may have been married to William Steel."

"Maybe. Maybe it's all true. But I'm telling you that Pat Lamone doesn't exist."

"But his family lived here," I say. "He went to school with Rory and Callie."

"Hey, I'm not calling you a liar," Jeff says. "All I'm saying is that on paper, there's no record of this dude."

"That doesn't make any sense."

"Sure as hell doesn't," Dad says, "but it's damned good news. If he doesn't exist, then he has no claim to the Steel fortune."

"There are only a handful of people, myself one of them," Jeff says, "who are capable of erasing a person from existence like this."

"Who are the others?" Dad says.

"Criminals," Jeff says. "They're criminals, Joe."

"Like you are?" Dad says.

"Hey, I make no bones about what I am. I'm good at what I do, and people like you give me good money to do it."

"I pay you good money to keep all my own information safe," Dad says.

"Which I do. Which I've done for you for the past ten years," Jeff says.

"Did you look any further?"

"Joe, you know me better than that." Jeff chuckles through the phone. "Of course I did."

"All right, then. Now we're getting somewhere. Who is this guy who says he's Pat Lamone?"

"His real name is Baby Boy Wingdam."

"Baby Boy Wingdam?" Dad narrows his eyes.

"Yep. His birth certificate, before he was adopted, doesn't show a first name. His birth mother never named him. Her name was Lauren Wingdam, and there's no father listed."

"So how did he become Pat Lamone?"

"He was adopted by a family with the last name Clark and named Daniel. I haven't figured out why yet, but his name was never legally changed on the books."

"So his name is Clark, then. Daniel Clark. Or maybe the Clarks changed his name to Patrick."

"Maybe. But his birth certificate says Baby Boy Wingdam."

"Why didn't it get changed?" Uncle Bryce asks.

"Got me," Jeff says.

"Not only that," Dad says, "but why did the Clarks change their name to Lamone? Maybe the Baby Boy birth certificate is a forgery."

"It's not a forgery," Jeff says. "Don't you think I know forgery when I see one?"

"I trust you, Jeff. It's not *your* talents I have an issue with. But these people—this human trafficking ring that we thought we wiped out twenty-five years ago—they've got a bone to pick with our family, and they will pick it in any way possible. And now, after how many years? Pat Lamone crawls out of some corner and claims to be a Steel relative? And his name isn't even Lamone? Something stinks here."

My mind has gone numb. Pat Lamone isn't Pat Lamone? He's Daniel Clark? Or rather, Baby Boy Wingdam?

"Dad," I say, "is Pat's claim through his adoptive side or his biological side?"

"Since I've never heard of the Clarks or the Lamones, I'm thinking it must be his biological side. We haven't taken his claim seriously enough to check it out so far."

"It must be through the father," Uncle Bryce says. "We don't know any Wingdams."

"Yeah, that's an odd name," I say. "Isn't a wing dam another name for a pier dam? A manmade jetty that diverts a current?"

"Yeah," Dad says. "But anything can become a last name."

"True enough," Jeff says. "My last name comes from my father's Native American side, but I'm pretty sure I'm not descended from an actual gray hawk."

"Just another question to answer," I say, more to myself

than to anyone else in the room.

"You got anything else, Jeff?" Dad asks.

"That's it. It's all sent in the encrypted file."

"Thank you. We'll be in touch if we need anything else. Payment will be sent in the morning."

"Always a pleasure, Joe."

Jeff's line goes silent.

Dad looks at Uncle Bryce and then at me.

We say no more.

* * *

I meet with Dad and Uncle Bryce again the next day, out in the grazing fields.

"Why out here?" I ask.

"Just a safety precaution," Dad says. "We check the office for surveillance equipment once a week, but this is just safer."

I regard our vast ranch, the livestock grazing nearby, the ranch hands doing their jobs.

Our ranch is a beautiful place. A place where we take care of our animals, raise grass-fed beef. Our animals aren't injected with hormones or fed industrialized food just to fatten them up. They have nice lives, for as long as they get to live on the earth.

I try not to think about it too much—the fact that they eventually die.

Dad taught us early on in life not to get attached to the livestock. Dogs and horses we could get attached to—those, we could love. But not the livestock. It would only lead to heartache.

"Our men combed both locations," Dad says. "Grabbed any evidence they could."

"Did they find anything?" I ask.

"Both were clean, except for one more red fingernail."

"Someone wants to implicate Brittany," I say.

"It would seem so," Dad agrees. "Brittany isn't as smart as she thinks she is."

"No, she's just a little bit sociopathic," Uncle Bryce says dryly.

"Brittany's the least of our worries," I say. "She's not the one who can get us arrested."

"We won't be arrested," Uncle Bryce says. "Your father and I have already seen to that."

"So what's next?"

Dad adjusts his Stetson. "We have the evidence, what was found, analyzed. We have the red fingernails, and we have the bones that belong to Patty Watson. We have the human femur, though its DNA hasn't been tested yet. In the meantime, the barns on both properties have been bulldozed, along with whatever was underneath them."

"You mean you didn't check?"

"I expect there were probably more bones."

"But Dad, if there were, then those bones belong to people. Missing people. We could at least give their families some kind of peace. Closure."

"I'm sorry, son. I wish we could. But the stuff is on our property. We had nothing to do with it, but it may not look that way in the eyes of the law."

"Have you asked Aunt Jade? Donny?"

"We haven't brought Jade into this mess. But yes, we checked with Donny. He agrees."

I shove my hands in my pockets. "So what now, then?"

"There was one more GPS coordinate that we didn't

check. So we sent our men out there and found basically the same thing. A couple of barns but nothing in them."

"Dogs?"

"The dogs have been moved at this point."

"So they know we're looking."

"They do. They know we found out what they're doing, so they'll be even sneakier now."

"Maybe they'll stay off our property," Uncle Bryce says.

"Probably. At least for now." Dad nods. "This isn't over. Not by a long shot. Not until we can find out who's behind it all and bring them to justice."

# CHAPTER THIRTY-SEVEN

**Rory**

Our first night in Grand Junction went well, but of course there were no agents waiting for us after the show.

Just as well.

I have a sour taste in my mouth after Selena Campbell and Sequoia McAllister.

I sit at the bar with the band after the show.

Several patrons come to visit us, tell us how great we were. We paste on our smiles, shake hands, even hug some of them.

We sell a few of our CDs. Well, a few of the band's CDs. I'm not on them.

"We should record a new CD," Jesse says. "With you, Rory."

"Maybe. Maybe I'll try to find the time."

"You know..."

"What?"

"The rest of the band and I... We were hoping that you'd consider joining us full time."

I can't say I haven't thought about doing so. But... "Are we going to go through this again? I have a full-time job, Jess."

"I know. I know you can't afford to stop teaching. It's just... You're such a draw. We might actually get a contract with an agent if you're around."

“I didn’t help last night or the night before.”

“Yeah, we got a couple of bad seeds. But we’ve played for agents before, and we’ve had their interest. Then we ultimately don’t get signed for one reason or another.”

“What reasons have they given?”

“Mostly that they didn’t have room on their roster for a rock band, but I remember this one time, there was an agent from LA who wanted to turn us into a boy band.”

I burst into giggles. “You’ve got to be kidding me.”

“I’m not. But we’re rockers through and through. So we declined.”

“Thank God. I can’t imagine you, Cage, Jake—and, oh my God, Dragon—in bright clothes bopping around the stage.”

“Being all NSYNC. Yeah, I know.”

“Did you consider it for a minute?”

“Maybe for a second. I mean, they were offering us a lot. They were guaranteeing us openings for some of the biggest boy bands out there.”

“But after that second, you got a clue, right?”

“Yeah. Although . . .”

“Although what?”

“That was before the fire, sis. If we got that same offer now . . . I don’t know if I could afford *not* to take it.”

“You’re not the only voice of the band, though.”

“Yeah, but Cage and Uncle Scott and Aunt Lena are in the same position we are.”

“Dragon and Jake?”

“I could get Jake on board. Dragon? He’s another story.”

“Oh my God, Dragon is *so* not boy band material.”

“Right?” Jesse shakes his head, chuckling.

I finish the water in front of me. “If it’s all right with you all, I think I'm going to head to bed."

"Yeah, I'm right behind you." Jesse turns to Cage, who's sitting on his other side. "Rory and I are heading to the hotel."

"Gotcha. We'll see you tomorrow morning."

Jesse and I walk to the car.

I'm hoping.

I'm hoping that maybe Brock has come to surprise me again.

We get to the hotel, and . . . no Brock.

Jesse and I head to our room, and I take the bathroom first. I shower, washing all the stage makeup off my skin, and go to bed.

I listen to the sounds of the shower, but before Jesse emerges from the bathroom, I'm asleep.

# CHAPTER THIRTY-EIGHT

### Brock

My phone buzzes.

It's early, but I'm already up, of course. Up with the sun, ready to go to work, and it's been a few days after dealing with everything.

It's Rory. My heart pounds at the sight of her name on my phone's screen.

"Hey, sweetheart," I say into the phone.

"Good morning."

"God, I miss you." I rake my hand through my hair. "Feels like we haven't seen each other in years."

"It's been a few days," she chuckles, "but I agree. I miss you too, Brock."

"I wanted to come surprise you again, but some weird shit is going down here."

"Don't worry about it. It's been strange here too. We've had two agents show up, both of whom only wanted to get laid."

"What?" A spike of jealousy shoots through my gut.

"Yeah. Don't worry. I'm a one-man woman now."

"You'd better be."

"I am. It still surprises the hell out of me, but I am."

"Are you kidding me? Me too. I was the biggest Rake-a-teer of all. But no longer."

"You better not be."

"Never again." I sigh. "Send me the information for your venue tonight."

She gasps. "You'll be there?"

"I can't make any promises, baby. But I'm going to try. I'm going to try like hell."

"It's a cute little bar in Grand Junction. They have a great sound system according to Jesse. Dragonlock has played there before. But it'll just be a concert. A performance. No chance of anyone being there to see us."

"Hey, there will be people there."

"Yeah. They're sold out, in fact."

"That's great!" But my excitement is short-lived. "Except I can't get in, then."

"Are you kidding me? I'll get you in. I'm with the band."

I roar into laughter. "Are you saying I'm a groupie?"

"You'd better be my groupie," she says.

"Always, sweetheart. And who cares about agents? You'll have a sold-out audience who paid to hear your angelic voice."

"Yeah. I'm trying to look at it that way. We do this for them, and for ourselves. Not to get famous, right?"

"You don't have to be famous to make a living."

"True enough. I would love for the band to get to a point where Jesse and the others don't have to do any part-time work."

"What about you?"

"I'm feeling hot and cold on it, to be honest. I gave up my opera dreams years ago, but this program you want me to put together… It's got me thinking. I still love opera. I still love musical theater. But I also love rock and roll."

"Are you interested in being a full-time rock singer?"

She sighs. "Brock, I just don't know."

"Well, you don't have to decide today, sweetie. All you have to do today is sing your heart out tonight. Because whoever hears you will fall in love with you."

"I don't know about that."

"Well… The only one who's truly allowed to be in love with you is me."

"And vice versa. Don't you forget it, either."

"Sweetheart, I'll never forget that."

After a few more "I love yous," we end the call.

Off to work for me, but my head isn't in the game. After a couple of hours, I let my assistant know that I'm done for the day. Then I drive into town.

To Doc Sheridan's residence.

I assume Pat's still house-sitting, because as far as I know, Doc and Brittany are still in Wyoming.

I knock on the door.

No answer.

I pound this time. "Lamone! Open up!"

Again, no response.

I check the doorknob, and it's open.

So I let myself in.

"Lamone, I know you're in here!"

Pat comes out of the kitchen wearing a T-shirt and jeans, no shoes.

"I can bust you for breaking and entering," he says.

"You said come in," I say.

"I did not."

"Funny. That's what I heard."

He raises a hand and then, apparently thinking better of it, drops it to his side.

"Well, now I'm telling you to get out."

"I don't think so. You invited me in. So we're going to have a little chat."

"I can't imagine what about."

"About a few things. About what you did to Rory and Callie, and all the evidence you may still possess."

"You'll never find it."

"Yeah, I think I will. Because your little girlfriend? Brittany Sheraton? She ratted you out like a canary."

Pat drops his jaw.

Yeah, I'm bluffing, but he's buying it.

"My father and I paid a visit to Brittany and her dad in Wyoming. We found out some interesting stuff."

"Hey, man. I don't have anything to do with what they're up to."

"Really? That's not what I hear."

"The bitch is lying."

"Then I guess it's your word against hers."

"No one will believe her. She's nuts, man."

Brittany is not insane. Sociopathic, maybe, but not insane.

But I can see why he wants to play that card.

"Here's what I don't get, Pat... If you think you're a Steel, and you think you're entitled to a part of our fortune, why would you take part in such heinous activities on our property?"

This time his eyes widen. Either he's a great actor, or he doesn't have a clue what I'm talking about.

I'm not willing to rule out the great actor part. Not just yet.

I already found out what a great actress Brittany is. But Brittany has a personality disorder. She's a sociopath.

Pat?

I'm not getting sociopath vibes from him. Just asshole vibes.

Gigantic asshole vibes.

"Have a seat," I say to him.

"Thanks, but I'll stand."

"Suit yourself." I clear my throat. "We take care of this town."

"You mean you *own* this town."

"I mean we take care of this town." I advance a step. "Don't try to put words in my mouth. You have no idea what's in my head."

Pat retreats a step. "And you have no idea what's in mine."

I scoff. "I have a pretty good idea."

"You don't. I'm not the kind of guy you think I am."

"Someone who drugs women and then violates them while they're passed out is a pretty bad guy, Pat."

"Violate? I never touched them."

"I'm not accusing you of rape. But drugging them, disrobing them, and shooting pictures without their explicit consent sure as hell *is* a violation."

"What if I told you that wasn't my idea?"

"I'd say you're a fucking liar as well as an asshole."

"It was all Brittany, man. Totally."

"Not buying."

"It was. I'm telling you, she's not right in the head. You have no idea. I'm not the villain you think I am."

"Actions speak way louder than words, but I'm sure I don't have to educate you on that."

"Brittany is—"

"I know exactly who Brittany is, and I think you know that I know, and you're willing to throw your little girlfriend under the bus."

"She's not my girl—"

"Shut the fuck up. I don't care if she's your girlfriend or not. I don't care which one of you fucks the other over. You can both die in prison, and I wouldn't shed a tear. That's not why I'm here."

"What do you want, then?"

"Do you have a copy of your birth certificate?"

He widens his eyes. "What the hell does that have to do with anything?"

"Maybe I'm just interested."

"Yeah. Because people enter my house unannounced all the time asking for my birth certificate."

"Maybe they should."

"Well, this may surprise you because I'm sure you Steels have documents lying around all over the place, but I don't keep a copy of my birth certificate on hand. This isn't even my house."

"Do you have one at home? At Mrs. Mayer's?"

"No, I don't."

"Would it surprise you to know that you don't exist?"

He shakes his head, wrinkles his forehead. "What?"

"Yeah. Patrick Lamone doesn't exist."

"Now *you're* the one who's gone mental, Steel."

"Actually, I haven't. You claim you're some kind of Steel heir, but on paper? Pat Lamone doesn't exist."

"I'm standing right here." He puts his fingers to his neck. "I'm pretty sure I have a pulse."

I'm well aware of the gun strapped to my ankle, but I am not my father. I will not resort to his tactics.

I can deal with Pat Lamone sans firearms.

"It's time to get real, Lamone. Tell me what you know

about your supposed connection to the Steel family."

"I don't have to tell you anything."

"Look. I don't like you. That's no secret. I don't like what you did to my cousin Diana, and I don't like what you did to Rory and Callie. But I'm willing to talk about it. I'm willing to entertain the notion that maybe you had a reason in your warped mind."

"Maybe I just don't like Diana. Or Rory and Callie."

"Or maybe you like them too much."

"The fuck?"

I close the distance between us. "You had the hots for Rory. She knew it then. Callie knew it. That's how they were able to manipulate you."

"I'm hardly the only guy who had the hots for Rory Pike in high school."

"True enough. What about Diana?"

"Diana is a different story."

"Tell me the story."

"None of your fucking business."

I draw in a deep breath to calm myself. "Pat, I think you're forgetting who you're talking to. I'm a member of the Steel family. The family you want to join. Level with me, make your case. We're not tyrants. If you have a valid claim, we'll share."

"Right." He scoffs.

"Give me any evidence you still have regarding Rory and Callie, and I'll make sure you're taken care of. Your grandmother too."

"My grandmother?"

"Sabrina Smith. The woman in the mental health wing at the hospital."

"How do you know about her?"

"Uh . . . we were there, remember? When you visited her? The night Frank Pike had a heart attack?"

"That's why you were there? Is he okay?"

"Like you care."

He says nothing. Just looks sheepish.

"Now level with me. Give me all the copies of those damned photos and tell me everything you know about your connection to my family, and I'll take care of things from there."

"You're a liar, Steel."

"I'm not a liar. You can take that to the bank."

"Fine. I still don't trust you. You've got stuff on me, I'm sure. I know you had this place searched. Mrs. Mayer's too. But your sleuths didn't come up with anything, did they?"

I'd honestly forgotten that we'd had our PIs checking out the two places, but if anything important turned up, Dad or Donny would have told me.

"I don't know," I say. "I haven't heard."

"Liar," he says again.

I curl my hands into fists. I don't like being called a liar. I take honesty seriously. Our whole family does.

"Call me that again, and I'll fucking put you on your back."

He opens his mouth, but I gesture him to be quiet.

"I'm not your enemy right now," I continue. "I'm trying like hell to find some common ground between us. I'll tell you what I know about your lack of birth certificate, but only after you give me everything you have on Rory and Callie." I take a step backward so I don't seem as threatening. "I'm serious. You want this to go away? You want my help? You need to make sure all those photos are destroyed."

He shoves his hands into his pockets. "I don't have any more photos."

"I don't like liars either, Pat."

"I don't expect you to believe me. I've been telling Rory and Callie the opposite, but it's not true. They found all of them. Brittany found out where they had hidden their safe-deposit key, and that's how I found it. I buried all the evidence I had—the last photos—underneath their box, figuring they'd never look there."

"But they did."

"Apparently they're smarter than I gave them credit for."

"Rory and Callie are both very smart, but so are you."

"Did you just compliment me, Steel?"

"I did. Which is why I don't buy it. I think you're lying."

"I'm not. I have nothing more to hide. Search this place again. Search my room at Mrs. Mayer's. Search my last known addresses. You won't find anything."

"What if I do? What if I already have?"

His eyes widen. "Then you're either a liar or it was planted."

I don't trust this man as far as I can throw him.

"I can tell you this: If those pictures ever see the light of day? Not only will you go down for child porn, you'll go down for a lot more."

He drops his mouth open. "What the fuck? Child porn?"

"Callie was underage in those pictures, dumbass. It's illegal for you to even possess them."

"I don't possess them. *They* do."

"Actually, they don't. They destroyed them."

"Man, you've got to believe me. I don't have any more. They got my only copies."

"You had better be telling the truth, because I *will* see you go down on child porn charges. And you know what happens to guys in prison who like little girls . . ."

"Oh my God, I'm not a pedophile."

"Doesn't really matter. Go down on child porn, and the guys in there will have certain preconceived notions about you."

"I'm totally serious, Steel. I don't have them. Look everywhere. Tear this whole house apart. I don't fucking care anymore."

Damn. He looks genuinely frightened. He's breaking out in a sweat, and he's trembling, raking his fingers through his hair. If I weren't such a skeptic, I might actually believe him.

Luckily, I *am* a skeptic.

"You'd better be telling the truth, because as we speak, I've got people looking everywhere. And I mean *everywhere*. If it weren't for other more pressing things going on, I would've done it long before now."

"You won't find anything. I promise."

"You'd better not be lying to me."

"I'm not. Rory and Callie found everything. I've got nothing."

"Then why did you tell them otherwise?"

"Because I had to make them believe I still had the upper hand."

"Why? Why would you want the upper hand with them? It's not like they can get you for poisoning Diana. The statute of limitations has passed."

"I know that, but your family can still get me."

"Did you know you might be a member of our family when you poisoned Diana?"

"I was a kid. I made a stupid decision."

"That's not answering my question."

He nods. "Yeah. I had gotten some anonymous tips."

"What do you mean *anonymous* tips?"

"I mean what I said. Anonymous tips. Emails."

"From what email address?"

"From a different email address each time. Whenever I tried to email them back, the emails bounced."

"Do you still have copies of those emails?"

"Yeah. I do. I have hard copies of everything."

"Good. I'm going to need to see those."

He sighs. "Fine. At this point, I have nothing to hide. I have no more photos of Rory and Callie. And apparently I don't even have a birth certificate."

"These emails you got when you were a kid, did they include a birth certificate?"

"No."

"Then why did you give them any credence?"

"I was a kid. I thought I might be related to the Steels. I didn't have to have the horrible existence I had. So I got pissed. Pissed at the Steels because you guys had everything that I might be entitled to."

"So you decided to poison one of us?"

"No. I decided to drug her. Maybe get her in a compromising position or something. Which didn't happen. I was just pissed. I was a pissed-off kid, and I sure as hell didn't mean to poison Diana."

"And you think that makes all of this okay?"

"Did I say that? I was pissed, and I did a stupid thing. Then Rory got me to confess, so I did another stupid thing. Have you never done anything stupid in your life, Steel?"

Plenty, but I never resorted to crime. Until a few days ago, that is, but I'm not admitting any of that to Pat Lamone.

"Not *that* stupid."

"Well, I bow to your superiority." He feigns a sarcastic bow.

"Stuff it, Lamone. You're not going to get anywhere being an asshole to me."

He opens his mouth. Closes it.

Do I actually expect him to apologize? No. He won't. I don't even care if he does. All I want is the fucking truth. If he *is* a member of our family, I want to know. And I want to make damned sure Rory and Callie are out of danger.

"You have any documentation about who you are?"

"All I know is that I was adopted."

"So you're not claiming that your parents are Steels."

"No."

"What are your parents' names?"

"Well, they're both deceased, but their names were Peter and Julie Lamone."

"Interesting."

"How so? At this point, what do I have to hide?"

"You tell me."

"I've told you. Look into me. Search everything. You won't find any photos of Rory and Callie. You won't find anything."

"And I won't find a birth certificate in your name."

"Maybe you won't. I have a driver's license. You want to see it?"

"No. But it may interest you to know that your name isn't Pat Lamone. It's Daniel Clark."

His jaw drops. "What?"

"Does that name sound familiar to you at all?"

"No. My name is Patrick John Lamone."

"Son of… Who did you say?"

"Adopted son of Peter and Julie Lamone."

"Who, you may be interested to know, also don't exist."

"Well, no, they don't. I told you that they're dead."

"You don't seem to be overly emotional about it."

"They've been gone for several years. Car accident. I miss them, sure, but I don't dwell on it."

"How much do you know about them?"

"They're my parents."

"Is there a reason why they may have changed their names?"

"I have no idea." He shakes his head. "Seriously, Steel, this is all news to me."

"And I'm supposed to believe that?"

"I can't make you believe anything. But it's the truth."

I like to trust my instinct, but my instinct is going against my head.

My instinct is telling me that Pat is telling the truth. But my head is saying that can't possibly be correct.

Usually my mind and my instinct are in sync, but not today.

"I need to see the hard copies of those emails. I suppose, since it was so long ago, you didn't think to check the IP addresses or anything."

"No."

"Why did it take you so long to approach the family?"

"I knew you guys wouldn't believe me."

"Yeah, I'm not sure we do."

"You've got to believe me, though. I had no idea my parents changed their names."

"And they're dead. So we can't ask them why."

"No."

"Convenient."

"Look, it's not convenient for me." He chokes up a little.

"They were my parents."

"That's not what I meant."

"Fine." He rises. "The emails are in a safe-deposit box in Grand Junction."

"Ah. That explains why our people didn't find them. What about the key? They should have found that."

He shakes his head. "I keep the key on me at all times, so they wouldn't have found it. I'm sure you'll want to come with me to fetch them."

"Absolutely."

# CHAPTER THIRTY-NINE

**Rory**

"Good news," Jesse says, handing out Mardi Gras masks to the members of the band. "It's masquerade night at the Dawn."

"Seriously, dude?" From Dragon.

"Hey, I gave you the only black mask they had."

Mine is pink. Freaking reddish pink.

"Seriously, Jess?"

"Sorry, sis, you get the girly one. We're playing the Y chromosome card."

I roll my eyes. "Fine."

"I don't like this any more than you guys do, but the manager says we have to wear them or we don't play."

"Don't we have a contract?" Jake says.

"We do. But why mess with it? It's just a stupid mask, and everyone else will be wearing them too."

"Okay, fine," Cage relents. "But do we have to wear them for rehearsal?"

"Of course not. Only Rory and I have to so we can see how they affect our peripheral vision. We have to play off each other."

I roll my eyes. "Great."

★ ★ ★

Later I get a phone call from Brock.

"Hey," I say, answering.

"Hey, sweetheart. I've got some good news for you."

"I could use some."

"I'm conducting another search, but I'm almost positive that Pat Lamone was lying to you. He doesn't have any more pictures of you and Callie."

"Really?" My heart leaps. "How are you so sure?"

"He basically told me I could search everywhere. That I wouldn't find anything."

"And you believe him?"

"I don't want to believe him, Rory, but something inside me is telling me that he's not lying."

"I trust you, Brock, but really?"

"I know. It's hard for me to believe too. But he was different today."

"You actually saw him in person?"

"Yeah. And I gave him some news that I don't think he was aware of."

"What's that?"

"It's a long story, and I don't want to mess you up before your concert tonight."

"I'll be fine. If you don't tell me, I'll just be wondering, and that will mess me up."

Brock sighs. "I shouldn't have said anything. But I found out that Pat Lamone isn't even his real name."

I nearly drop the phone. "What?"

"Yeah. First of all, he was adopted, and his claim to the Steel fortune seems to be through his birth parents, not his adoptive ones."

"Wow. Really?"

"Yeah. And he was aware that he was adopted, but what he wasn't aware of is that his adoptive parents changed both his and their names. Their real last name is Clark, and Pat's is Daniel Clark."

"Why would they do that?"

"I don't know," he says, "and they're both dead now, so we can't ask them."

"Wow."

"You're telling me. I don't want to lay anymore of this on you. I want you ready for your performance tonight. You never know who might be in the audience."

"Nobody at this place," I say. "Besides, it's masquerade night, so no one will recognize us anyway."

"What?"

"Yes. We all have to wear these ridiculous Mardi Gras masks. Fun stuff."

He laughs. "Well, you'll still rock the place. And you'll still be the most beautiful woman out there, even if half of your face is covered."

"I love you, Brock."

"I love you too, sweetheart. I can't wait to see you."

"Ditto."

"I have to go. Rock the town tonight."

"I'll give it a try."

* * *

A couple of men in the back catch my eye when the stage lights go down after our first set. They're wearing masks, of course, so it's impossible to tell who they might be, but they look slightly familiar. One is very blond, and the other is dark-haired.

They watch me intently. And then they seem to move their focus back and forth from Jesse to me.

Probably nothing.

I take my mind off them and concentrate on the second half of our show, going through it in my mind as I douse myself with water.

"You two sounded great," Cage says to Jesse and me. "I'm not sure I've ever heard you so on fire."

I take another drink of water. "Thank you."

Jesse nods. "Yeah, we seem to be really in sync, sis. I'm not sure we sounded this good since… Have we ever?"

We really do sound good together. That Christmas concert will be a smash with him next to me.

"I don't know," I reply. "But you're right. Something is different up there. I wonder if it's this whole thing with Dad. We're both trying to focus so hard on the music so we don't think about him."

"God, I'd hate to think that was it," Cage says. "Uncle Frank needed to have a heart attack to get you two in sync like this?"

"I'm not doing anything different," Jesse says. "It's all Rory. You've been amazing during this entire tour. You're rocking like you've never rocked before."

Is it? I doubt it, because Jesse is rocking the house. But if I'm the one who's different… What has changed since the last time we sang together before this mini tour?

One word.

Brock.

I'm in love, and Brock helps me to see myself as I truly am. I'm no longer an operatic mezzo, and that's okay. Maybe I'm a rocker at heart.

But honestly? Why label myself? It's okay to love both rock and opera. But in truth? The reason I'm looking forward to the holiday concert isn't to sing opera. It's to sing musical theater with my brother, and maybe we'll add some rock as well.

"Who are those guys in the back?" I ask my brother and my cousin. "They look familiar to me, but I can't place them."

"Which guys?" Cage asks.

"All the way in the back. They look kind of unassuming, wearing baseball caps, but one has long dark hair and the other long blond hair. Why do they look so familiar to me?"

Cage squints. "For God's sake..."

"What is it, cuz?" Jesse asks.

"I'm not sure. But we'd better make this next set count."

I swallow. "Cage..."

"Are they agents?" Jesse asks.

"Just make it fucking count."

Nothing like putting some pressure on us. I wish I hadn't asked.

"Five minutes!" the stage manager yells.

Five minutes until we're back onstage, making music. Trying to impress those two guys in the back whose faces I partially recognize.

"Damn," I say to Jesse. "Now I'm nervous as hell."

"Channel it. You can do it. You've been performing your whole life."

"Right."

He's not wrong. I *have* been performing my whole life, and I performed to many accolades back in Snow Creek. But the last time I performed live specifically to impress someone was for an audition in New York. I had killed it... or so I thought.

Even when I felt everything had gone great, I only found out later that I had blown it.

Every time I've auditioned for something that counts, I've blown it.

I take a quick trip to the bathroom. My makeup still looks pretty good, and I pat some powder on to reduce the shine. I sweat onstage under the harsh lights and because we work so hard when we rock. But stage makeup doesn't melt for anything. Clothes look good.

*Breathe in,* I tell myself. *Hold it. Breathe out.*

I repeat the exercise two or three more times.

Then I gaze in the mirror.

And I look at myself.

I try to look at myself through Brock's eyes.

He thinks I'm beautiful, but he sees more than just my beauty. He sees my depth. Funny that a womanizer like Brock Steel sees me for who I truly am.

People change.

Brock is no longer a womanizer.

And I? I am no longer an opera singer.

I'm a rocker.

Man, I never thought this day would come. I've always loved singing with my brother in the band, and it gave me a chance to perform that I wouldn't otherwise have had. But in the end? I always thought I was an opera singer at heart. A classical singer. Perhaps a musical theater singer on a different day, but at heart, classical.

No longer.

The opera world didn't want me.

Perhaps the rock and roll world will.

I stick my chest out, breathe in again. Stand tall, my spine straight.

I will show them tonight.

Whoever those men are, I will show them that Rory Pike can rock.

★ ★ ★

Back onstage, I take my position. I'm the only one in the band who doesn't also play an instrument, so I can concentrate fully on my vocals. Jesse plays second guitar and also sings. But I wonder . . .

We still have a few minutes.

The crowd is cheering because we've gone back onstage.

I turn to my brother. "Can Jake take over for you? Do we need two guitars?"

"I've always played, sis."

"What if the two of us concentrated fully on the vocals? What if we really sang our hearts out for these people?"

"I can walk and chew gum at the same time," Jesse says.

"I know that. But if we really should be impressing these dudes . . . Did Cage ever tell you who they are?"

"Nope. He wouldn't budge on that. Says he's not sure."

"And agents don't normally come here."

"No, not normally."

"Then tonight doesn't really matter," I tell him. "Let's experiment. You and I sing. That's what we do."

"Why is this so important to you?"

"I don't know," I say in all seriousness. "Except that we are singers. Sure, I play a little piano and you play a little guitar. But our voices are our instruments. Let's show them off."

"I don't get what you're saying," he says.

"It's just a feeling, Jess." I grab his forearm. "Trust me. Put your guitar down and tell Jake he's pulling double duty. And you and I . . . We can just *sing*, Jesse. We can do what we were created to do. We sing."

He shakes his head at me. "You're serious."

"I am. Call it a feeling. Call it women's intuition. Call it whatever the hell you want to call it. But let's try it. Let's just sing. The two of us. Focus on the words and the music and the melody and the harmony. Let's just freaking sing."

Jesse draws in a breath. "Okay. Let's do it." He walks over to Jake, talks to him for a few seconds, and then removes his guitar strap and sets his guitar to the side of the stage.

He returns.

The owner of the place, Journey Blake, takes the mic. "Back again for their final set, please put your hands together for Dragonlock!"

# CHAPTER FORTY

**Brock**

After a lengthy phone call with my father, I'm able to breathe a sigh of relief.

All evidence of the GPS coordinates has been destroyed, and our guys did a flyover of all our property, and there aren't any other barns that we didn't know about.

To be sure, we're going to have every square inch of our property traced by foot as well, but that will take some time. For now, we can be nearly one hundred percent certain that there is nothing linking us to the trafficking organization.

And if Pat Lamone is to be believed, there are no more copies of those pictures of Rory and Callie out there.

This is good news.

Two of our problems are solved.

But bigger problems still remain.

We don't know who these criminals are, but we can assume they are somehow related to the original human traffickers who Dad and his brothers took down twenty-five years ago.

Why else would they be using our property? Why else would they be trying to implicate us?

Then, of course, there's all the documentation we found under the floorboards at Brendan Murphy's place.

The research Callie found, proving that we do—in a way—

own this town.

The pumpkin diamond ring, traced to my grandmother, but the initials engraved inside it are LW. Who is LW?

And what do we do with Doc and Brittany Sheraton?

Man, our family needs a break. A big damned break.

Brittany needs help. Big-time help. How can you have someone committed against his or her will? I begin a Google search when—

The doorbell rings. Sammy barks.

I rise from the kitchen table, where I'm working on my laptop, go to the door, and gaze through the peephole.

Seriously?

I open the door.

"What the hell are you doing here?"

Pat Lamone stands outside, his hands shoved in his pockets. "I need to talk to you."

I begin to close the door. "I think we said all that needs to be said earlier."

"Hey, I was serious when I said I don't have anything more regarding Rory and Callie. If they destroyed what they found buried, then everything is destroyed."

"So why are you here, then?"

"There's something else you ought to know."

"Something else you couldn't be bothered to tell me earlier?"

"Yeah. I mean you kind of caught me off guard."

"For Christ's sake." I hold the door open. "Make it quick. Rory is performing with Jesse's band tonight in Grand Junction, and I want to catch the second set."

Normally I would offer someone a drink when they show up at my house, but that's not happening tonight. I don't even ask him to sit down.

"What is it?"

His hands are still shoved in his pockets, and his facial features are tense. "I used to think, once I found out I might be related to the Steels, that you guys would come out of the woodwork and rescue me from my shitty life."

"You kind of made that impossible when you poisoned one of our own."

"I told you. I didn't mean to poison her."

"What did you think would happen when you laced her drink with PCP and meth?"

"I thought she'd get high."

"This was Diana Steel. Our family doesn't do drugs. She was a freshman in high school, and she had no tolerance."

"Well, I was a junior in high school. I'm not saying it's an excuse, but I wasn't thinking clearly either."

"You made it pretty clear that you resented the fact that the Steels had everything and you had nothing, when you might actually be related to us."

"Right. I was seventeen years old, Brock. What the fuck did you expect?"

"I expect a seventeen-year-old guy to know better than to put drugs in a fifteen-year-old girl's drink."

He says nothing.

"Anything else? Because I've heard this before."

"Yeah. That's not why I came here. I . . . I no longer care about your fortune."

I raise my eyebrows.

He drops his gaze. "Okay, that's not true."

"I didn't think it was for a minute."

"But I care more about my grandmother, who's a complete mess."

"Who is she?"

"Her name is Sabrina Smith. I didn't even know about her until a couple of years ago. All I knew was that I was adopted, and I might be related to the Steels."

"And who is Sabrina Smith exactly?"

"Like I said, she's my grandmother. My biological grandmother. And she suffers from some serious mental illness."

"I figured that out when I saw she was strapped down."

Pat's eyebrows rise. "How do you know she's strapped down?"

"Oh, save it. That night at the hospital, when Frank Pike had his heart attack, Donny and I followed you. And once you left, we paid your grandmother a little visit."

"You went into her room?"

"Yeah, we did. And do you really want to go there, Pat? After everything you've done?"

He doesn't reply.

"I thought so."

He shuffles his feet. "Like I said, I only found out about her a few years ago. So I sit with her. I ask her questions."

"And has she ever answered you?"

"Sometimes she says a few garbled words. None of it makes any sense."

"What kind of garbled words?"

"If they made sense, I'd tell you."

"Would you? Do you know her diagnosis?"

"I'm not technically a relative. I'm a blood relative, but legally my parents are the Lamones. Or as you say, the Clarks."

"So"—I clear my throat—"you say you care more about your grandmother than our fortune. What are you here for, then?"

"I've thought a lot about this. I've been thinking about it

ever since Callie and Rory found the evidence against them that I buried. I've told you before, that was all of it, so now I have nothing."

"Nothing to extort money from us with. Right. Got it."

"For God's sake, Steel."

"Give me a break. You expect me to be all lovey-dovey *Hey, newfound cousin* after all you've done?"

"No. I don't expect any of that."

"Continue, then."

"I'm willing to sign a document. A document relinquishing any claims I have to any of the Steel money."

"Okay, but I'll have to check my driver's license first. Make sure I wasn't born yesterday."

"Well, sure," Pat says. "I do have a condition."

"I was pretty sure you would."

"I want your family to take care of my grandmother. She's a ward of the state right now, and she needs help. Like I said, I don't even know what her diagnosis is."

"I certainly can't find out what it is. We're not her family."

"You can find out."

He's right. We can. But hacking into medical records is a huge invasion of privacy. I didn't particularly like it when Dad and Uncle Bryce did it to Brittany. Though, I'll admit, I'm glad we have the information.

"All right. Let's say, for the sake of argument, that I can find out. I can get Sabrina Smith's medical records, and I can find out her diagnosis, and perhaps I'm able to help her."

"Your mom is a renowned psychiatrist," Pat says. "One of the best in the nation."

"She is, but number one, she's retired, and number two, she specializes in childhood trauma. Not geriatric trauma."

"Still, she's the best. She could treat my grandmother."

"From what I could see, your grandmother is comatose."

"It's a medically induced coma. For her own protection."

"How old is she?"

"In her eighties. I don't know her exact birthdate."

"That's easy enough to find. We'll pull her birth certificate. Why haven't you done that?"

"I did."

"Let me guess... She, like you, technically doesn't exist."

"Bingo." Pat meets my gaze.

"Interesting. Someone has gone to a lot of trouble to erase you and your grandmother from existence."

"I know. I thought it was odd that my grandmother's birth certificate couldn't be found, but when you came to me earlier today and told me I didn't have a birth certificate... Well, it got me to thinking."

"So now you're thinking."

"Yeah. I just want to know who I am, Steel. If I'm a Steel, great. I won't take any of your cash. Whether I'm entitled to it or not. But I need this woman lucid. I need the information she has trapped inside her head."

"How do you know you're even related to her?"

"Well... I..."

"Oh, spit it out. Do you really think it's worse than anything else you've done?"

"All right. I paid one of the phlebotomists to get me a blood sample from Sabrina. Then I ran a DNA test. I'm definitely her grandchild."

"I see."

"I've offered to do a DNA test to prove I'm a Steel as well."

"I know that. But as we've told you, a DNA test, when we're talking about a half sibling from three generations back, may not be conclusive."

"But it could show *something*. It could show that I'm at least related in some way."

Funny. If I were Dad and Uncle Bryce, I would have gotten the DNA test right away. But for some reason, they haven't pushed it.

Damn, they're still keeping secrets.

Well, I'm done with this.

It's time to figure things out.

"There's one more thing," Pat says.

"What's that?"

"When I had the DNA tests run on my grandmother, it matched with some DNA on file elsewhere."

"How do you know that?"

"The person I hired to run the test has access to the criminal databases."

"And . . .?"

"All he would say is that Sabrina Smith is an alias."

"Let me guess. He wants money."

"Bingo," Pat says again.

"Fine. How much does he want? I'll gladly pay it."

"Ten grand."

"Pocket change."

Pat stiffens.

Yeah, that was a cheap shot, but what the fuck?

Pat pulls his wallet out of his pocket, opens it, and hands me a card.

"Here you go. Give him a call, wire the money, and he'll give you the name."

"Consider it done."

# CHAPTER FORTY-ONE

**Rory**

Jesse and I walk to the front of the stage, he without his guitar this time.

Jake begins on guitar, Cage on keyboard tonight instead of bass, and then Dragon on drums.

Our intro, and then—

Jesse and I, in perfect harmony.

And damn . . .

It's magic onstage.

The high. It's almost effervescent in its intensity. And Jesse . . . I see it on his face. Letting go of the guitar has freed him in a way I've never seen him before. He throws himself into the music, vocalizes. And his voice . . .

The deepness of his baritone, combined with my alto that can even extend into the male range.

I don't go into my head voice at all for this set, and man . . . It's freeing.

In that moment, I leave opera behind forever.

We do a few covers, and then we move to original pieces. Cage writes all the music, and he, Jesse, and Dragon write lyrics.

I've never been a composer, but I used to write poetry.

I'm going to write some lyrics. Have Cage set them to music.

Perhaps I've found my true calling now.

This silly pink mask helps me. Jesse and I, both masked, break out of our molds.

I free myself from the chains that have bound me to opera.

And I sing...

I throw myself into it, become one with it, relish the harmonizing.

I sing with my brother. We sing to the accompaniment of Cage, Jake, and Dragon.

I sing to the audience as they cheer, whistle, enjoy every minute of this performance.

I simply sing.

An encore. And then another.

The audience continues clapping, cheering, whistling, yelling *encore*.

But we never do more than two encores.

We leave the stage, and I head straight to the ladies' room.

# CHAPTER FORTY-TWO

**Brock**

"This is Brock Steel," I say into the phone. "I'm looking for Amos Dugard."

"You found him. Are you one of *the* Steels?"

"Guilty."

"What can I do for you?"

"You can tell me who Sabrina Smith's DNA belongs to. You ran it for Pat Lamone a while back."

"Ah . . . I guess I don't have to ask if you can pay."

"I can pay. But you're going to have to give me the name first."

"Not going to happen, man."

"Then don't expect to see any money out of me."

"Wait, wait. What if you send me half first?"

"Five K?"

"Right. Five K."

"So you can steal five thousand dollars from me? I don't think so."

"I've got to get something."

"You'll get your ten grand. I'm a man of my word. But not until I get the name and any accompanying documentation."

"For Christ's sake."

"Look, Mr. Dugard. The information isn't doing you any

good sitting on your computer somewhere. Give it to me, and you get ten grand."

"I just have to give it to you first."

"That's right."

"I don't know you from Adam."

"Actually, you do. My name's not Adam. It's Brock. Brock Steel. Operative word being *Steel*."

Silence for a moment, then— "For God's sake. Fine. I'll send it encrypted to your email address."

"Now we're talking."

"How quickly can I get the money once you send it?"

"All I need is your cell phone number, and you'll get it instantly."

We exchange information, and within a few minutes, the information comes up on my computer.

I run the encryption file and take a look.

The results of the test show that Pat Lamone is indeed a grandchild of this woman.

Sabrina Smith.

Whose DNA matches someone named . . .

Dyane Wingdam.

Wingdam.

Now we're getting somewhere. She really *is* Lamone's grandmother . . . if she has a daughter named Lauren.

"Lamone!" I yell from the kitchen.

He walks in.

"Does the name Dyane Wingdam mean anything to you?"

"Should it?"

"I have no clue, but she's your grandmother."

"She is?"

"Yep, and she's got a rap sheet a mile long. Felony forgery, bank fraud, insider trading . . ."

"Has she done time?"

"Not according to this, but it's easy enough to find out."

Pat rolls his eyes. "Great. I'm not only descended from someone who is a complete nutcase, she's also a criminal."

"The apple doesn't fall too far from the tree."

"Cheap shot."

"Hey, I get that you're not the one who injected Rory and Callie with those drugs. That's on Brittany. But you're the one who took off their clothes and violated them, took photos of them in compromising positions."

"I was a kid."

"Do I look like I care? Even kids should know better."

Pat looks at the floor. "What now? What about this woman? Do we have a deal?"

"I'll have to check with my father. But if you're willing to relinquish any claim on our money in exchange for us taking care of this old woman who can't possibly live much longer, I'm pretty sure I can say we have a deal."

"Good. Let me know when you know for sure."

"I will. Now get the fuck out of my house. I have a concert to get to."

# CHAPTER FORTY-THREE

## Rory

I remove the pink mask and regard myself in the mirror once more.

And I see someone different. Someone different from who I saw only an hour before when I was in here.

I'm Rory Pike.

I'm a rocker.

I smile. My makeup is still flawless, and right now I need a couple gallons of water. I toss the mask in the trash, wash my hands, leave the restroom, and walk to the bar.

"Water," I say. "The biggest one you have."

The bartender smiles behind his silver mask. "Coming right up. Man, you guys were hot tonight. On fire."

"Thank you," I say.

He turns to fetch my water.

"On fire's an understatement."

I jerk at the low voice next to me.

"You guys scorched this place," he continues.

I turn. One of the men I saw from the back sits on the stool next to mine, and he's taken off his mask as well. His long black hair is pulled into a low ponytail, and a Minnesota Twins hat sits on his head.

"Thank you."

"What's your name?" he asks.

"Rory. Rory Pike."

"Nice to meet you, Rory." He holds out his hand. "I'm Jett Draconis."

My eyes nearly pop out of their sockets.

No wonder those guys looked so familiar.

Jett Draconis is the lead singer and guitarist for Emerald Phoenix. They're huge. And the blond? He must be Zane Michaels, secondary vocalist and keyboardist for the band.

*Breathe, Rory. Breathe.*

"Wow," I say, trying not to let my voice shake. "It's a pleasure. A real honor. I'm a huge fan."

"The honor is mine," he says. "As of tonight, I'm a huge fan of yours as well."

He's not coming on to me. He wears a wedding band on his left hand, and the love story of him and his wife, Heather, is well known in rocker circles.

No, this isn't a come-on. This is a true compliment.

"Who's the guy you sang with?" Jett asks. "The two of you have an amazing sound together."

"Probably because he's my brother. We come from the same gene pool, so our voices probably mix well."

"I'd like to meet him." Jett smiles. "I'd like to meet the rest of the band as well."

The bartender slides a large glass of ice water in front of me. I down half of it in one gulp. Then I turn back to Jett.

"Absolutely. I know they'd love to meet you too."

"Where are they?"

"If I had to wager a guess?" I smile. "I'd say they're somewhere being greeted by a drove of adoring fans."

"Why aren't you with them?"

"As much as I do like adoring fans, I'm actually in a very serious relationship right now. Besides, this is their night."

"I'd say it's your night as much as theirs."

"Thank you. Thank you very much. It took me a while to get here, but maybe this is where I belong."

"Rory, this is *exactly* where you belong. What do you mean it took you a while to get here?"

"I began as an operatic mezzo-soprano. But New York didn't want me, so I hung out a shingle and taught piano and voice in my small hometown. Rock was always Jesse's thing."

"Jesse?"

"That's my brother. Jesse Pike."

"So you're not a rocker."

"I am. I came to that conclusion just tonight. I'm not an operatic mezzo. I'm not a classical singer. I'm a rocker. Through and through."

"Glad to hear you say that, because you sure as hell look the part." He smiles. "And that voice . . . It's like Ann Wilson on steroids. Or if Karen Carpenter had been a rocker. That's you, Rory. That's you."

I return his smile. "I'm not sure I'm worthy of that compliment. Those women were two amazing vocalists."

"You're worthy. I don't say things like that for my health. And as you can see"—he waves his left hand at me—"I'm happily married, so I'm not trying to get into your pants."

I laugh. "Not that I don't find you attractive. I mean, you're Jett Draconis. But that's a welcome relief after the last two agents who approached us after the show."

"They tried to bed you."

"Yup, both of them. But at least one of them was honest. She said she wasn't interested in signing any new acts, but she wanted a threesome. Can you even imagine?" I shake my head, shuddering.

"Ah… Selena."

"Yeah, Selena Campbell. Do you know her?"

"Kind of." He laughs. "She's our agent."

Warmth floods my cheeks. "Oh… geez."

Jett takes a drink. "She's great at her job. You said yourself that she was honest."

"I suppose I can give her that."

"She likes sex. She likes both men and women. And she especially likes threesomes."

"I gathered."

"But she's crazy smart in business. Emerald Phoenix owes her a lot. I hope she didn't scare you away from trying to secure representation."

"Of course not. I mean, if you vouch for her…"

"I do. And I'm sure she loved you, but her book is full right now."

"She did say we were great, and I didn't get the feeling she was blowing smoke up my ass."

"She wasn't. In fact, it's because of her that I'm here tonight."

I raise my eyebrows. "So she *did* like us."

"She did. And you *are* great, but a lot of bands are great."

"Oh." I try not to slump my shoulders. Here it comes. The brush-off.

"What took you to the next level, though, was when your brother put down his guitar and sang with you."

"Oh? You liked that?"

"Are you kidding? The two of you are magical together."

"Oh my God!" A huge smile splits my face. "I told him we would be."

"That was your idea?" Jett raises his eyebrows.

"It was."

"Rory, you took that band from great to mind-blowing."

"Simply by taking my brother off guitar?"

"Your brother's voice… Like I said, your two voices just go together. And man, can you guys rock."

Cage approaches us. "Hey, Ror."

"Cage, oh my God. How come you didn't tell me this was Jett Draconis?"

"I wasn't sure myself."

"Jett, this is my cousin, Cage Ramsey. He's our bassist slash keyboardist."

"Man, is it great to meet you." Cage holds out his hand.

Jett takes it. "Those were some mean ivories you were tickling, dude. I was telling Zane you're as good as he is."

Cage's eyebrows nearly fly off his forehead. "Are you jiving me?"

"No. Anyone who knows me knows I don't jive. You guys were amazing. Every one of you. The guitarist, the drummer. Every one of you freaking rocked it."

"Man, this is like a dream come true," Cage says. "I'm a huge fan."

"Well, like I was telling Rory here, likewise. As of tonight, I'm a huge fan of yours as well."

"What can I get you?" the bartender asks Cage.

"Whatever you have on tap. And something for my friend here."

Jett shakes his head. "Nope. Everything the band wants is on my tab tonight. Because I want to talk to all of you."

I freeze. Quite literally. I want to say something, but my mouth won't move.

"Sure, man," Cage says. "What do you want to talk to us about?"

"We'll get to that. For now . . ." He motions to the blond man—Zane Michaels—who's talking to a few women on the other side of the bar.

Zane ends his conversation and comes over. "Hey," he says. "Man, you guys were great."

I'm about ready to faint, but at least my lips have unfrozen.

"Zane Michaels," I say. "I'm a big fan."

"Likewise . . ." He grins. "This is where you tell me your name."

"Rory. Rory Pike."

"And I'm Cage Ramsey, keyboard and bass."

"Damn. That was some fine playing."

"Thank you."

"So yeah, Jett, have you asked them about our idea?"

"Not yet. I want to talk to the whole band."

"Yeah, awesome. Where are the others?"

"Dealing with adoring fans," Jett says, "according to Rory here."

"Yeah," Cage says, "and don't expect them to be out here anytime soon."

"Why aren't you back there with them?" I ask.

"Because I saw you here at the bar with Jett. I wanted to see if I was right."

"You were."

I hop off my stool. "I'll go get the rest of the band. I know they'll want to meet and talk to you guys."

I head backstage, where indeed, I find my brother, Dragon, and Jake talking to a group of six women.

"Hey, guys," I say. "You need to come to the bar."

"We're kind of busy here, sis," Jesse says.

"Trust me," I say to him. "You want to come with me. Now."

★ ★ ★

"Guys, I'd like you to meet Jett Draconis and Zane Michaels," I say. "Gentlemen, this is my brother, Jesse, our lead guitarist, Jake Michaels—no relation, I'm sure—and our drummer, Dragon Locke."

Jett raises his eyebrows. "Dragon Locke? Seriously? The band's name?"

"That's right," Jesse says. "It was too cool of a name not to use."

"Is that your real name, man?" Zane asks Dragon.

"Says so on my birth certificate," Dragon says in his dark voice.

"Fantastic," Jett says. "Zane and I need to talk to you guys about something, but it's kind of noisy in here. It's a little chilly outside. Is there anywhere else we can talk?"

"Sure," Jesse says. "We can go backstage. It's a little quieter back there."

"Let's do it." Jett hops off his stool.

We head backstage, and my heart has finally quieted down to its normal rhythm.

What on earth do they want to talk to us about?

I'm almost scared of the possibilities.

"Okay," Jett says when we're all seated in a circle of folding chairs.

"Yeah?" Jesse says.

"Here's the thing: Emerald Phoenix is going on tour in

January. Right after the holidays. It's an overseas tour. UK, France, Spain, Portugal, Belgium, and the Netherlands. Plus a homecoming tour hitting twelve major cities in the States afterward."

"Yeah," Jesse says. "I read about that."

"The band that was supposed to open for us, Potato Soup, had to cancel. Two of their members were in a car accident."

I swallow. No way. He's not about to suggest—

"Zane and I have been scrambling, trying to come up with a band who can fill in. We think we may have found them."

# CHAPTER FORTY-FOUR

**Brock**

Damn the traffic!

A semi overturned on the highway to Grand Junction, and we're down to one lane. It's slow going, but I'm determined to get to the Dawn.

At this rate, I'm going to miss the show.

Oh well. I've heard Rory sing with the band before, and I'll hear them again. The most important thing is getting a room at the hotel so Rory and I can be alone tonight.

I have so much to tell her, but that can wait until after we've had some fast and furious fucking.

Damn.

Who the hell is Dyane Wingdam?

Whoever she is, apparently she was once either married—or at least had a kid with—William Steel.

Unless she's Pat's grandmother from the other side.

I suppose I should've asked him that, but I'm not sure he would even know.

I still don't trust the asshole.

Minutes tick by, and I finally get past the blocked lanes.

I gun it into Grand Junction.

# CHAPTER FORTY-FIVE

## Rory

None of us say a word.

Seriously, you could hear a fucking pin drop in here.

"So... Are you at all interested?" Zane asks.

Jesse's jaw drops. Then Cage's. Then Jake's. Then my own.

The only one who doesn't look surprised is Dragon. The expression on his face almost never changes.

"So I take that as a yes?" Jett says.

"Wow, that..." I say. "We all... What a surprise."

"We came here at the request of our agent, Selena Campbell," Jett continues. "She heard you guys the other night and thought you might have something. We didn't expect you to be as good as you are."

"Thank you," Jesse says.

"Who's your agent?" Zane asks. "We should talk to them."

"We're self-managed at the moment," Jesse says.

"I already told Jett we're not represented," I add.

"We were hoping to be represented by now," Jesse says, "but we had to cancel some major gigs in California because of a fire that destroyed Rory's and my family's property."

"I get it. You need to be there for your family," Jett says. "I've been there, man. You've probably read all about my brother's troubles. Let me tell you this. If you sign with us, go on tour with us? You'll be able to help your family a lot."

My heart starts beating again.

This could be just what we've been hoping for.

Callie is marrying Donny, so she'll be able to help, but this way… Jesse and I might be able to help as well. And I won't have to depend on Brock for it.

But a tour. All that time away from home.

Away from Brock…

"I think I can speak for the band," Cage says. "We're totally interested."

"Great. That's great."

"I said the band," Cage says. "I can't speak for Rory."

"You're not part of the band?" Jett asks.

"I am," I say with certainty. "I think I just realized that tonight."

"What are you talking about, sis?" Jesse asks.

"It was between sets when I was in the bathroom. And that's part of the reason why I asked you to give up your guitar for the last set. You and I—our voices work together, Jesse. We should both be singing exclusively."

"I'll agree with that," Jett says.

"But more than that," I continue, "I think I finally let go this evening. I was having so much fun singing with the band, and I was thinking about Dad, and how lucky we are that he's alive. And I was thinking about Brock, and how I'm in a relationship that could change my life. And I realized that *I've* changed. And I let go of it, Jess. I thought I had let go of my opera dreams years ago, but I hadn't. Never truly. Not until tonight. I embraced this side of me. I embraced rock and roll."

"Right, you mentioned opera." Jett says. "That explains a

lot. Did you know my background is in opera too?"

"Really?" I say.

"Yeah, really. Rock was never my dream either. And Zane here—he was a concert pianist."

My jaw drops. "Oh my God . . ."

"Yeah. We got into rock because we weren't making any money in classical," Jett says. "We found a benefactor who sponsored us."

"Who we're no longer with, thank God." This from Zane.

"It's okay," Jett continues. "It's okay to leave one part of your life behind for another. Especially when maybe the other is what you were meant for all along. You're a rocker, Rory. You have a voice that rivals Karen Carpenter's, but you can rock like Joan Jett and Chrissie Hynde combined. And you sure have the look as well."

"You might be surprised to know that I don't normally wear thigh-high boots with spikes," I say, smiling.

"You should," Zane says. "You're fucking hot."

"That's my sister you're talking about," Jesse says.

"Jesse, he didn't mean anything by it."

"No, man, I didn't. Besides, I think the lady said she's in a relationship?"

I smile. "I am. In a really good one, and I'm happy."

"That's great to hear," Jett says. "When you know, you know, right? That's how it was with Heather and me."

I nod. "Yeah. When you know, you know."

Zane clears his throat. "So Jett and I don't mean to put pressure on you guys, but we're going to need an answer, and we're going to need it soon. Time is of the essence here, since Potato Soup backed out. Through no fault of their own, of course, but we need an opening act, and we'd like it to be you."

"And rest assured," Jett says, "that we think you're up to the challenge. We like our openers to be on the same level that we are, so we don't make this request lightly."

"Wow," Jesse says. "We're really honored, you guys."

"Then honor us further," Jett says. "Say yes."

My mind is racing. Dad is still in the hospital, and Brock . . . Brock is dealing with so much.

"How long will this tour last?" I ask.

"Six months," Jett says. "So yeah, you need to be sure. Once you sign on the dotted line, you can't back out. There just isn't time."

Six months.

Six months away from Brock.

I don't know if I can handle it.

"We're willing to give you a signing bonus," Jett says. "Since you have to decide so quickly."

Jesse nods. "And how much might the signing bonus be?"

"Ten grand for each of you," Zane says.

More money than either of us has ever seen at one time.

Of course, mere pennies to the Steels.

But this is money we earned. Jesse and me. And it could help our family while we're gone.

"Then, of course, you'll get your percentage from the tour," Jett says. "That's paid twice a month."

"What's that percentage?" Jesse asks.

"Twenty percent for the opening band. After expenses."

"So that means your band gets eighty percent?" Jesse says.

"Yes," Jett says. "We're the main attraction of course, but I can tell you this. Most of the venues are already sold out."

"So what exactly might this twenty percent add up to?" Jesse says.

"More money than we've ever seen," I say.

"Right. I want to hear numbers, though." Jesse shifts his hands in his pockets.

"Our share of ticket sales is usually around a hundred thousand dollars per concert," Jett says. "The share for the bands, to be precise. You'd get twenty percent of that, which is twenty K."

"Four K for each of us," Jesse says.

"Right, and it's an even four," Jett says, "because we take all expenses off the top first. Plus, there's merchandising. We make more in merchandising than we do in ticket sales."

"Yeah, but you're a known entity," I say. "We're brand-new."

"Once the crowd hears you? They're going to want your merch," Zane says.

"But those are costs we have to front," I say. "What if we can't?"

A throat clears behind me. "You can."

I turn.

I know that voice.

# CHAPTER FORTY-SIX

## Brock

"Brock!" Rory launches herself into my arms. "What are you doing here?"

"I couldn't stay away from you any longer."

"How much of the conversation have you heard?"

"Enough to know I don't want you to give this up."

"Hey, guys," Rory says. "This is my boyfriend, Brock Steel."

"You're kidding me," I say. "Emerald Phoenix?"

"Jett Draconis," Jett says, holding out his hand. "And this is Zane Michaels."

"Wow. I've seen you guys in concert three times. I'm a huge fan. You rock."

"Great to meet you. So you're one of *the* Steels? The Colorado beef barons?"

"Guilty," I say, my eyes widening. "Though I'm not sure we've ever been called that before."

"Brock," Rory says. "You're not going to believe this, but Jett and Zane have invited us to open for them on their next tour."

"Seriously?" My face splits into a wide grin. "That's amazing, sweetheart. I just heard the part about you needing money to front some merchandising costs."

"Yeah," she says, "but we don't have any."

"You do now," I say. "I'd be proud to invest in your band."

"We're not taking your money, Steel," Jesse says.

"Who said anything about taking my money? I just said I'll *invest*. I put up the money, and I get a return just like you guys do."

"I'd be gone for six months, Brock," Rory says. "Beginning in January."

Okay, I hadn't thought of that. I wrinkle my forehead. "Six months?"

"I know. I don't want to leave you for that long."

"So come along," Jett says. "My wife comes with me."

"It's not that simple," Rory says. "Brock has responsibilities to his family business."

"You know what?" I say. "I think a six-month vacation sounds like heaven."

"You mean you'd come with me?" She kisses my lips. "Seriously?"

"Sweetheart, that still gives my family a month and a half to clear up the other business." He smiles. "Besides, haven't I always said I'd follow you anywhere?"

"You have. I just never thought I'd *go* anywhere."

"So let me get this straight," Zane says. "You *are* a member of the band then, Rory? Because I've got to be honest with you: You're a big part of the draw. The sound you and your brother make together, it's charmed."

Rory meets my gaze, her brown eyes full of love and devotion. If I asked her not to go, to stay with me, she would. Which is exactly why I'd never ask her. This is her time. She's been here for me, and now she needs to shine, and damn it, I want to be there to see it.

"Yes," she says, her gaze not wavering from mine. "I'm part of the band."

"I love you, my little rocker," I say.

"I love you too, Brock. So damned much."

Our lips lock for a moment, and she opens for me, lets me sweep my tongue into her mouth.

We kiss for a moment, until throats clear behind us.

Rory breaks the kiss and wipes her mouth. "Sorry."

"Don't be sorry on our account," Jett says.

"I was thinking more about my brother."

Jesse smiles. "Sis, if this guy makes you happy, then I'm happy. If I can get used to Callie and Donny, I can get used to just about anything."

"When does the tour begin?" I ask.

"The first of the year, after the holidays," Zane says.

"Good," I say. "You'll still be able to do your holiday concert."

Rory bites her lip. "Could I ask you guys a favor?"

"What's that?" Jett asks.

"It's a huge favor, and we can't pay you anything."

"Just ask, babe," Zane says.

I shoot some darts at him with my eyes for the *babe* comment.

"How would you like to play for no money at all in a cinema in a small town?"

Rory, Rory, Rory . . . I've got to hand it to my woman. She has more balls than most men I know.

"We just happen to be free until the tour," Jett says. "We might be able to accommodate you."

Rory shines. "You know any Christmas songs?"

Zane laughs. "We know them all."

"It might give you a chance to stretch your operatic muscles as well," Rory says. "I'm going to be singing a couple of arias, but it'll mostly be musical theater pieces with Jesse."

"Rory," Jett says, "it would be an honor to sing with you."

Happiness flows through me. Happiness that has nothing to do with me but with the woman at my side.

She's glowing. Actually fucking glowing, as if the roof opened up and the sun is somehow shining through her.

"Just one thing, sweetheart," I say to her.

"What's that?"

"It wasn't my intention to bring this up in front of your brother and everyone else, but if I'm going to accompany you on a tour around the world, I'd like to do it honorably. As your husband."

# CHAPTER FORTY-SEVEN

**Rory**

My jaw drops.

I was so upset when I found out I wasn't pregnant.

But now?

If I were, I wouldn't be able to take this great opportunity. I'd be nearly nine months along by the end of the tour.

It's definitely time to get a diaphragm. Because I need to go on this tour. I need to see if Jett and Zane are right about me. About Jesse. About the band.

Everything happens as it should.

Perhaps a performing career *is* in my future. It's just not the one I thought it would be.

Sometimes, life throws you a surprise.

Life threw Brock to me, and now I can't imagine my life without him.

Now? Life threw me another surprise. I'm not an operatic mezzo-soprano. I'm a rocker. A rocker through and through.

And it feels right.

All of it feels so *right*.

"I would love to be your wife, Brock." I brush my lips against his.

He pulls something out of the pocket of his dark-brown leather jacket.

"I grabbed this earlier. I just had a feeling."

It's a red velvet box. A ring box.

My hands fly to my mouth.

"My mother gave this to me. It belonged to her grandmother on her mother's side."

I gape at the ring. It's a pink stone that gleams in the artificial light of the bar.

"It's gorgeous. I've never seen anything like it."

"It's a star sapphire, but it's not as gorgeous as you are," Brock says. "Not by a long shot. But I'd like you to wear it, and I'd like you to be my wife, Rory."

I tremble as I hold out my hand, and he slips the ring on my left ring finger.

I gaze at its beauty. "It's a perfect fit."

"My mother knew," Brock says. "Somehow she knew. Her intuition has always served her well in her profession and also as a mother. She knew that you were my one and only, Rory. She knew you were my forever."

Our lips meet then in a searing kiss, and in that moment, we're alone.

Jesse and the band, Jett Draconis and Zane Michaels, the bartenders and waitstaff, our fans . . . They've all disappeared.

The bar is empty, and only Brock and I exist.

Our tongues tangle, and I pull him to me tightly.

We kiss and we kiss and we kiss, until—

Applause rings out and breaks the spell.

But it's okay.

Because I'm here, and Brock is here.

Jesse is here. Cage, Jake, and Dragon are here.

Jett Draconis and Zane Michaels are here.

And Dragonlock is going on tour with Emerald Phoenix.

With the money we'll make, Jesse and I will be able to help our family. We'll recover from the fire, and we'll come back stronger than ever.

Things are falling into place.

Even Brock's family has solved part of their mystery.

But there's still a lot more to solve.

I will help. Soon I'll be a Steel, and I will be happy to help in any way I can.

Brock and I break our kiss.

"I love you," I say softly.

"I love you too, sweetheart. Forever."

# EPILOGUE

### Ava

My mother and father got married on Thanksgiving twenty-five years ago.

Twenty-five years with the same person.

It's unimaginable to me.

I'm a Steel by birth, but I've never felt like a Steel.

I don't want my family's money. I like being on my own. I opened my bakery and sandwich shop with my own money—money that I earned, not money from my gigantic trust fund, which, even though I gained control of it when I turned twenty-one three years ago, I've never touched.

I'll never touch it if I can avoid it.

Don't get me wrong.

I love my family. All of them, without condition.

I just don't want their money.

I'm kind of the black sheep of the Steel family. Or rather, the pink sheep, if my hair color makes me who I am. So I like pink hair. Sue me. I can pull it off.

My little sister, Gina, thinks I'm crazy. She's gorgeous, of course. Looks just like our father, Ryan Steel, who's the pretty boy of the Steel family. Gina has his dark hair and light-brown eyes that are fringed with those ridiculously long lashes.

I look more like our mother, Ruby Lee Steel. I have her

brown hair, lighter than Dad's, but of course I color it. I also have her blue eyes. That's where our similarities end, though. I'm not nearly as pretty as Mom is.

I'm just me.

Ava.

Simply Ava, who loves to bake and who's damned good at it, if I do say so myself.

I learned at an early age from my aunt Marjorie, who's a trained chef. I'm supposed to be meeting with her now, as we're planning Mom and Dad's twenty-fifth anniversary party.

It will be huge and lavish and at the main house, where Uncle Talon and Aunt Jade live.

Just like all the Steel parties.

And man, we Steels *love* to give parties.

I'm running late, of course, because I got sucked into a Tarot reading with some of my online pals.

Gina rolls her eyes at me whenever I pull out the Tarot deck, but that's fine. I don't consider it fortune telling or witchcraft or anything. I simply use it to tap into my own intuition. Plus, I enjoy it.

I'm about ready to log off when my phone dings with a text.

*Darth Morgen is alive.*

Huh?

I wrinkle my forehead and check the number. I don't recognize it.

Darth Morgen? Is this some kind of *Star Wars* reference?

*Who is this?*

No reply, until—

*Darth Morgen is alive.*

O . . . kay. Whoever sent this message probably mistyped a number. It's not meant for me. Still, I'm curious, and I want some guidance.

I shuffle my deck and pull a single card.

The hierophant.

I jerk slightly.

Not because the hierophant represents anything that concerns me but because in the ten years I've experimented with the Tarot, I've never drawn this card in a reading for myself. Others, of course, but not myself, which always made sense. The hierophant can represent conformity and group identification.

That's not me. Not Ava Steel.

I'm the Steel who didn't use her sizable trust fund to open my bakery in town. I'm the Steel who colors her hair and wears a lip ring.

Definitely not a conformist.

But . . . a hierophant is also someone who interprets secret knowledge and seeks a deeper meaning.

*Darth Morgen is alive.*

Secret knowledge? A deeper meaning?

Was this message meant for me after all?

CONTINUE THE STEEL BROTHERS SAGA
WITH BOOK TWENTY-FIVE

# MESSAGE FROM HELEN HARDT

Dear Reader,

Thank you for reading *Scorch*. If you want to find out about my current backlist and future releases, please like my Facebook page and join my mailing list. I often do giveaways. If you're a fan and would like to join my street team to help spread the word about my books, please see the web addresses below. I regularly do awesome giveaways for my street team members.

If you enjoyed the story, please take the time to leave a review on a site like Amazon or Goodreads. I welcome all feedback. I wish you all the best!

Helen

**Facebook**
Facebook.com/HelenHardt

**Newsletter**
HelenHardt.com/SignUp

**Street Team**
Facebook.com/Groups/HardtAndSoul

# ALSO BY HELEN HARDT

**The Steel Brothers Saga:**
*Craving*
*Obsession*
*Possession*
*Melt*
*Burn*
*Surrender*
*Shattered*
*Twisted*
*Unraveled*
*Breathless*
*Ravenous*
*Insatiable*
*Fate*
*Legacy*
*Descent*
*Awakened*
*Cherished*
*Freed*
*Spark*
*Flame*
*Blaze*
*Smolder*
*Flare*
*Scorch*
*Chance*
*Fortune*
*Destiny*

**Blood Bond Saga:**
*Unchained*
*Unhinged*
*Undaunted*
*Unmasked*
*Undefeated*

**Misadventures Series:**
*Misadventures with a Rock Star*
*Misadventures of a Good Wife* (with Meredith Wild)

**The Temptation Saga:**
*Tempting Dusty*
*Teasing Annie*
*Taking Catie*
*Taming Angelina*
*Treasuring Amber*
*Trusting Sydney*
*Tantalizing Maria*

**The Sex and the Season Series:**
*Lily and the Duke*
*Rose in Bloom*
*Lady Alexandra's Lover*
*Sophie's Voice*

**Daughters of the Prairie:**
*The Outlaw's Angel*
*Lessons of the Heart*
*Song of the Raven*

**Cougar Chronicles:**
*The Cowboy and the Cougar*
*Calendar Boy*

**Anthologies Collection:**
*Destination Desire*
*Her Two Lovers*

# ACKNOWLEDGMENTS

I had a ton of fun with *Scorch*! Not only are Brock and Rory one of my favorite Steel couples, but I got to revisit Jett Draconis and Zane Michaels from *Misadventures with a Rock Star*! Be sure to give that one a read if you haven't already.

Huge thanks to the always brilliant team at Waterhouse Press: Audrey Bobak, Haley Boudreaux, Jesse Kench, Jon Mac, Amber Maxwell, Michele Hamner Moore, Chrissie Saunders, Scott Saunders, Kurt Vachon, and Meredith Wild.

Thanks also to the women and men of Hardt and Soul. Your endless and unwavering support keeps me going.

To my family and friends, thank you for your encouragement. Special shout out to Dean—aka Mr. Hardt—and to our amazing sons, Eric and Grant. Special thanks to Eric for giving *Scorch* a much-needed edit before I handed it in to Scott at Waterhouse.

Thank you most of all to my readers. Without you, none of this would be possible. I am grateful every day that I'm able to do what I love—write stories for you!

We'll see Brock and Rory again when the band goes on tour, but in the meantime, there are still mysteries to solve... and a new couple to welcome into the Steel universe!

# ABOUT THE AUTHOR

#1 *New York Times*, #1 *USA Today*, and #1 *Wall Street Journal* bestselling author Helen Hardt's passion for the written word began with the books her mother read to her at bedtime. She wrote her first story at age six and hasn't stopped since. In addition to being an award-winning author of romantic fiction, she's a mother, an attorney, a black belt in Taekwondo, a grammar geek, an appreciator of fine red wine, and a lover of Ben & Jerry's ice cream. She writes from her home in Colorado, where she lives with her family. Helen loves to hear from readers.

Visit her at HelenHardt.com